Have You
Seen Her

Lisa Hall

ONE PLACE. MANY STORIES

HQ
An imprint of HarperCollins*Publishers* Ltd
1 London Bridge Street
London SE1 9GF

This paperback edition 2019
1
First published in Great Britain by
HQ, an imprint of HarperCollins*Publishers* Ltd 2019

ISBN: 978-0-00-821501-9

MIX
Paper from
responsible sources
FSC™ C007454

This book is produced from independently certified FSC™ paper
to ensure responsible forest management.

For more information visit: www.harpercollins.co.uk/green

Printed and bound in Great Britain by
CPI Group, Croydon CR0 4YY

PR[...] L

'This is an unrelenting and scarily plausible story weaved expertly around some very real characters. Good luck putting it down . . .'
Heat

'Compelling, addictive . . . brilliant!'
B A Paris

'A dark, compelling read that demands to be read in one sitting.'
Sam Carrington

'An addictive read.'
Closer

'This is a fast-paced book, and with twists up until the final page, you won't regret investing in it.'
Woman Magazine

Lisa Hall loves words, reading and everything there is to love about books. She has dreamed of being a writer since she was a little girl and, after years of talking about it, was finally brave enough to put pen to paper (and let people actually read it). Lisa lives in a small village in Kent, surrounded by her towering TBR pile, a rather large brood of children, dogs, chickens and ponies and her long-suffering husband. She is also rather partial to eating cheese and drinking wine.

Readers can follow Lisa on Twitter @LisaHallAuthor

Also by Lisa Hall

Between You and Me
Tell Me No Lies
The Party

To Nat, Charch and Christie . . .

#solesisters

PROLOGUE

The fire crackles as the flames leap into the frigid November air, sending out showers of sparks. The wooden pallets that have been piled high by volunteering parents, eagerly giving up their Saturday afternoon, crumple and sag as they burn. The guy – the star of this cold, clear Bonfire Night – is long gone now, his newspaper-stuffed belly and papier mâché head only lasting a matter of seconds, the crowd cheering as his features catch alight, feeding the frenzy of the flames.

My breath steams out in front of me, thick plumes of white that match the smoke that rises from the bonfire, but I am not cold, my hands are warm and my cheeks flushed pink. The crowd of parents, teachers and children, five or six deep in some places, that gathers in the muddy field behind the school are transfixed as the first of the fireworks shoots into the sky, before sending a spectacular display of colours raining down through the night air. I watch as she keeps her gaze fixed onto the display, the heat of the bonfire casting an orange glow across her features, her hat pushed back on her head, so her view isn't obstructed. For a moment I feel a tiny twinge of guilt – after all, none of this is really her fault – before I remember why I'm doing this, and I bat it away impatiently.

All I need to do now, is wait. Wait for the realisation to dawn on her face, for the fear to grip her heart and make her stomach flip over as she realises what has happened. For her to realise that Laurel is gone.

CHAPTER 1

'Here.' Fran thrusts a polystyrene cup of mulled wine into my hand, fragrant steam curling into the cold November air. I don't drink – not even cheap mulled wine with the alcohol boiled out of it – something I've told her repeatedly for the past three years that I've worked for her as a nanny, but she never takes any notice.

'Thanks.' I cup my hands around the warm plastic and let the feeble heat attempt to thaw out my cold fingers. Another firework shoots into the air, blue and white sparks showering across the sky, and a gasp rises from the crowd. Fran sips at her wine, grimacing slightly, before pushing her hat back on her head so she can see properly. She fumbles in her pocket, drawing out a slightly melted chocolate bar. 'I got this for Laurel,' she says, the foil wrapper glinting in the reflected glow from the giant bonfire behind the cordon in front of us.

'Laurel?' I say, frowning slightly. Laurel is a nightmare to get to bed if she has sweets this late in the evening, Fran knows that. Although, it'll be my job to tussle Laurel into bed all hyped up on sugar, not Fran's. I glance down, expecting to see her tiny frame in front of us, in the position she's held all evening. She dragged us to the very edge of the cordon as soon as we arrived at the field behind the school, determined that we wouldn't miss a second of the Oxbury Primary School bonfire and fireworks display.

'Yes, for Laurel – you know, *my* daughter,' Fran says impatiently, thrusting the chocolate towards me. She follows my gaze, and frowns slightly, biting down on her lip, before she opens her mouth to speak. 'Where is she?'

I turn, anxiously scanning the crowds behind us, the faces of parents, family members and teachers that have all come out in their droves to watch the display. Laurel isn't there. She isn't in front of me, in the tiny pocket of space she carved out for herself, and she isn't behind me either. I turn back to Fran, trying to ignore the tiny flutter in my chest.

'I thought she went with you?' I say, the cup of mulled wine now cooling quickly in the chilly night air, a waft of cinnamon rising from the cup and making my stomach heave.

'With me?' Fran's eyes are wide as she glances past me, searching for Laurel.

'Yes, with you.' I have to stop myself from snapping at her, worry nipping at my insides. 'You said you were going to get us a drink and pop to the loo, and Laurel said, "Hang on, Mummy, I'm coming with you."'

'She did? Are you sure?'

'Well, reasonably sure,' I say, a delicate twinge of frustration whispering at my breastbone. 'I mean, I saw her follow after you, because I shouted out to her to keep hold of your hand.' There are hundreds, if not thousands of people here tonight, the display well known in the small patch of Surrey that we live in. It's a regular annual event arranged by the PTA, and it's well attended every year.

'She didn't,' Fran whispers, her eyes meeting mine as the blood drains from her face. 'She didn't hold my hand. She didn't catch up with me at all.'

I feel sick at Fran's words, her fingers gripping my forearm, digging in vice-like. Trying to crush the rising unease that makes my stomach do a tiny somersault, I take a deep breath, peeling Fran's fingers from my arm and taking her hand in mine.

'Don't panic,' I say, trying to keep my voice level and calm, 'she must have just wandered off. There are people on the gate; no one would let her walk out on her own, she's only little.'

Fran nods, her face a sickly shade of white. 'We need to look for her, I need to find her. Surely, she can't have gone too far?' She drops my hand and starts to shove her way past the crowds of people hemming us in. I follow after her, ignoring the tuts and frowns from others. Finally, I break free of the crush and catch up to her, as she begins to run across the field towards the bank of portaloos, slipping and sliding in the mud that coats her designer wellies.

'Wait, Fran,' I gasp, 'wait. We need to . . . to think for a minute. We need to think about this logically, about where she might be.'

'She was following me to the loos, that's what you told me,' Fran says, her eyes frantically scanning the field behind me, 'I'm going to look there, maybe she did follow me, maybe she's got locked in one of them, maybe she's banging on the door now and no one can hear her.' Another burst of fireworks erupts in the sky with a popping noise, as she pulls her arm away from me, staggering slightly.

'OK,' I nod, 'good idea. You check the loos, I'll go and ask at the barbecue area. See if they've seen her – she might have asked for you if she couldn't find her way back to us in the crowd.' Fran has hammered it home from the

5

first day I began working with them, that if Laurel gets lost she must find a policeman, or security guard — someone in authority — and ask them to find her mummy. Laurel knows the rules. Fran gives a sharp nod, but I can see her mind is already on getting to the portaloos, and she turns and starts to run towards the row of green plastic cabins. I gaze after her for a moment, a whicker of fear making my pulse beat faster, making my feet stick to the ground for just a minute before I begin the walk over to the barbecue area. I hurry as fast as I can, but the field beneath my feet is a slurry of mud, thanks to three days of constant rain, and straw, laid to soak up the mud, which is now a thick, sludgy, slippery mess.

Heat, a thudding bass from the DJ system in the 'bar' area (a tent, with a trestle table full of wine and beer bottles), and the acrid scent of barbecue smoke assaults my senses as I approach the table, and I have to swallow hard before I can speak.

'Hi.' My voice is drowned out by the crappy music, and the pop of fireworks exploding over my head. 'Hey!' I shout.

'Hello, darlin', what can I get you? Burger? Sausage?' The burly guy behind the table turns to me, hot dog roll in hand. It's my second visit to Pete the Meat tonight, the local butcher (and local lothario, if the rumours are true).

'No, no thank you.' I shake my head, 'I'm looking for a little girl – she's got lost. Have you seen her?'

'What's she look like?' There is a smear of tomato ketchup across the sleeve of his white coat, a slash that looks like blood against the clinical whiteness, and my mouth goes dry.

'She's four, um . . . about this high.' I hold my hand at about waist height. 'She's got blonde hair, and she's wearing a pink coat, pink wellies and a sparkly silver bobble hat.'

'Can't say that I have. Let me ask the others.' He turns and shouts to the two teenagers that work behind him, slicing rolls and folding napkins, before turning back to me. 'Sorry, darlin', we haven't seen her. We'll keep an eye out though, yeah?'

'OK. Thank you.' I try and muster a smile, before turning back to the field. I scan across the crowds, my eyes seeking out that distinct glittery bobble hat in the dark but to no avail. Spying the admissions table, where three PTA mums sit all bundled up against the cold, I start to hurry towards them, cursing the mud for hampering my progress.

'Hello, hi.' I am breathless with the effort of trudging through the churned-up mud as I reach the table. 'Can you help me? I'm looking for a little girl.'

'Is she lost?' A caramel blonde woman, wearing an expensive waxed jacket and perfect make-up speaks first, her eyes widening as her hand with its long, manicured nails flies to cover her mouth.

'Yes, I think so . . . I mean, she followed her mum to the loo and . . . look, we can't find her, her name is Laurel Jessop, she's four . . .'

'Laurel?' One of the other women gasps, strands of her dark hair sticking to her lip gloss as she jumps to her feet. 'I know Laurel, she's a friend of my daughter, Daisy.' As she says the words I recognise her as the woman my friend Jessika nannies for.

'Yes, Laurel. Please, have you seen her? She's going to be frightened if she's wandered off and she can't find us.'

7

My fingers knit together anxiously as I look from one to the other, my feet itching to get back to the field, to start looking for Laurel. The third woman, pale and mousy, who I recognise from the school gate but can't match to a child looks up with wide eyes but says nothing, her fingers pausing briefly in their tidying of admission tickets.

'We haven't seen her,' Caramel Blonde says, 'and we wouldn't let a little one out on their own. Oh my gosh, this is terrible.' She turns to the dark-haired woman, Daisy's mother, an accusatory tone creeping into her voice. 'I told you we should have set up a lost children zone.'

'Please . . .' I say again, 'are you absolutely sure she hasn't been past here?' Even as I say the words I know Laurel hasn't – she would have stopped and asked Daisy's mum to help her find us, as per Fran's strict rules.

'Absolutely sure,' the woman says firmly, shouldering her way past Daisy's mother to come and stand next to me, her eyes scanning the field. 'Right. Where's Mr Abbott? The head will need to know about this – we have a process to set in place when a child goes missing. You two,' she turns to the women next to her, an officious air about her now, as though she's used to taking charge, 'you need to get this gate closed off before things finish and people start to leave.'

Daisy's mother starts nodding frantically in agreement, twisting her hands together as she looks anxiously between the open gate and the hordes of people watching the fireworks burst over our heads, panic starting to creep across her features. The mousy woman tidying the tickets whispers something, but before I can ask her to repeat it, there is a huge cheer as the grand finale of the fireworks goes off, and to my horror I see people start to turn to depart, gathering up small children with their glow sticks, stumbling over discarded polystyrene cups and sweet wrappers as they make their way through the field back towards the still open gate and the darkened lane that leads out and away towards the main roads.

'Anna!' Fran careers across the field, her feet almost sliding out from under her, her hat pushed right back on her head. Her eyes are glittery, and her cheeks flushed, and I think at first that it's all OK, that Laurel was just locked in the loo after all. 'Did you find her?'

My heart sinks. Fran is flushed from her frantic searching, not because it's all over.

'Anna? Did you find her?' Fran repeats, and I shake my head.

'No. No one has seen her. I checked with Pete at the barbecue station, and I asked the PTA mums at the admissions table, but none of them have seen her.'

'Fuck.' Fran pulls her hat off and shoves her hand through her glossy black bob, her eyes combing the scene behind me, as people now flood towards the open gate. 'LAUREL!' she shouts, grabbing my hand and pulling me back into the field, back into the thick of the dispersing crowd. 'LAUREL!' We both take up the cry, and a thick knot of fear rises up in my chest as the thought skitters across the back of my mind that maybe, maybe Laurel hasn't got lost.

'Mrs Jessop? Mrs Smythe on the PTA tells me we have a missing child. Is that right?' Mr Abbott, head teacher at Oxbury Primary appears in front of me as I struggle to keep up with Fran.

'I'm not Mrs . . . yes, she's missing. Laurel . . . her name is Laurel,' I manage to stutter. 'We can't find her.'

'Right, try not to panic, the chances are she's just wandered off somewhere.' His voice is calm, but his brow is creased with concern. 'Where did you last see her?' I ramble on about Fran getting drinks and using the bathroom, before impatiently pushing past him and catching up to Fran, who is yanking open the doors to the portaloos again.

'I thought maybe I missed one,' Fran sighs. 'I thought she might have gone in there after I checked. Did you ask the people who were serving at the bar?'

I glance towards the bar area, where Mr Abbott is talking to the parents and helpers behind the table, gesturing across the field with one arm. Behind him I see the PTA mums gathered at the now closed gate, a crowd of people waiting to leave bottlenecking in front of them. 'The head teacher, Mr Abbott, is talking to them now.'

'The head? He's looking for her too?' Fran looks up at me, a look of blind panic behind her eyes. 'Dominic!' she shouts suddenly, her hand flying to her mouth. 'Dominic was meant to be here . . . what if he turned up and saw her . . . maybe she was cold, and he took her home?'

'Maybe,' I say doubtfully, but Fran is already fumbling in her coat pocket, dragging out her mobile phone and dialling Dominic's number. 'He's her dad after all,' she says, phone clamped to her ear. 'I mean, why wouldn't he take her home . . . and he wouldn't think to ring me, not that I would have heard it even if he had . . .' she trails off before she hangs up without speaking. 'Voicemail,' she says, bitterly.

Mr Abbott appears by her side and gives us both a tight smile, as we hear the sound of Laurel's name being called in an announcement over a loudhailer.

'Mrs Jessop.' I point at Fran and he turns to her. 'I've spoken to a few of the parents over at the bar area, but none of them have seen Laurel. We have implemented the first stages of our missing child process. All exits have been closed for the moment, and several people have already volunteered to start searching the immediate area for any sign of Laurel. What time did you last see her?'

'I don't know . . . the display had started, I think. Anna?' Fran turns slightly, throwing the question to me, her eyes already looking past me, still searching the field for any glimpse of Laurel.

I have no idea. I haven't checked the time all evening, and my heart thuds in my chest, a frantic double beat that makes my breath stop in my throat for a moment.

'I'm not sure,' I say. 'Just after the fireworks started?' Mr Abbott flips his wrist and checks his watch.

'So, she's been missing for around half an hour now?' He frowns, and I feel sick – I hadn't realised how long it had been, it feels like seconds ago and a hundred years all at the same time since I last saw her. 'OK, I think perhaps it's time we made a phone call . . . I think we need to get the police involved.'

I turn to Fran, and see my own fear written all over her face.

'I'll do it.' She gulps hard, and slowly pulls her mobile out from her pocket again, tapping in the numbers with shaking fingers, her face illuminated by the glow of the screen.

'Police, please. It's my daughter . . .' Her eyes find mine and I watch as she blinks slowly, pushing a thick, heavy tear out and over her pale cheek. 'She's gone . . . I can't find her. I think someone has taken her.'

11

CHAPTER 2

Pulses of blue light flash as the patrol cars pull up across the entrance gate to the field, illuminating the faces of the families still waiting to go home. There are three of them, parked haphazardly across the entrance to the field, blocking the way out. Just the sight of the blue lights, seeing the dark uniforms of the officers stepping out of the cars, is enough to make my nerves jitter and my hands shake. I've spent the last five years doing my best to avoid any interaction with the police, at all costs. I have no choice tonight, though. I watch as the taller of the first two officers leans down to listen as Caramel Blonde says something, pointing in our direction. While others have started searching the field for signs of Laurel, the head teacher has kept Fran and me here, not far from the bank of portaloos, up to our ankles in mud, telling us that we need to stay put to make it easier for the police to find us. And now, they are here.

'Oh God.' Fran lets out a little moan as two of the police officers make their way towards us, pressing her fingers up towards her mouth. 'I didn't think they'd actually come . . .' She turns to me with a look of panic on her face. 'I thought we'd find her – I thought we'd find her and there'd be no need for them.'

'It's OK,' I say, wanting to reassure her but she's usually so unapproachable that I find it hard to break the habit of keeping myself back a little.

'Mrs Jessop?'

Fran says nothing, and I give her a little nudge.

'Yes,' she says finally, turning a tear-stained face to the police officer in front of us. 'That's me.'

'I'm DS Wright. You rang us – said you couldn't find your daughter. Do you want to tell us what happened?'

The woman's voice is low, and I have to strain slightly to hear her. Fran starts to recount the evening, starting from when she arrived at the field. Laurel had been excited about the bonfire all week, it had been all she had talked about, and I'd ended up leaving the house with her half an hour before we'd needed to, arranging to meet Fran at the field so she could finish getting ready in peace. Laurel had tugged on my hand all the way along the lane to the entrance, not even stopping for Mr Snow's house at the top of the pathway – an older gentleman, who was often in his garden in the afternoons, and Laurel liked to pause and chat to him for at least five minutes, seeing as he quite often had lollies in his pocket. I think about the way she rushed along the pavement, excitement making her squeeze my hand, before she pulled away, eager to be the first in the gate and I feel my heart constrict in my chest. What if she'd fallen? What if a car had come speeding round the corner and almost hit her? Would I have held her hand a bit tighter then? Would I have made sure she was in my eyeline for the entire evening, instead of assuming that she'd caught up with Fran?

'. . . and she just wasn't there, was she, Anna?' I am shaken out of my thoughts by Fran's voice speaking my name.

'And you are?'

'Anna.' I look over at DS Wright's colleague, a slight woman with short blonde hair and a smattering of freckles across her nose, who stands poised with a small black notebook, as Wright waits for my answer. 'Anna Cox. I'm . . . I'm Laurel's nanny.'

'And you brought Laurel here, earlier this evening?'

'Yes. I walked here with her while Fran was getting ready. Laurel was excited, she wanted to get here as early as possible.'

'And then . . . what? Can you run me through exactly what happened – when you first realised that Laurel wasn't where you expected her to be?'

I see Fran glance in my direction as I open my mouth to speak, to repeat exactly what she has just told them. 'Fran was going to the loo, and to get us a drink. Laurel said she was going as well, and she ran off after Fran. But then Fran came back, and Laurel hadn't caught up with her.' Guilt lies heavily in my stomach. *Why hadn't I watched? Made sure she reached Fran, kept my eyes on her until she grabbed her hand?*

'Thank you, Anna.' The police officer seems satisfied with my comments, scratching away jotting down my words in her notebook. 'So, it sounds as though she's wandered off, lost sight of Mum. We've got the exits closed now and we're looking for her, OK? She can't have got far – we'll find her.' She gives me a brisk smile, before walking away towards her colleagues, leaving Fran and me alone, the chilly night air taking on a sinister feel as Laurel's name is shouted again and again into the dark.

I'm not sure how long it is before DS Wright walks back over to us, her face pensive. She stumbles over an uneven patch in the muddy ground, her sturdy black shoes sliding as she almost loses her footing. Righting herself, she brushes a splash of mud from her black trousers, before stopping in front of us.

'What is it?' Fran says, almost shoving me aside to get close to the police officer, her hand reaching out before falling to her hip. Her voice is hoarse from shouting Laurel's name, and as I swallow I realise my throat is also raw. 'Did you find something? Did you find Laurel?'

'Mrs Jessop . . . Fran.' DS Wright speaks slowly, calmly, before she turns her gaze to include me. 'As yet, we haven't found any sign of Laurel in the immediate area, but we are still carrying out a full, intensive search. In the meantime, there are just a few things that I would like to ask you about.'

Fran says nothing, her face pale, so I nod instead. 'Yes, of course. We'll answer any questions you have, won't we, Fran?'

'Great, thank you.' DS Wright pulls out her notebook, rifling through the pages until she finds what she's looking for. 'So, Laurel went to catch up with her mother – with you, Fran – is that right?'

'Yes.' I nod again, as Fran crushes a tissue to her nose, tears spilling over and running down her cheeks. 'But I didn't actually see her catch up with Fran.' Just saying the words makes me feel sick.

'But you're sure she went in that direction – towards the portaloos?'

'Yes, yes I'm sure.' *I am sure – aren't I?* Guilt and worry converge to make me doubt myself, to doubt the picture

I see in my mind's eye of Laurel running towards the back of Fran's coat, as she weaved her way slowly through the crowds.

'And you didn't notice anything out of the ordinary, either before or during the bonfire? Nobody hanging around that shouldn't have been? No one who seemed overly interested in Laurel?' Her eyes settle on my face and I feel a slight sweat break out across my forehead, despite the cold night air, as though it is me under investigation, me who has done something wrong.

'No. No one. Although, there were people starting to arrive as we walked up the lane, so I don't know that I'd . . .' I was going to say, *I don't know that I'd have even noticed,* but I can't bring myself to say it out loud.

'And what about Laurel's father? Fran says that he was supposed to meet you all here this evening?'

'He was,' I say, frowning slightly, 'he's a surgeon – a heart surgeon at the hospital in South Oxbury – but he didn't make it here, obviously.'

'I tried to get hold of him,' Fran says, a frown to match my own creasing her forehead. She pauses for a moment and blinks hard. 'I called him a few times, but it just kept going to bloody voicemail.' She presses her lips together and looks away, wrapping her arms tightly around herself.

'It was sort of a big deal, tonight . . .' I say in a low voice, 'he works really long hours, but he'd promised Laurel that he would make it.'

'Can we try him again?' The blonde officer who spoke to me earlier has arrived to stand next to her colleague, and she looks to DS Wright for confirmation.

'I'll do it,' I say, glancing at Fran. She looks white, the blue lights still pulsing in the background giving her face a sickly sheen every time they pass over her features. 'I'll call him.'

I call his number, my fingers fumbling with the phone, but I don't know if it's through shock or simply the cold. Just as it did for Fran, the voicemail kicks in within a couple of rings.

'Dominic? It's Anna. Can you call me as soon as you get this?' Fran is talking to DS Wright, so I step away slightly, hanging up the phone and scrolling down to the number I am only to call in strict emergencies. This counts, I think to myself, this definitely counts as an emergency. It starts to ring, and I press one finger into my ear in order to hear better, as I feel the blonde officer's eyes on me – DC Barnes, I think Wright called her. I turn my back and wait for the call to be answered.

'Theatre,' a gruff voice barks into the receiver.

'Oh, hello,' I say, gripping the phone tightly as I try to keep my voice steady, 'I need to speak with Mr Jessop, please, it's rather urgent. Can you tell me if he's in theatre, or is he available?'

'Mr Jessop?' There is a pause on the line and a murmur of voices faintly in the background, and I imagine the nurse glancing at the whiteboard, then asking her colleague, checking to see which theatre he might be in. 'Sorry, he's not on this evening. His list finished at five o'clock.'

Shit. Where the hell is he? He promised Laurel that he would be here tonight, and I assumed that he had got

17

caught up with work – after all, that's usually what happens with Dominic. I glance over to where Fran is holding a tissue to her nose, her other arm wrapped tightly around herself as if cold. DC Barnes takes a step towards me, and I hold up one finger as the phone in my hand buzzes, relieved when DS Wright calls her over and I don't have to worry about her listening in.

'Dominic?' I pause. 'You got my message? Fran's been trying to get hold of you for ages.'

'Oh, Jesus.' I hear him exhale, a long, deep sigh, and imagine him sat in his car, his big, luxury Porsche Cayenne that neither Fran nor I are ever allowed to drive, or maybe at home, knowing he was going to be late and miss the bonfire, waiting for us to get back so he can put Laurel to bed. 'Look, Anna, if she's getting you to call me just so I answer and then she can take the phone and chew me out, I'm hanging up now, OK?'

'No, Dominic, it's not . . . it's not that.' My mouth is dry, and I wish I could take it back – I wish I had left it to Fran, or one of the police officers here to make the call.

'What is it, then? I know I missed the fireworks, but . . . I'll talk to Laurel tomorrow and make it up to her. It wasn't my fault . . .'

'Dominic, I called the hospital, looking for you.' Whispering, I grip the phone tightly in my hand, feeling the skin stretch over my knuckles, and turn back to where Fran is waiting. I raise my voice again. 'It's Laurel. She's gone missing.'

As I speak the words out loud to Dominic, I see Fran almost visibly stagger slightly, as if my words have cut her, her hands covering her mouth as if to hold in a scream.

Mr Abbott appears at her side to clutch her by the elbow and keep her steady.

'What? What's happened? Where is she? Are you still at the field?' Dominic fires questions at me, one after the other, barely giving me time to respond, before he tells me he's on his way and hangs up on me abruptly. More police officers are arriving, and there is a sense of urgency now humming in the air. Mr Abbott has rounded up several more volunteers who are already beginning to search the field more thoroughly, and I hear Laurel's name being cried repeatedly into the frosty night air.

'She'll be getting cold.' Almost as though she read my mind, Fran comes close to me, her voice quiet. 'And she's not keen on the dark either. Remember that time the bulb went in the nightlight in the middle of the night and she woke up? We all thought she'd been . . .' Her voice trails off and she gives a tiny huff of wheezy laughter, that catches in her throat. 'Is Dominic coming?'

'Yes. He got held up.' I don't mention my call to the hospital. My hands are freezing now, and I shove them deep into my pockets, my fingers touching something cold and plasticky. I snare whatever it is between my fingertips and draw it out, only to see a tiny doll, like the little Polly Pocket dolls I used to have as a child. Mr Snow gave it to Laurel as we passed one morning on the way to school – it had blonde hair, and a pink jacket, and he told her it looked exactly like her – I assumed it must have belonged to one of his grandchildren. It certainly wasn't new. Laurel must have sneaked it into my pocket without me noticing. I curl my fingers round it and feel the soft plastic stick slightly to my palms.

'He's always held up.' Fran's voice jolts me back to the present. 'Maybe if he'd actually bothered to turn up this evening this never would have happened.' She gives a little sob and presses the back of her hand to her mouth again, as her eyes comb over the field, watching the figures of volunteers sliding across the mud, all shouting Laurel's name.

'Fran? Anna?' Someone else approaches now, a stranger, but I can tell immediately that he belongs to the police. There is something about his manner, the way he carries himself, that tells me he is important. He introduces himself to Fran, but I don't catch his name, only the words, '. . . senior investigating officer.' With a pang, I remember the last time I heard those words. *It's different this time*, I think, *I can't be blamed this time.*

'We're doing everything we can to find Laurel – due to the length of time she's been missing now we've put in a request for a helicopter to join the search, but for the moment I think it's best for yourself and Ms Cox to return to the house,' he is saying, a hand on Fran's elbow to guide her towards the waiting police vehicle.

'What? No!' Fran wrenches her arm away, sliding a little in her wellies. 'Laurel is out here somewhere. Shouldn't I be here? Waiting, in case they find her?'

'Mrs Jessop,' the officer's voice is low and soothing, and Fran stops dead, biting back whatever she was going to say. 'We've got our finest team out searching for Laurel – the best thing you can do is go home and wait.'

'Fran, listen,' I say, still slightly unnerved by Fran's display of emotion this evening. I'm not used to it – she is usually reserved to the point of occasional rudeness, and to see her so open, so exposed, makes me feel uncomfortable. 'I think it makes sense for us to go back to the house . . . what if Laurel has wandered off and she's made her way home and you're not there?'

'Do you think so? DI Dove . . . do you think she might be at home?' She turns to face DI Jayden Dove, hope written across her face.

'It's possible. We have already dispatched a team to the house just in case.' He tries to force a smile, but it doesn't sit right on his face. 'DS Wright and DC Barnes will take you home.' *He's lying*, I think, the thought closing around my heart like a cold fist, *he doesn't think Laurel is at home at all*. I try to force the thought away and tap Fran lightly on the arm.

'Come on,' I say, 'if she is at home, she's going to want a cuddle and a hot chocolate.' And I lead her slowly towards the police car, trying to squash down the familiar feeling of dread that rises up, threatening to consume me.

Laurel isn't there. Of course she isn't, I knew deep down that she wouldn't be and I think Fran knew that too. She is quiet as we step into the hall, DS Wright shadowing us as we enter the slightly chilly living room. The curtains are open, a shaft of moonlight slicing the room in two before I switch on the overhead light and slide my coat off. I take Fran's coat and usher her into an armchair, before returning to the hallway to hang the coats. I slide the little doll from my coat pocket into the back pocket of my jeans. As I reach up to the coat pegs, the sound of the front door opening makes me jump and I gasp, dropping Fran's Ralph Lauren jacket on the floor.

'Dominic,' I place my hand over my racing heart, 'you made me jump.' He looks terrible, his silver hair standing on end as though he has been pushing his hands through it, his face pale and eyes ringed with dark circles.

'Is she here?' His voice is desperate, and he grips my forearms tightly, eyes boring into mine. 'Is Laurel back?'

'No,' I stammer, trying to pull away from him, 'she's not. The police are through there.' He lets me go and I gesture towards the living room.

'OK. OK.' He shoves his hand through his hair again, before rubbing his palm across his mouth, twelve hours' worth of stubble scratching his skin. 'Anna, did you tell anyone I wasn't at the hospital? Did you tell Fran?'

I frown, shaking my head. 'No, I didn't get a chance to. As soon as I hung up DI Dove told us we should come back here. Why?'

'Nothing.' He takes a deep breath. 'Just . . . don't, will you? Don't say anything just yet. I don't think Fran would understand . . . I'll tell her later, when things are . . . you know.'

'Right.' I don't know how I feel about this and I waver for a moment, before I decide I have to let it go, for now anyway. Fran will be furious if she finds out, and I know the focus for all of us should be on Laurel and getting her home safely. I go to speak, to tell him that I'll keep it quiet for now, but he's already pushing past me, headed to where Fran sits in teary silence on the sofa.

'Dominic.' She gets to her feet as he enters, and at first I think she's going to shout, or hit him, fury crossing her face before she crumples into his arms. 'She's gone, Dom. Laurel's gone. Someone has taken our baby.'

CHAPTER 3

I wake with a jolt, without even realising that I have
dozed off. It must have only been for a few minutes, as
I had watched the sun rise a couple of hours ago and
now its light inches its way through the open curtains to
create a warm puddle of gold on the parquet flooring.
I shift, stiff and uncomfortable from spending the night
scrunched into an armchair in the front room, my eyes
gritty and sore.

With a rush the events of the previous evening come
back to me and I force my stiff body round, placing my
freezing cold feet on the floor, the wood warm beneath
my bare skin. We had all been questioned separately, but
informally, over the course of the evening about what had
happened and what we had seen, and it had left me feeling
almost drunk with tiredness, reliving those terrifying first
moments when I looked down and Laurel was gone. My
head aches, and I wince as I sit forward, taking in the scene
in front of me.

Everyone is pretty much in the same position as they
were last night, when Fran told me roughly to go to bed,
that there was nothing I could achieve by staying up.
I had refused, wanting to be there if any news came in,
wanting to know if Laurel was OK, but her voice had
a familiar hard edge to it, one that she uses to remind

me that she is the boss, that she is in charge, not me. Instead of doing as I usually would and hurrying away upstairs to my room, I had folded myself into the hard, uncomfortable armchair in the corner of the room, for once daring to disobey Fran. Dominic had given me a tiny smile of solidarity as he watched me tuck my feet up underneath me, making it quite clear that I wasn't going anywhere, that I would stay awake all night. Obviously, exhaustion had overtaken me at some point, even if it had only been for a few minutes.

Now, my head throbbing so hard it makes me feel queasy, I look to the tableau in front of me. Fran still sits curled into the huge, squashy sofa, while Dominic stares out of the front window. As I follow his gaze I see DS Wright pacing outside the front of the house, mobile phone clamped to her ear. Both parents look exhausted and grey, with slight wrinkles that I've never noticed before appearing at the corners of Fran's eyes.

'I take it there isn't any news?' I ask.

'No.' Fran shakes her head and dislodges a tear that runs slowly down her cheek. 'Nothing.' The door swings open and a tall, slim girl appears. She gives me a small smile, before asking if anyone would like some tea.

'You remember DC Barnes, from last night,' Fran says, her voice dull, as she leans down and picks up the mug of tea, now stone-cold, that I left by her feet an hour or two ago. 'Apparently as well as a DC, she's a "family liaison officer".' I can hear the quote marks she puts around the words.

'Would you like a hand in the kitchen, DC Barnes?' I ask, the atmosphere in the living room suffocating me in the few short minutes I've been awake again. She smiles her thanks and I follow her through into the huge, clinically clean kitchen where she looks around for the kettle, confused when she can't seem to find it.

'Here.' I lean past her to the sink, turning on the boiling water tap. 'No need for a kettle.'

'Oh, fancy!' She throws tea bags into the mugs laid out on the counter and starts to fill them. 'Enough with the DC stuff for now,' she says, raising her voice over the sound of rushing water. 'Just call me Kelly. So, you're Anna? Laurel's nanny?'

'Yes.'

'Have you worked for the Jessops for long?'

'About three years,' I say, thinking back to the day I got the job. I wasn't sure if I'd even turn up for the interview, after what had happened before. I didn't think I was cut out for nannying, not anymore, but working in a bar wasn't for me as I had soon discovered, and a chance meeting with an ex-boyfriend, where he revealed that an old friend of his was looking for a nanny, meant that I decided to bite the bullet and take a chance. 'Laurel was a year old when I started working here. It doesn't seem like that long.'

'And how is it?' Kelly slides a hot mug of coffee towards me and leans against the counter, her blonde hair falling over one eye.

'It's OK. Good, I mean. I enjoy it.' I sip at the coffee. 'Laurel is a little sweetie. It wasn't meant . . . It was only supposed to be temporary, a stopgap, you know? But . . . I liked it. So, I stayed.' I'm more attached to Laurel than I ever thought I would get. I was conscious in the beginning that I shouldn't let myself care for her too much, that it was

25

bound to go wrong. Now look what has happened. I take another, bigger sip of coffee and let it scorch my tongue.

'What about Fran and Dominic?' Kelly asks, her eyes never leaving my face. 'How are they to work for?'

'Oh, you know,' I shrug, but she gives a nod as if to say, *go on.* 'Mostly fine. Fran is a bit . . . highly strung at times. She's an actress, she's always busy learning lines, meeting directors, that sort of thing, so things can get a little stressful for her. Dominic isn't here a lot of the time. He's always at the hospital.'

'So, neither of them is about much?'

I think for a moment. 'Not as much as they'd like, maybe. Fran loves being with Laurel, she just isn't able to much of the time, not with auditions and meetings and things. And Dominic . . . well, he has to put his patients first quite often.'

'And how are they together? Do they get along OK?'

'Most of the time. Everyone has their ups and downs, don't they?'

'And what about you? Have you got a partner, boyfriend, significant other?'

'No,' I let out a little huff of laughter, 'definitely not. I spend all my time with Laurel.'

'So, did you live in the area before you started working here? Or did you move here especially?'

I snap my head up from where I am staring into my coffee and meet her gaze. I should have known that she wasn't simply being friendly, I need to remember that she's not my friend – she's only here to do a job. I could kick myself for letting my guard down.

'Am I being questioned?'

'No,' Kelly says, a faint blush rising in her cheeks, 'nothing like that. I'm sorry. I just wanted to get a feel for how things are usually in the house. Obviously today it's tense, and everyone is under a lot of strain. I don't think Fran has taken too kindly to my being here.'

I let out a long sigh of relief. 'She doesn't mean anything by it. It's simply the way she is. Prickly.' I let out a tiny huff of rueful laughter. Fran is unpredictable at the best of times, and I often find myself walking on eggshells around her in case I inadvertently do something to upset her. Frequently I find myself making the wrong decision – taking Laurel to the park for half an hour on Saturday mornings after Fran has come home late, in order to let her have a lie in, only to come home and find her pacing the kitchen, demanding to know why Laurel wasn't there when she woke up, or all the times I've bathed Laurel and put her to bed, only for Fran to waltz in earlier than expected and then demand to know why Laurel wasn't kept up to see her. You don't always know which Fran you're going to get.

'Did you know them before you worked for them?' Kelly asks, before looking away. 'Sorry. I'm honestly not interrogating you. I just need to get a feel for things, it's an important part of the investigation. You know we need to do everything we possibly can to find Laurel.' She gives me a reassuring smile and I stare into my coffee cup, shaking my head.

'No, I didn't know them. I'd never even heard of Dominic, although apparently he's top of his field and well known for what he does.'

'But you grew up round here?'

'No.' I'm puzzled now. 'Why do you ask?'

'Sorry.' She gives me a proper smile now. 'It's just that you look familiar, and I thought maybe we went to school together or something. You must have one of those faces.'

'That'll be it.' I manage to force the words out, the blood freezing in my veins. 'We definitely don't know each other.' I slide off the stool the moment Dominic pokes his head around the doorframe, his face grave.

'Anna? DS Wright wants to talk to us all. Can you come in?'

I nod, and follow him through into the living room, my heart starting to thunder in my chest. *Has there been a development? Or has DS Wright found out what I so desperately wanted to keep a secret?*

DI Dove is standing in front of the log burner, his hands clasped in front of him as I totter into the room on shaking legs. DS Wright looks small and frail next to his large frame. Fran still sits huddled up on the sofa, her face pale and drawn, already looking thinner, diminished somehow.

'OK,' DI Dove speaks, his voice a rumbling baritone that matches his dark, brooding looks. Italian, I think, or maybe Spanish. 'I think we all know that now we are looking at the very real possibility that Laurel hasn't simply wandered off. That someone else might be involved in her disappearance.'

There is a little squeak, and Fran presses her hands to her mouth, as Dominic sinks onto the cushion next to her, wrapping his arm around her shoulder, trying to pull her in towards him. Sitting alone on the armchair opposite, I feel cold and sick, the headache I woke up with still pounding away at my temples.

'We had people searching the field well into last night, and again since early this morning, and we have yet to uncover anything that might lead us to Laurel, or give us some idea about what might have happened to her. We still have a team of volunteers down at the site, all willing to continue the search and we have officers doing door-to-door questioning to see if anyone saw anything that might be of use.'

'Well, that will help, won't it?' Fran asks, a note of desperation creeping into her voice. 'Someone must have seen something, surely? It's not like Laurel could just vanish into thin air!' Her voice rises to almost a shriek and she cuts off abruptly.

'There isn't any CCTV footage along the lanes that lead to the field, which is not ideal, but this is a fairly close-knit community and I'm hoping that someone will have seen something, and even if it seems insignificant, that they'll report it to us.'

To me, this doesn't sound terribly hopeful at all, and the mention of CCTV makes my heart sink. The field is well away from the main roads, surrounded on all sides by tiny country lanes that lead miles into the surrounding areas of Surrey. An abductor could have travelled for miles in any direction before being picked up on a CCTV camera. Laurel could be anywhere.

'We'll also need to have a team of officers search the house,' Dove says, as Dominic gets to his feet.

'What? Why?' Dominic demands, as Fran stands, reaching out a hand to him. 'She didn't go missing from here, did she? Why would you need to search our house?' He is bemused, looking between the two investigating officers, as Dove tries to explain that it's all part of the process.

'Dominic, please,' Fran cries, 'please sit down and let them do their job. Please.' Her voice breaks, and Dominic sits back down next to her, pulling her tight, even though her shoulders are rigid. I say nothing, my mind working overtime at the thought of there being a search of the house.

'Is there anybody I can call for you?' Kelly has slipped quietly into the room. 'Anybody who you might like to come and sit with you, your parents or . . .'

'No,' Fran says shortly, shaking her head. 'I haven't seen my father for years, and my mother lives in Dubai. There's not a lot she can do from there.' Despite her faded pallor, and the way she wrings her fingers together, there is a hint of the old Fran in her clipped tone.

'What about Polly?' Dominic asks.

'Polly?' Fran snaps back at him. 'Don't be so bloody ridiculous!'

'Sorry, can I ask . . . who is Polly?' Kelly asks, as I look on in confusion. I have no idea who Polly is either.

'Polly is Fran's sister,' Dominic sighs, scrubbing a hand over his eyes.

'Yes, my sister, who Dominic can't bear.' Fran gets to her feet. 'In fact, Dominic can't bear her so much that I lost contact with Polly years ago – just to make Dominic happy.'

'Oh, come on, Fran, that's not strictly fair . . .'

'Mr and Mrs Jessop.' DS Wright's voice cuts through the thick, tense atmosphere. 'Please.'

Fran sits back down, on the edge of the armchair, out of Dominic's reach. 'The last I knew Polly was living somewhere in the Scottish Highlands, but that was ages ago. My mother keeps in contact with her, Polly regularly goes over to visit her.'

'Right. Anna? Anyone you want to contact?' DS Wright turns to me and I shake my head slowly, trying my hardest not to shrink away from her gaze. There is no one, not right now. 'Seeing as we don't have any leads so far, I wanted to ask you if there is anyone you can think of who might want to . . . who might have a grudge against you? Who might have taken Laurel. Anyone suspicious hanging around, anyone you may have felt uncertain about?'

'No one that I can think of,' Dominic says, a deep V appearing between his brows as he frowns. Dominic wouldn't notice anyone hanging around though, I think, he's never here. As the words float through my mind Fran speaks.

'How would you know, Dom? I mean really, how would you know? You're always at the hospital.'

'There hasn't been anyone hanging around,' I butt in, before they start sniping at each other again. 'I'm the one who spends most of my day here, at the house, or out and about with Laurel and I'm certain I haven't seen anybody unusual or suspicious hanging around.'

'Well, what about Pamela?' Fran throws out, spitting the words at Dominic from across the room. The air between them is so thick you could cut it with a knife, and I hope that neither DI Dove or DS Wright thinks that the atmosphere here is always like this, even though sometimes, it can be.

'Jesus Christ, Fran, you're clutching at straws! Don't be so . . . God.' Dominic gets to his feet and starts pacing as the police officers say nothing, only watch.

'Clutching at straws!' Fran cries. 'Of course I am, Dominic! My child is missing! My daughter is out there, somewhere, with God only knows who . . .' Her voice cracks and she covers her face with her hands. Kelly moves towards her, and Fran stiffens as Kelly's arm goes around her shoulders.

'Sorry . . . who is Pamela?' DI Dove asks quietly, clearly accepting the heightened emotion in the room as he seems completely unfazed.

'No one,' Dominic says, 'no one important, or relevant. She's an ex-girlfriend.' He suddenly sounds very tired. 'I went out with her before I met Fran. She's nobody, I haven't had anything to do with her for years. Look, I think I want to go down to the field, see if they need any help with the search.'

'Mr Jessop, I'd really appreciate it if you could stay here at the house, just for . . .'

'No! I'm sorry, but no. Am I under arrest? Can you legally stop me from leaving my house, right now?'

'No, we can't but you must understand . . .'

'No, *you* must understand. You've torn my house apart, you're asking us the same questions over and over . . . you should be *out there* looking for my daughter, not here, questioning me. So, if you'll excuse me, I *am* going out there to search for Laurel, whether you people like it or not.' He shoulders his way past DI Dove, who frowns but says nothing.

'I'll come with you,' I say, jumping at the chance to get out of the house, to get away from the cloying, claustrophobic atmosphere that has swallowed up every fitting and all its inhabitants. Plus, I am eager to get out there, to be doing something constructive to help bring Laurel home.

Grabbing a coat from the rack and snatching up my mobile, I step out into the cold, fresh November morning, thinking as I do so that when I last left this house, Laurel was clinging tightly to my hand, bubbling over with excitement and now . . . well, now who knows where she can be? Fighting off the exhaustion that tugs at my bones, I fall into step with Dominic, who marches on towards the field in silence, and I inhale the crisp air, hoping to clear my head. I need to find Laurel, before it's too late. I can't let something awful happen again. It can't happen again.

CHAPTER 4

My mobile buzzes in my pocket, and I pull it out to see seven text messages from Jessika, my nanny friend, three missed calls, and several texts from numbers that I don't recognise. I shove it back in my pocket without opening them, realising I have fallen behind and Dom is now several paces in front of me. I consider asking him about the previous evening, asking him where he was when he wasn't at the hospital, but he marches towards the fields at a brisk pace.

I take long strides in order to catch up. Finally, I draw level with him. His face is grim, his eyebrows knitted together and his mouth a harsh line scored into his face.

'Dominic?'

'What?' He turns back to me, that angry, desperate look still etched into his features. His face softens. 'Sorry, was I going too fast for you? I just . . . I just want to get there, you know? I should have been there last night.'

'That's what I wanted to ask you – about last night.' I slow right down, a stitch in my side making me wince. 'Where were you? You said you'd be here . . . and you weren't at the hospital. And you asked me not to say anything to Fran.'

He stops abruptly, before turning to face me. 'That is none of your business, Anna.' His voice is cold, and it sends icy shivers down my spine. Dominic has never spoken to me this way before. Clearly, I have overstepped the mark, but he carries on before I can apologise. 'Wherever I was last night had nothing to do with Laurel, do you hear me?' He takes a step towards me, grabbing me by the upper arms, and I draw in my breath in a hiss of pain as his fingers dig tightly into my flesh through my jacket. 'Are we clear on that? I've told the police where I was, and that's the end of it. I don't want to hear another word, OK?' He lets me go, and I rub at the tops of my arms before I give a slow nod.

'OK. I'm sorry.' I swallow, fear making my throat dry. 'I never meant anything by it. I'll forget about it.'

'Thank you.' Dominic strides off again, not even attempting to temper his pace so that I can keep up this time. I watch him for a second, as he hurries past Mr Snow's house, onwards towards the school, his head bent, and I run his words over in my mind again before I start to follow him. *I'll forget about it.* I'll try, but it will be difficult to forget the way his eyes flicked up and to the right, as he said he'd told the police where he was last night: up and to the right – a classic sign that someone is lying.

As we approach the field, a police officer directs us towards the school hall, that backs on to the fields a little further along from where the bonfire was held. There are people everywhere, and I hear Laurel's name as groups gather together, some prepared with bottles of water and backpacks, as if in for the long haul. There is a sense of urgency in the air, underwritten by something else, something that if I had to name it, I would say was panic. Things like this don't happen in places like Oxbury.

I lose Dominic as he forges ahead, which I think is probably for the best – I don't think I can cope with the now strained atmosphere between us – and as I step into the hall I pause for a moment. The familiar smell of school dinners – cabbage, with an underlying, vanilla-y hint of lumpy custard – assaults my senses, and there is a rousing babble of chatter that dies momentarily as people notice me enter the room.

'Anna!' The caramel blonde woman from the PTA rushes towards me, her arms outstretched. The other mother from the PTA admission stand last night hangs back, hesitant, as though she wants to come over but daren't.

'What's going on?' I look around, puzzled by the sheer number of people in the hall and on the field outside. Quite a few had hung around last night to help search, and while I'd thought it would be similar today, this has the air of . . . organisation.

'We've set up a search station . . . well, I have.' She fusses at her hair, smiling with perfect white teeth on display. 'The police are sending volunteers to us, and then we are directing them to start their part of the search, as arranged by the officers in charge. I've got someone making up posters and we're even having T-shirts made up with Laurel's face on . . . you know, *Have You Seen Her?* et cetera, et cetera.'

'Right,' I say, my eyes still roaming the room. I can't see Dominic anywhere, and I wonder for a brief moment how he feels about all of this. I know that I feel overwhelmed by it all. 'I'm sorry, I can't remember your name?'

'Lola's mum. Cheryl.' She looks a bit put out, and I smile to soften the blow. 'Is Fran here?' She cranes over my shoulder, looking towards the door. 'I thought she might like to see what we're doing, the effort the community is making.' She gestures around the room, and I see a man with a large camera around his neck talking to one of the other parents. I shrink back, sure that he must be with the local press.

'No, she's not. She's stayed home,' I say, spying Jessika on the other side of the room, 'will you excuse me?' I push past, ignoring her as she calls something after me, and make my way across the crowded hall, keeping my head lowered as I pass the man with the camera. It's started to empty out slightly, people moving towards the double doors with polystyrene cups of coffee in one hand, crumpled posters bearing Laurel's face in the other.

'Jess!' I call out, before she can join the hoards leaving the hall. Jessika Lewis is the one friend I have in Oxbury. She is nanny to Laurel's best friend, Daisy, and we met in the park one warm summer's day when the girls were tiny. She turns to face me, biting her lower lip.

'Oh God, Anna. Are you OK? I've texted you like, a million times.' Her arms reach around my skinny frame and pull me tightly towards her in a hug.

'Sorry, I only just saw the messages . . . what are you doing here?' I say. 'Where's Daisy?'

'Technically it's my day off, so I thought I'd come along and see if I can do anything to help find Laurel. But then Claire turned up here anyway, and brought Daisy along with her, so I'm pretty sure I've only got an hour or so before Madam calls me over to take Daisy back to the house.' She gives a little jerk of her head behind her, and I see Daisy sitting at a low table, colouring in, while Claire buzzes around behind her, posters in hand. 'Cheryl Smythe somehow organised all of this, overnight, single-handedly.' She points, and I realise that she's talking about the caramel blonde woman. 'It doesn't take long for word to spread around here, you know that, and everybody wants to be involved.'

Somehow this doesn't surprise me – Fran and Dominic are the closest Oxbury gets to a celebrity couple. Thanks to Dominic's success as a surgeon and Fran's bit parts in a couple of BBC historical dramas everyone knows who they are.

Jess must see something in my face, as she says, 'I meant *help*. Everybody wants to help, not *be involved*. Come on,' she takes a look over her shoulder to make sure Claire is still otherwise occupied, 'I've been assigned the far end of the field – I'm sure no one will mind if I have an extra pair of hands.'

As we turn to leave the mousy woman from the PTA, the one whose face I can't put a name to, is standing close behind me, and I almost step on her foot as I swivel round.

'Oh God, sorry.' Holding up my hands I go to move past her, but she lays a hand on my arm. Her nails are bitten down to the quick, her fingers thick and rough looking.

'How is Fran?' There is a slight West Country twang to her voice. 'Is she OK? Is there anything I can do for her? I haven't seen her for a while, but you know . . . I want to let her know I'm here if she needs me. Tell her, won't you? Tell her Ruth, from the PTA, is here if she needs her.'

'Um . . . OK. I'll let her know.' I have no idea if Fran knows this woman – Fran rarely does the school run, so I'd be surprised if she would recognise her, and anyway, even though I know her from the PTA I still can't think which child belongs to her.

'Anna, come on, we have to get started.' Jess tugs on my arm and we walk out of the stifling hot hall, the cold air outside hitting me like a slap in the face.

As we cross the path and step onto the wet straw that marks the entrance to the field, the area where last night the PTA stood guard to ensure no small children escaped (although that didn't seem to work so well, did it?), I realise that I am still wearing yesterday's clothes. As well, I'd shoved my feet into trainers, not wellies. Although the sky last night was clear, meaning a frosty start to today, the rain that has fallen all week long along with hundreds of feet marching through the field has led to more sloppy mud, with a thin crunchy shell of frost on top. There is a damp mist in the air, the kind of cold that seeps right into your bones, and already my feet are cold. My shoes slide awkwardly on the mud as I follow Jess.

There are maybe thirty other people combing the edges of the field where the grass leads into the wooded area that surrounds the lake beyond it. I see others heading out of the gate, presumably to search the lane. I look around, but I don't see Dominic.

'Are they looking anywhere else?' I ask. I hadn't felt able to ask DI Dove for any information this morning, or indeed last night, not in front of Fran and Dominic. After all, Laurel isn't my daughter, as Fran regularly goes to great lengths to remind me.

'Mainly the woods this morning, I think, and then out into the lane,' Jess says, her cheeks pink with the cold. She's remembered to put wellies on, at least. 'They said the main area of the field was searched last night, but they want to search again in daylight. Police are going door-to-door through the main road to the village this morning as well, I believe. Hopefully someone saw something that might point them in the right direction.'

We reach the edge of the woods, the rough path in front of us splitting in two just a few yards into the bushes. Jess stops and points to the left. 'I'll go that way, you take the right-hand path. Meet back here in an hour?'

'OK. Jess . . .' I say, panic starting to beat in my chest as I look towards the thick overhang of trees above me. It's winter, and the branches are bare, but they reach towards each other, tangling their limbs together leaving dark, sinister shadows across the mulchy forest floor. 'What am I looking for?' I blink rapidly, to fight back the tears that spring to my eyes.

'Oh, Anna.' Jess reaches for my hand, clasping it in her gloved palm, transferring warmth to my cold fingers. 'Anything – anything at all that doesn't look right. Bushes that have been flattened, any signs of . . . disturbance.' She blinks hard. 'The police gave us a talk when we all arrived at the hall, told us what sort of things we should be looking out for. We'll find her, Anna, I'm positive we will.'

I give her a watery smile and wish that I shared her conviction. She steps away, on to the left-hand fork of the path and I turn to the right, keeping my eyes trained on the ground for the first few feet, anxious in case I miss something. Then I realise that some of the tree branches are shoulder or even head height to Laurel, and I might have missed something that may have caught on the bony fingers of the branches.

I retrace my steps back to the edge of the wood, a flash of colour catching my eye as I reach the outskirts. It's Dominic's yellow ski jacket, and he paces backwards and forwards a little way from the entrance to the woods, mobile phone clamped to his ear, his breath escaping in tiny clouds of vapour as he speaks. I slide my thin frame behind the nearest tree, straining my ears to try and hear what he's saying. He paces the same route over and over, shoving a hand through his hair until it sticks up in short silver spikes, but it's no good, I'm too far away to hear him.

I start to creep backwards, into the shadows of the woods, when a branch cracks under my trainer, and Dominic looks up. He starts to walk towards the woods, when whoever is on the other end of the line says something he clearly doesn't like. He hangs up with an angry curse and stares at the phone for a moment as if wondering whether to throw it at the nearest tree. After the way he reacted earlier, grabbing me when I mentioned his whereabouts last night, I can't help but feel nervous – but he tucks the phone into his back pocket and walks off towards the hall. I let out a shaky sigh of relief and edge back onto the path, my eyes combing every branch.

The damp, mulchy path squelches underfoot as I get further into the wooded area, muddy water leaching up from the leaf litter and soaking my white trainers. This far up there is a large expanse of woodland before the lake, and I am glad that I don't have to search near the water. The thought of finding something that belongs to Laurel close to the edge of that dark, dank, silty water makes my blood run cold. As does what I see in front of me next: a pile of leaves, clearly recently disturbed, their wet, smelly undersides exposed to the open air, filling the area with the scent of decay.

As I edge closer, I see they have been carved into ruts, as though something (or someone, my brain hisses) has been dragged through them. *As though two tiny little feet have been pulled through the wet, mulchy mess*, a voice whispers in the back of my mind. I raise my eyes to follow the line of rutted leaves towards a diamond mesh fence that runs along the perimeter of the woods, separating it from the field behind. The diamond mesh fence that has clearly been cut, to reveal a small opening. Perfect for the size of a small child.

Heart thumping, a wash of nausea making me feel dizzy, I hesitate, unsure whether to shout for Jess, or take a closer look. *It might be nothing*, I whisper to myself, running my tongue over dry lips. I step close to the fence, careful not to place my feet anywhere near the drag marks, and peer into the field beyond. I see nothing at first, until I slide through the opening in the fence and into the field. The damp grass near the fence has been flattened down, and a trail of bent stems lead away from the fencing towards the other side of the field – as though someone has walked a path through the longer grass. I look behind me, telling myself that if Jess is in sight I'll call her over, but there is no one. From here, I can't even hear the searchers calling Laurel's name. Stepping to one side, so I create my own path, I follow the trail over the slight hill, stopping short as I see where the path of flattened grass leads to.

A camp. There are eight or nine caravans parked up on the far side of the field, no doubt having forced their way in by cutting the padlock off the gate on the other side. It's happened more times than anyone cares to mention in Oxbury; the travellers' arrival usually gets reported to both the police and the council within hours of them pitching up. Nice middle-class people from Surrey don't want travellers in their midst. Obviously, this time the police have been too busy to come out and move them on, and if they only arrived last night there's a chance that no one else has even noticed them yet. I force my feet on towards the camp, ignoring the flip of my stomach as I get closer, nervous at having to speak to them. The only experience I've had of them before was when one of them threatened to smash up the Co-op after he got caught pinching bacon, while I was buying sweets for Laurel. As I get closer, I see two men standing outside one of the caravans, both turning to face me as I get within talking distance.

'Hello,' I say, my mouth dry again. They are both tall and well-built, their skin tanned a dark brown, roll-up cigarettes dangling from their mouths. Neither of them wears shirts with sleeves despite the cold, and I see the tattoos on one of them ripple as he raises a hand to push his hair back from his face, his dark curls dotted with droplets of water from the mist.

He speaks, his voice rough. 'What d'yer want?'

'I'm looking for a little girl,' I say, running my tongue over my lips. 'She went missing from the fireworks party in the field over there last night,' I point behind the trees, 'there's a huge search operation being organised by the police.'

With an anxious glance at his friend, the tattoo guy speaks again. 'We don't know nothing.'

'Are you sure you haven't seen anything? No one coming through here last night . . .' I break off, about to mention the drag marks and the cut in the fence before common sense catches up with me.

'We said, we don't know nothing.' The second, slightly smaller guy takes a step towards me and I flinch a little, hating myself straight away for looking so weak. Adrenaline shoots through me, leaving my knees wobbly. 'Get lost.'

'OK, thank you. Forget it, I'm going. Sorry,' I babble, almost falling over myself to get back through the fence to where other people are. I'm intent on finding a police officer to explain about the drag marks, then I can go home and check on Fran and wait for Laurel, and *forget* about the intense, intimidating stare that these two guys laid on me. And I *would* forget, only . . .

I stop, something moving in my line of vision, something that makes my breath catch in my throat. I see it again, from the corner of my eye, the thing that made me stop in my tracks and I turn my head a fraction towards the caravan immediately behind the two men.

'I'm going,' I say again, holding my shaking hands up in surrender, as they both take a step towards me, my heart thumping double time in my chest as I try and process what I just glimpsed. The back of a head, at the window of the caravan. A tiny, blonde head, with a high ponytail, that I'm sure I last saw being stuffed into a sparkly silver bobble hat.

CHAPTER 5

I manage to walk calmly away, resisting the urge to run until I reach the mesh fencing and I am sure I am out of sight of the two travellers. I squeeze my way hurriedly through the tiny gap, the sharp cut edge of the fence slicing into my fingertip, catching my jacket as I go. *Shit.* I've probably contaminated a crime scene now as well. My shoes sliding on the damp, muddy forest floor, I rush back towards the field, branches grabbing at me, my hair falling over my face and my breath coming in short hitches that strike up the stitch in my side again. Coming out of the woods I look around, hoping to see a police officer, or Jess at the very least, but everyone seems to be tied up, busy with their own searches so I push on towards the school hall.

Falling through the double doors, I call out, 'Is there a police officer here?' A sob catches in my throat and I have to work hard to swallow it back down, not wanting to lose it in front of the volunteers.

'Oh gosh, you need to sit down, here, come this way.' The mousy woman from the PTA appears by my side, her hand grabbing at my forearm and tugging me towards a chair. 'Let me help you.'

'I don't need to sit down.' I shake myself free impatiently, trying to see over the tops of people's heads to catch a glimpse of DI Dove, or perhaps Dominic.

'Anna? There you are.' Jess appears from the throng of people that have edged their way towards me. 'I waited for you and you never came . . . look at the state of you. Oh God, you're bleeding!' She grasps my hand tightly. 'What happened?'

I glance down at the mud that cakes my shoes and splatters up the legs of my jeans. A thin trickle of blood stains my fingertips where I caught myself on the mesh, and there is a long rip in the arm of my jacket from the fencing. I can feel the sweat break out over my skin again. 'A police officer, Jess. Are there any still here or are they all doing the door-to-door?'

'I'm here,' a voice says behind me, and I turn to see DI Dove.

'Oh, thank God.' I resist the urge to throw myself on him in relief. 'I found something, out there on the other side of the woods.'

'OK,' Dove pulls me to one side, away from prying eyes and straining ears. 'What did you find? Tell me.'

'At the edge of the woods – where it meets Briars Meadow – the fencing has been cut. There are drag marks . . . I crawled through it, and they're there . . .'

'Whoa, not so fast.' DI Dove waves his hand up and down in a gesture designed to slow me. 'Who is there?'

'The travellers,' I say, my breathing finally calming. 'There are eight or nine caravans, all parked in the field, in the usual spot. There are drag marks, like feet, leading to the cut in the fence and then the grass is all beaten down as though someone has walked through there. But that's not it. I saw her.'

'You saw her? Who? Laurel?' A spark gleams in his eye and I see why he is a detective – he loves the thrill of the chase.

'I think so. I saw her hair. It's in a high ponytail, she was sitting in the window of one of the caravans. I'm sure it was her. You have to go! You have to go and see if it really is her!' My voice rises, and several people glance our way. There is no sign of Dominic, and I hope that they find him before someone tells him I saw something. DI Dove looks around, one hand on my shoulder.

'We need someone to take you home,' he says, as I shake my head.

'I can take her,' a voice pipes up, and it's her again, the mousy woman.

'No, I'm not leaving. I need . . . I want to be here when you bring Laurel back.'

'Anna, it might not even be Laurel. And I need you to be with Fran, she's on her own . . . I mean, Kelly is there, but it's best if either you or Dominic stay with her. Just in case.' *Just in case there's bad news.* That's what he means. Reluctantly I give a slow nod, just as Jess arrives at my side.

'Come on,' she says, giving a curious glance in DI Dove's direction. 'I have to take Daisy back to the house anyway, she's getting bored. She keeps asking where Laurel is.' Her mouth turns down. 'Best to get her out of here.'

I let Jess lead me out of the hall, away and towards the lane, watching as Dove calls over another police officer, waving his arms and gesturing. There is a flash of yellow as Dominic appears from behind the building and sees Dove, changing his course to walk over to the policeman. Jess follows my gaze.

'Let's get you back,' she says, one hand on my arm, one holding tightly to Daisy.

'I should stay,' I insist, eyes fixed on Dominic as Dove talks at him, hands moving as he shakes his head, clearly telling Dominic to stay where he is.

'You can't,' Jess says firmly, 'Dove told you to leave . . . and he's right. Someone needs to be with Fran, whether it is Laurel or it isn't, and better it's you than some police officer that she barely knows.' *Especially if it isn't Laurel*, I think, letting Jess guide me away. I can't imagine how Fran will react if it turns out that it isn't her after all.

Jess leaves me at the front gate, smiling at Kelly who has stepped outside to the garden to have a cigarette. She smiles sheepishly back, as if ashamed to have been caught on a break.

'I'll be fine, Jess, you go.' I step back, waggling my fingers at Daisy. Jess looks uncertain, but I nod at her enthusiastically. 'Honestly, I'll be fine. Kelly's here. You go.' I want her gone before Fran looks out the window and sees Daisy. I can't imagine that she'd want to see her daughter's best friend, not when her own child is gone. If I'm honest I'm finding it hard enough to see Daisy without Laurel beside her, and I am relieved when Jess finally turns to leave.

'Are you OK?' Kelly lets out a stream of smoke, picking a tiny piece of tobacco from between her teeth, and I have to struggle to stop my mouth curling up in disgust. The smell of cigarette smoke always puts me on edge. 'I've spoken to DI Dove.' So, she does know what's going on over at the field. 'I haven't told Fran yet. I was waiting for you to get back. I thought she might need you.'

'I'll tell her,' I say, 'I don't mind. No offence, but it might be better coming from me than from you. She knows me.

She trusts me.' *When it suits her.* Kelly wavers for a second before she gives a small nod.

'OK.' She stubs out her cigarette and throws the butt into the black bin. 'Let's head back in.'

I don't have any choice but to agree, and my heart feels as though it's lodged in my throat as I slide the door handle down and step into the front hallway. The house is cool, chilly almost, and I realise that the heating timer has probably switched off, and Fran hasn't noticed. I peer into the living room, expecting to see her tucked into the huge grey Conran sofa, the plush corded material etching lines into the skin of her bare feet as she sits with them tucked up beneath her, her pose of the last twelve hours, the light from the Tiffany lamp casting a yellow glow across her face. But the living room is empty, with only the faint scent of Fran's perfume on the air. I step along the hall into the kitchen, thinking that maybe she's making a cup of tea, but the light airy room is also empty.

'Shall I?' Kelly nods her head towards the sink and I shrug. I don't want any more tea – it feels as though all we've done since we got home last night is drink tea.

'Fran must be upstairs. I'll go and get her.' Lightly I make my way up the wide staircase to my little box room, a tiny bubble of hope blooming inside me at the thought that Laurel might be back home with us soon. Fran must have finally gone up to get some sleep, I think to myself, before muffled voices come from the room above me, the attic room that Fran and Dominic converted into their huge, spacious bedroom before Laurel was even born. Stealthily, I creep up the tiny staircase, telling myself that I'm going to knock and make sure that Fran doesn't need anything.

But my hand doesn't tap on the door. Instead, I find myself pressing my ear to the wooden panel, holding my breath in order to be as silent as possible.

'No. No, honestly, it's all going to be fine,' I hear Fran say, as her footsteps pace across the wooden floorboards. 'I don't know why . . . look, it will be OK. I promise. I can deal with this. I'm OK on my own.' More pacing, her voice becoming indistinct as she steps away from the door, presumably towards the windows that face the back garden. I lift a hand and tap the door lightly before she discovers me.

'Fran?' I push the door open, seeing her hand slide her phone into her pocket. 'Is everything OK? I thought I heard voices?'

'Well, I wouldn't say I'm OK.' She gives me a tight smile. She still looks terrible – her skin washed out and grey, and her eyes puffy – but she has given her lashes a lick of mascara, and her lips shimmer with a faint, rosy glow, achieved from a tube of lip gloss. 'I was just . . . I was talking to my mother.'

'Oh?' I don't know what else to say. Fran very rarely mentions her mother. She told me once, rolling in after a late-night boozy wrap party, that she didn't get along too well with her mum. That it was her mother's fault that her father had left them, taking his generous bank balance with him.

'She offered to fly over here. Although what she can do to help I don't know.' Fran shakes her head, sadly. 'I don't want her fussing over me. It'll simply be easier if she stays where she is. And anyway, Dominic won't want her here.'

I don't know where to look, so I stare at my feet as I shift them uncomfortably on the spot. Although Fran and

I have lived in the same house for three years, and Fran entrusts her daughter to my care every day, we are not friends. Although I share this house with Dominic, Fran and Laurel, this house isn't my home and I am not really a part of the family. Fran is prickly, aloof, and quite clear where the boundaries lie between us. She is my employer, and I am her employee. This Fran, the Fran that speaks openly, that shrieks at Dominic in fear, that exposes her emotions is a stranger to me.

'Well,' I say, for lack of any other response, 'shall we go downstairs? Kelly is making some tea . . .'

'More tea.' Fran tries to muster a smile and fails miserably, before heading for the door, her movements sluggish and slow as if she is weighed down with exhaustion. I follow after her, my socked feet slipping on the polished oak staircase. Kelly is placing three mugs of tea on the table as we enter the kitchen. Fran slides into the nearest chair and wraps her hands around a mug as if to soak up the warmth.

'Fran,' I say, my stomach full of butterflies. *Please let Laurel be coming home.* 'I went to the field this morning . . .'

'Yes, I know.' For a second I catch a glimpse of the old Fran – brittle, impatient Fran – before her shoulders round and she almost seems to shrink in her chair. 'I assumed . . . wait. Did something happen?' Her eyes flick between me and Kelly and all of a sudden, I can't tell her. I look at Kelly, and she takes the hint.

'Fran, there's something I should let you know. Something was found in the meadow behind the field.'

'What?' Fran's voice has a tremor to it that almost sounds false and I feel a tiny bubble of inappropriate nervous laughter prick in my chest. 'What did they find?'

51

'I saw something,' I step in, the chill of the house settling into my bones, and I wish I'd thought to flick the heating back on. 'In the meadow . . . there are caravans parked up there. I saw a blonde girl sitting in the window of one. I told Dove and he's gone there now, I mean, the men I saw were dark, all black hair and tanned skin, so why would there be a blonde girl with . . .' I trail off, as the blood drains from Fran's face.

'So, she could be there? She's in the meadow?'

'We don't know.' Kelly lays a hand on Fran's arm, who pulls away as though burnt. 'Officers have gone to the scene and as soon as they know something, they'll tell us.'

Fran nods, but stays silent, her fingers creeping to her mouth as she starts to nibble at the skin around her cuticles. 'Where is Dominic?'

'He's there,' I say, 'I left him there, with the police.'

Fran lets out a long sigh. 'I'm sure he'll find somewhere more important to be on his way home.'

I look away, not knowing what to say, as Kelly also turns and reaches for the mugs, even though no one has touched the tea. Fran slides a hand towards her pocket, before catching herself and raising her fingers to her mouth again. I wonder if she is thinking about calling her mother back, about telling her she's changed her mind and she does want her to come.

The next half hour drags as we wait for news, Fran's eyes closing as she sits at the kitchen table, a puddle of sunlight highlighting the reds in her dark hair, the skin round her nails now ragged and sore. The crash of the front door opening jolts all of us back to life, and Fran and I both jump to our feet as DS Wright and Dominic enter the kitchen.

'Where is she? Where is she, Dom?' Fran looks frantically past him, trying to edge away and head towards the front door, but he grips her tightly by the upper arms.

'Fran,' he says, his voice breaking, 'stop for a moment. It wasn't her. It wasn't Laurel.' She sags against him, and he pulls her into a tight embrace before he raises his eyes to mine. 'Someone made a mistake. It wasn't our girl.'

CHAPTER 6

There is a crushing sense of disappointment at Dominic's words, heightened when Fran shoves Dominic from her and rushes from the room.

'I'll go after her,' Kelly says, a grim look on her face, as Dominic sinks into the nearest kitchen chair.

'I'm so sorry.' I feel the mistake as if it were an actual physical pain, a shaft of hurt piercing my skin. And not just mine – it seems I got everyone else's hopes up for no reason. 'I really thought . . . the hair, it was the hair. She was wearing it the same way Laurel wears it, and it was the same shade . . .' I trail off, the bitter taste of failure thick on my tongue.

'It was a genuine mistake,' DS Wright says, 'and better that you raised it with us, because it could have been Laurel.'

'It was their daughter,' Dominic says wearily in a husky voice, his head resting in his hands. 'It was their own little girl. She takes after her mother – blonder than you, Anna, she was. Up close she looked nothing like Laurel.'

'The drag marks were caused by them,' DS Wright tells us, 'apparently the girl sneaked out through the cut fence to watch the fireworks. When they found her, she didn't want to leave. Had a paddy by all accounts, and they ended up dragging her back to the caravans. They only arrived yesterday evening, a little before the bonfire started. Officers had already spoken to them late last night and told them to move on today.' Her face twists in something like disapproval.

'I'm sorry,' I whisper again, 'I don't know what to say.'

'There's nothing you can say.' Fran has appeared back in the doorway, faint smudges of mascara beneath her eyes revealing she has shed yet more tears. 'It was a mistake, Anna. You weren't to know that it wasn't her. Us sitting here crying isn't going to help get Laurel back, is it? DS Wright – is there anything else you can tell us?'

I blink back tears, frantically trying to rid myself of them before they fall. Fran is right, sitting here crying won't get Laurel home to us. Although slightly forced, Fran seems to be trying to channel her usual brisk self, and I guess that is the only way she can cope with what is happening in this house right now – to try and keep control of events the way she always does. I can imagine her sitting upstairs, beating herself up, punishing herself for her emotional outbursts and hating herself for losing control.

'Well,' Wright says, pushing her dark hair away from her face and gratefully accepting the hot tea that Kelly thrusts in her direction – she's good for refreshments, if nothing else – 'we have made some headway following the initial door-to-door enquiries.'

'Really?' Dominic lifts his head and gazes around the kitchen. 'Why are we only hearing about it now?'

'As you can understand, checking out the possible sighting of Laurel became our priority, and I have only just received the most recent updates from the team that are carrying out the enquiries.'

'So, what is it?' The words tumble out before I can stop them and Fran stares at me, putting me back in my place without saying a word. Laurel is *her* daughter, not mine. Wright doesn't appear to notice though.

'There has been a report of a child matching Laurel's description getting into a car along the lane from the bonfire last night, at a time that corresponds to when Laurel went missing.'

'What?' Fran whispers, her face a chalky white. She licks at her lips and raises a shaky hand to her mouth to wipe at it.

'Obviously, we are taking this witness very seriously, and we will be investigating further,' DS Wright says, glancing between myself, Fran and Dominic, as though wanting to make it absolutely clear that this could also be another dead end.

'Tell us what happened. Tell us who saw it and exactly what they think they saw.' Dominic is on his feet, fingers gripping the edge of the table tightly, so tightly that his knuckles are white.

'A resident of the area looked out of the window at approximately eight fifteen last night, supposedly to watch the fireworks display, and saw a young girl getting into a car not far from the entrance to the display. She describes the car as an "off-roader" which we are taking to mean an SUV. Officers are with the lady now, showing her pictures of different vehicles to see if she can narrow it down for us. At the moment an SUV, possibly dark in colour although she can't be sure, is all she can tell us.'

'And what about the driver?' Dominic says, a sheen of sweat sparkling on his forehead, in the patches where his silver hair has started to recede. 'Did she see who was driving it? A man? Woman? Did she see anything?'

'She says it was too dark to see who was driving, and to be honest, she didn't really think anything of it at the time. All she saw was a small girl, wearing a pink coat, climbing into the back seat of a dark car.'

'How can she be sure it was Laurel?' Fran asks, her voice barely above a whisper. She clears her throat, making a harsh, raspy sound that seems too loud in the thick silence of the kitchen. 'I mean, Laurel wouldn't get into a car, would she?' She looks to me and I shake my head, reluctantly. 'She wouldn't go off with a stranger. I know my daughter, DS Wright, and she wouldn't willingly get into a stranger's car, not after everything I've taught her.'

'She might, though,' I say, unable to keep the words in, knowing that I'm about to effectively tell the police that I know how Laurel would react to this situation better than Fran would. 'Sorry, Fran, I don't mean to contradict you, but she might. Laurel is a very friendly, outgoing child.' I think about the way she stops to greet Mr Snow every afternoon, the way she always has a smile and a wave for everyone, regardless of whether she knows them or not. 'And she's only little. If a stranger told her that you had said she was to go with them, there's every chance that she might have got into a car.'

'We don't know for certain that it was Laurel,' DS Wright says, as Fran turns an icy-cold gaze on me, her eyes narrowed. I don't know which is worse – the idea that Laurel might have got into a car belonging to somebody she doesn't know, or that it isn't her and we are still no closer to finding her. 'But I have to ask you if you know anybody who might have a dark-coloured SUV?'

'No. We don't know anyone who has a dark-coloured SUV. And she wouldn't have got in it anyway.' Fran's nostrils flare as she speaks, deliberating turning her face away to let me know that she is in charge of this, not me, that I shouldn't have dared to contradict her.

'Of course. As I said, officers are working with the witness concerned, and as soon as I have anything more to tell you, I will.' A shrill ring pierces the air, and DS Wright excuses herself to answer the call. I let out a breath that I haven't even realised I've been holding.

'Do you mind if I . . .' I wave a hand towards the staircase, and Dominic gives a little shrug. I need to step away for a moment, away from the tension, the words that lay between all of us, unsaid. The blame that I feel lies on my shoulders for mistaking that girl for Laurel and raising everyone's hopes. I escape to my tiny box room, pausing only briefly on the landing to turn the heating back on. Dominic is behind me and I let out a little gasp of shock.

'Sorry, you startled me,' I say, pressing my hand to my chest, feeling my heartbeat thud rapidly beneath my palm.

'Sorry.' He looks a little sheepish. 'I only wanted to say . . . you did the right thing just now. Speaking up to say that you thought Laurel might have got in the car.'

'Oh. I just . . . I didn't mean to . . .'

'Really, Anna, it was the right thing to do. I saw the look Fran gave you when you said it, and I . . . look, you know how she is.' Our eyes meet in a look of understanding. *Yes, I know how she is.* 'This is really tough on her, and she's probably going to take a lot of it out on you, but I understand that it's tough on you, too. You can talk to me, if you need to.'

'Thank you.' I feel a faint blush start to creep up my neck, relief that perhaps I am not on my own through this starting to flood my veins.

'And if you think of anything – anything at all that might help find Laurel – in the meantime just come to me.' Dominic pats the top of my arm and turns to head back down the stairs to Fran.

My room is freezing cold, the weak wintry sunlight streaming in through the window not enough to warm the room at all. I'm not sure if it's the temperature of the room, or the fact that Laurel is missing that makes me shiver, my arms stippled with goosebumps. My stomach twists, as I think of her again, running after Fran, the way I turned back to the fireworks display before I saw her catch up. *Why didn't I keep my eyes on her, just for a few seconds longer?*

Clothes litter the end of my bed, from where I tried on and discarded several different outfits before leaving last night, settling on the blue and white striped top I still wear now. I sniff under the armpits and grimace, before tugging it over my head and dropping it into the laundry pile. I need a shower, and clean clothes. My blonde hair hangs limply around my shoulders, and the tops of my feet are splattered with tiny flecks of mud where my trainers didn't cover them.

Listening out as I step on to the landing, I hear the murmur of voices below as I go into the bathroom and lock the door. The hot water thunders down over my hair and I let go of the tears that I've held at bay since this morning. Salty trails stream down my cheeks, mixing with the hot water from the shower, and I gasp as my nose clogs, the steam catching in the back of my throat.

I love Laurel. It's something I find hard to admit, even to myself. I've been in a situation before where I let myself become attached – *and look how that ended*, I chide myself. I swore that this time, it would merely be a temporary stopgap until I could find something else, a different job where I could simply turn up from nine to five and then go home and not think about it again till the morning. But I got lured in by Laurel and her familiar baby smell, right at the beginning. It is second nature to me to comfort her as she runs to me, not Fran, when she falls and hurts herself. She fell a few weeks ago, as she ran in from the garden, the paving slabs wet and slippery underfoot. Fran and I had been stood in the kitchen, both of us hearing the thud as she went down and then her thin piercing shriek. We'd rushed outside together, Fran pushing past me to get to her first, her arms outstretched ready to pick her up, but Laurel had shrieked louder and shaken her head, reaching her arms out to me, for me to scoop her up and carry her inside. Fran had shrugged it off, but I'd seen the look of fury on her face when I had lifted Laurel up, her head fitting naturally into the hollow of my shoulder as if she were my own.

Spending all that time caring for her, making sure she is happy, looked after, it was inevitable that I would get attached in the end. And now, it's happening again, just as it did before. I take my eye off the ball for a few seconds and everything comes tumbling down.

*

Fran is lurking outside the bathroom when I slide the lock back and pull the door open, making me jump, and I almost drop the bundle of dirty laundry I am carrying. I can only hope that the thunder of the water drowned out the sound of my sobbing, although the redness around my eyes will still give it away.

'I'm going to try and get some rest,' she tells me, her face closed. I don't blame her. I don't think she slept at all last night and her face is pinched with exhaustion. Plus, she is clearly still annoyed with me for what I said – it's probably best for both of us to be in separate rooms for a while. 'Get Dominic to wake me up if . . . anything happens.' She glances down towards the bundle in my arms. 'What is that?'

'Just the laundry.' I have collected up my own dirty clothes, as well as the bundle in the bottom of the laundry basket. It's not my job to do the laundry; Fran has a cleaner every day that takes care of it, but I feel as though I am lost at sea without Laurel to occupy me.

'No, that.' She points at something sticking out of the bottom of the bundle, that I can't see from the position I am holding it in. 'Give it to me.' She tugs, and the clothes fall out of my arms, all over the hall carpet. Fran is clutching a scrap of lilac cotton to her face, that I recognise as the nightdress I took off Laurel yesterday morning before I put her in the bath.

'No one said you could take this!' Fran cries, tears shining in the corners of her eyes. 'No one said you could do the laundry! Just leave it! Put it all back!' She holds the nightdress tight against herself, rocking slightly as she cries.

'Fran? What's going on?' Dominic thunders up the stairs, concern pulling his eyebrows in to a deep crease in his forehead. 'Anna?'

'I was just . . .' I stutter, too frightened to say anything more. There is something primal, something horrifying, about the way Fran wails, the noise chilling the blood in my veins.

'She was going to wash Laurel's clothes!' Fran cries, before burying her face in the soft washed cotton again, her shoulders hitching.

'I'm sorry, I didn't think . . .' Of course, Fran wouldn't want me to wash Laurel's clothes, how could I be so stupid? 'I only wanted to help.'

'Leave it, Anna. Fran, come on. I'll take you upstairs.' His tone curt, Dominic puts an arm around his wife, guiding her gently towards the stairs that lead to the attic room. Fran turns to stare at me over one shoulder, and I look down, not wanting to meet her gaze, ashamed that I could be so thoughtless.

I grab my laptop and slide down onto the floor, my back against the radiator as I wait for it to boot up. The incident with Fran has left me feeling drained and shaken, and I wish I could sleep, but I know I won't. My mind is too busy turning over the events of the past few hours, the vision of Laurel climbing into the back of a car etched on my brain. As I wait for the laptop, my mobile buzzes. It's Jess. Again. She's messaged several times since I left her, and I can't ignore her any longer.

'Jess?'

'Anna. Just wanted to check you're OK? This morning was pretty emotional.' *Understatement of the year.*

'I'm OK. Well . . . you know.'

'I'm guessing it wasn't Laurel then?'

'No. It wasn't. I made a mistake, a massive one.' I close my eyes, thinking of that blonde head bobbing in the window of the caravan. I'd been so sure.

'Have you been on Facebook today?' Jess asks, a note of trepidation creeping into her voice.

'Not yet. Why?' I pull the laptop back towards me and log into my Facebook page. 'Oh.' The first thing that comes up in my timeline is a page entitled 'FIND LAUREL JESSOP'. I click on the page and Laurel's face fills my screen. My heart does a little double skip in my chest as I start to read the opening post.

'Jess, who did this? Was it you?'

'No, it was Cheryl Smythe. She's been rather busy since yesterday evening, don't you think?' I can picture Jess rolling her eyes as she speaks.

'Do you think this will help?' I am scrolling down the page, scanning my eyes over the posts. They are all incredibly supportive, some offering ideas as to what may have happened to Laurel, others suggesting places to search. There is a post from eight o'clock this morning, from Cheryl, informing people that the school hall will be the main point of contact for all search volunteers – which explains why it had been so busy this morning.

'It can't do any harm, can it?' Jess says. 'I mean, look at how social media has worked before. Lots of people have been found thanks to thousands of others all sharing the same image. I just thought that I should let you know in case Fran hasn't seen it yet.'

I don't know how Fran will react to the page.

'Thanks, Jess.' I hang up, and push myself to my feet, my stomach rumbling. It's almost mid-afternoon and I haven't eaten since one of Pete the Meat's dodgy barbecue burgers last night, and despite feeling as though I could never feel hungry again, my stomach is telling me otherwise. Deciding to make a few rounds of sandwiches – as far as I know neither Fran nor Dominic have eaten today either – I head into the kitchen, only to find Dominic, Fran and Kelly all sitting at the kitchen table. There is no sign of DS Wright and I assume she's gone back to the investigation.

'Sorry, am I interrupting?' I say, glancing from one person to the next and wondering if I should head back up to my room, even though I desperately what to hear what is being said.

'Not at all.' Kelly gives me a brief smile. 'Now, as DS Wright was saying earlier, we are still pursuing the information we have been given regarding the SUV, and news of Laurel's disappearance has reached the national press. We're not too sure who contacted them, but it was to be expected in a situation like this.' A knife twists in my chest at hearing Laurel referred to as a *situation* and my eyes flick towards Fran, who sits blank-faced, her hands clasped together on the table in front of her. 'We believe that our next course of action should be to hold a press conference to answer questions, to keep the press on our side.'

'Ah, no,' Dominic says, raising one hand. 'I don't think so. I don't want . . . I don't think a press conference is a good idea.'

'What?' Fran says, her eyes wide. 'Why not, Dom? Don't you want to find Laurel?'

'Of course I do,' Dominic snaps, 'but you know what happens with a press conference?' He turns to Kelly, who sits there calmly, waiting. 'You know, don't you? They'll all be scrutinising us! They'll be saying that we had something to do with it!'

'Don't be so ridiculous. No one would think that. We have to do it, Dom, if it means that we can get Laurel back.' Fran taps her fingers on the table top, long nails scratching at the wooden surface, a noise that sets my teeth on edge.

'Look at all the other times it's happened!' Dominic shouts. 'All the other criminals who stood there on television, telling the world to *please, just give their little princess back*, and then all the time it was them!' His voice breaks, and he slumps back down into the chair. 'I don't want that, Fran. I don't want people thinking we're guilty of something we're not.'

'Dominic,' Kelly lays her hand gently on his, 'I promise you, people don't think like that. This is the best chance we have of keeping the press on side, and we'll only reveal the things that we need to right now.'

The doorbell gives its piercing ring, making all of us jump. I pull away from where I lean against the kitchen counter. 'I'll get it.' There is a dark silhouette in the glass as I approach the door, and when I pull it open I am stunned to hear a cacophony of voices, flashbulbs going off in my face, and more than one iPhone shoved under my nose as questions are shouted at me, relentlessly one after the other.

'When was the last time you saw Laurel?'

'Who are you to the family?'

'Can we speak with Fran and Dominic?'

The press has arrived.

CHAPTER 7

Pushing open the door to the school hall I slide my way in, grabbing the first available seat at a table tucked into the corner. It's busy, the air buzzing with conversation as volunteers bustle about, some of them wearing T-shirts with Laurel's face on, and obviously, the talk is all of the same topic. *Laurel.*

It was a complicated mission to get here this morning, one which involved creeping along the path that runs through the back garden and sliding through the battered wooden gate at the end, cap pulled down low over my forehead so that the press didn't see me. My heart skips as I think about the potential fallout if a picture of me appears on the front page of a national newspaper. Thankfully none of the hurried snaps they took on Sunday evening as I opened the door made it to the pages of the newspapers. It'll be OK. I've changed my hair, lost weight. I'm barely recognisable as the old me anymore. That's what I tell myself anyway, but you can never be too careful.

Hence that's why I am sitting on my own in the school hall, the hub of the volunteer search centre, instead of accompanying Dominic and Fran to the television appeal. Fran protested at first when I said I didn't think I should be there. My mouth went dry with panic that she would demand an explanation as to why I didn't want to go, but

I was forgetting that the old Fran isn't here anymore, that we're dealing with this new, raw, broken Fran. She gave in almost immediately, too tired or too fragile to argue when Dominic agreed that I should stay home.

So, I watched them both leave this morning from the window, peering out from the between the blinds as Dominic chivalrously helped Fran into a waiting unmarked car, as DS Wright got into the driver's seat, as they drove away towards the main road – the few greedy, grasping press who haven't already left for the appeal chasing after them – before hiding myself away in here.

I keep my head down as I wait for the appeal to start, but it doesn't stop someone hovering in the periphery of my vision, and I look up to see the woman from before. Ruth, I think she said her name was. She stands to one side of me, close enough that I can smell soap on her skin, a harsh carbolic scent.

'Hello,' she says in a hushed voice, 'are you here to watch the appeal?' She doesn't wait for me to respond before she carries on talking. 'Fran looks ever so frail, doesn't she? I saw her getting in the car this morning. I hope she's eating enough, I did send her a few text messages, but she hasn't replied yet. But I'm cooking lasagne when I get home and I'll bring it over. She needs to keep her strength up, you know. It's a terrible feeling, losing someone like this. Losing a child.' Her words tumble out one after the other, as if she is worried I'll stop her from speaking before she's said all she wants to say. *Fran must know her from somewhere.*

Someone makes a shushing noise, as Fran's face fills the huge projector screen that has been wheeled into the hall, a nameless parent hooking up their laptop so we can all watch the appeal. Her eyes are bloodshot and her cheeks are pale, apart from two spots of colour that flare high on each. The woman is right, she does look frail. I turn to agree, but she has moved off, across to the other side of the hall. The man sat behind the laptop fiddles with the keys, turning up the volume, and the newscaster's voice fills the hall.

'... *not seen since Saturday evening, at the annual fireworks event hosted by the Oxbury Primary School. Police are searching ...*'

Don't they say the first twenty-four hours are the most important in a police investigation? That in the case of child abduction if the child isn't found within three hours there's a higher risk of harm? It's Wednesday now, and over seventy-two hours since anyone last saw Laurel. I close my eyes and wish I'd waited at home to watch the appeal, instead of out here, but the thought of sitting alone in that chilly, too-bright house, with none of the warmth that usually fills it, had made me want to cry and I had to get out. There is an essence, a vibe, that is missing now Laurel isn't there, something that only Laurel brings. Now, sweat prickles at the back of my neck, as the air in the hall feels thick and stifling, and I feel scrutinised by the people around me, even though I know it's probably all in my head. *But I've been here before, haven't I? Watched by every member of the public, opinions forming before they even know the truth, making their decisions based on the lies printed by the media, guilt forming a hard ball in my stomach.* I straighten up in my chair, as if trying to convince myself that this time it's different.

'Still managed to put her make-up on,' a woman sitting behind me sniffs to her companion under her breath.

I bite my tongue hard, in order not to say anything – I should have known that some will only be here to find out what's going on; after all, that's only human nature, isn't it? And, of course, people will be judging Fran and Dominic (*and you,* a spiteful voice whispers in the back of my mind) – look at how we all jumped on Kate and Gerry McCann – and the fact that Fran has managed to smear a slick of palest pink lipstick over her mouth and a smudge of concealer under each eye will only make people judge her even harder. If you knew her, I think viciously, internally, if you knew her then you'd see the black circles under her eyes that push through the thin layer of concealer, you'd see the new tiny lines at the corners of her eyes and alongside her mouth. The force with which I think these thoughts is a surprise to me, I never would have believed that I could have felt protective over Fran – sharp, spiky, demanding Fran.

Someone shushes, and a hush settles over the hall as we all strain to hear the appeal. On screen, Fran and Dominic sit behind a table, their hands clasped tightly together. Fran sits up rigidly in her chair, her mouth a grim slash carved into her porcelain white skin. DI Dove leads the appeal, his voice thick and dark like hot rum, as he goes over Fran's story of the events of Saturday night. My heart catches in my throat as he talks about Laurel, what she was wearing, where she was last seen. It feels like forever but is realistically only a few minutes before Dominic begins to speak.

'Please,' his voice is scratchy, but he almost seems relaxed compared to Fran, whose shoulders are somewhere up around her ears. 'If anyone has seen Laurel, please, please contact the police. If you think you might have seen something, anything, no matter how insignificant . . . it might not seem like anything much, but it might just bring our little princess home to us.'

'Someone must know something.' Fran's eyes are dry, but her voice is thick with tears. Her hands squeeze tightly around the soft toy she holds – one I recognise as Bom, a tired, worn-out tiger that has seen better days. Laurel has had it since she was born, and she refuses to sleep without it. I swallow down the lump in my throat. How has Laurel slept without Bom for the past two nights? 'Someone must know where she is.' She glances away from the camera, before pressing a tissue to her mouth as if to hold in a sob.

DI Dove holds up a hand as a buzz of chatter begins, the press already itching to ask their questions.

'Yes?' DI Dove points and a disembodied voice floats from somewhere off screen.

'Will you be extending the search area now beyond the immediate vicinity of where Laurel was last seen?'

'We will. We have been made aware of some information that may help us to narrow down a route that whoever took Laurel may have taken.'

'Do you have any names?' someone shouts out, and the entire school hall seems to hold its breath. I feel as though I haven't taken a full breath myself since Fran and Dominic took their seats in front of the press. I am so relieved that I stood my ground.

'When we have a name that we can release, we'll let you know. One more question,' DI Dove says sternly, taking a quick glance towards Fran and Dominic. Dominic seems to be OK, holding his own although his jaw is tense, but

Fran looks fragile. She rearranges her features, trying to hide her emotion as best she can, and I wonder if she's calling into play her drama training in an attempt to hold things together. Despite her best efforts, her face has lost any colour it might have had, leaving her cheeks a now familiar chalky white, her dark fringe lying starkly against her forehead. The tiny slick of pale lip gloss she smeared on glistens on her mouth as she moves her head slightly, to glance at whoever is off screen. Kelly, I presume, there to give support.

'Did you have anything to do with your daughter's disappearance?'

The question is asked, and the room falls silent. I feel light-headed, the room swaying slightly around me. I pull at the scarf, loosening it away from my hot skin.

'Shiiiittttt,' a young lad in a bright yellow high-viz jacket whispers under his breath as he leans against a table, coffee in one hand, a poster bearing Laurel's face in the other. On screen, the room erupts, as Dominic gets to his feet.

'Are you kidding me?' He shoves his chair back. DI Dove frowns before following suit. Fran says nothing, only blinks as her façade cracks and tears spill over her cheeks. She presses the tissue to her mouth again, Bom lying limply in the other hand.

'Enough.' Dove raises his hand, as Kelly appears on screen to usher Fran and Dominic away from the baying press. 'No more questions. The appeal is over.' He turns and follows Fran and Dominic from the room and the screen cuts back to the anchor in the newsroom. There is a shocked silence that fills the hall for just a few moments, before the conversation resumes, although more quietly than before.

Feeling sick, I sit back in my chair, poking a finger into the leftover foam in the bottom of my coffee cup. I don't want to go home now, not after that, even though I know it will be a while before the Jessops return. The atmosphere in the house will be even more suffocating, especially as Dominic didn't want to do the appeal in the first place.

'Do you mind if I sit here?' A voice rouses me from my thoughts and I look up to see a tall, fair-haired woman standing in front of me.

'Sure. I'm going anyway.' I shrug and lean down to pick up my bag. I'll go for a walk, leave it a while before I head back to the house.

'Don't go on my account,' she smiles at me, and I think I recognise her from somewhere. 'It's raining hard out there. There's plenty of room for both of us.' I glance out of the window and she's right. Rain streams down the glass, obscuring the small groups of people headed back out to resume the search for Laurel. It's either go straight home or get soaked.

'OK.' I sink back down into my chair and pick up my phone, hoping she'll get the hint. She doesn't.

'God, it's awful, isn't it?' she says, gesturing towards the projector screen. The anchor is still talking, Laurel's photo in a tiny square next to her head. 'You just can't imagine it.'

'No,' I say, blandly, still staring at my phone, scrolling through the messages from Jess (*'Where r u? Are u going to the appeal? I am at home if u want to watch here* ☺ *let me no ur ok'*), and from a couple of the other nannies from the toddler group I used to take Laurel to (*'So sorry Anna,*

72

call if you need anything. Anna, this is Beth, pls let me know if I can help in any way'), and others that share the same underlying tone – *thank goodness it wasn't* me *this happened to.* The woman is still talking, despite my giving her the cold shoulder. If she carries on, I'll have to leave.

'I think I recognise him, you know? The dad?' She pauses, one hand on her chin, as she looks up at the screen again, and realisation starts to dawn.

'You're a bloody journalist, aren't you?' I say, anger bubbling up in my chest. 'How dare you? Don't you think we've got enough to deal with without you lot snooping around, pretending to be friendly?' I get up and grab my bag, throwing it over my shoulder.

'No, wait!' she says. She's taller than me, and she stands so that I'd have to force my way past her if I want to go. 'I'm not a journalist, I swear. Please, sit down.'

I pause, wavering. I really don't want to leave yet, not with the rain still pouring and the atmosphere at home. It's like she can tell that I'm not sure, as she smiles, showing off perfectly even white teeth.

'Please,' she says again. I lower myself back down into the chair, warily. 'Let me get you another coffee – just to say sorry for taking your table, and making you think . . . you know.'

'OK.' I nod, and she hurries over to the urn, returning quickly with another cup of vile, lukewarm coffee.

'I'm not a journalist, I promise,' she says, as she sips at her drink, wincing slightly at the taste. 'It's . . . it's horrifying, isn't it? I'm sure I recognise the father from my school days – Dominic, isn't it? It's scary to think that this could happen to someone you know.'

'Yes. It's terrifying,' I agree, not wanting to elaborate on anything. I'm not sure if she realises I'm Laurel's nanny. 'For all the community.'

'He was always very smart at school,' she goes on, 'one of the clever ones. He was in my year, but I didn't really know him. I didn't know he'd moved here.'

'Why would you?' I ask, curious now, at meeting someone who knew Dominic as a child.

'Oh, you know. This is a small community, believe it or not. No different to living in a village. Most people know most things, if you get what I mean.'

That's not the impression I've had of Oxbury in the three years I've lived here. I've had the impression that everyone keeps to themselves where possible, unless something really juicy happens, then everyone is fair game. I keep my mouth shut.

'You're the nanny, aren't you? I saw you at the school, on Sunday morning. When they were searching for Laurel.' So, she does know. The woman sitting across from me doesn't meet my eyes. 'Sorry – I probably should have said.'

'And you're definitely not a journalist?' I raise my eyebrows disbelievingly.

'No! God, no.' She gives a small laugh. 'Would that I had such an exciting job as that. I work in the library! No, I remember Dom from school, and I just wanted to check in, I suppose. I'm Ella, by the way. I used to live around here . . . God, years ago, I've only recently moved back to the area myself. I . . . I lost a child before and I know how excruciating the pain can be.' Her brown eyes cloud over and she blinks rapidly.

'I'm sorry,' I say, my skin prickling uncomfortably. What can you say to that?

'How is Dom?' she says, dabbing at her eyes briefly.

'As well as can be expected.'

'I bet Laurel is a lovely little thing, isn't she?' She laughs. 'I can well imagine her, just like Dom. How are Dom and Fran holding up as a couple?'

'She is lovely,' I say, then, 'Um . . . OK, I guess.' I don't mention the snippy, angry comments that are flying backwards and forwards between them, the heavy aura of tension that fills the room when they are both there together. 'Why don't you send a card or something? I'm sure Dominic would appreciate hearing from an old friend.'

'I don't think so,' she shakes her head, 'I don't think Dom would even remember me. Gosh, it's almost two o'clock. I'm so sorry, I have to dash. Meeting.' She rolls her eyes and necks the last of her coffee. 'Nice to meet you, Anna.'

'Wait—' I call out. 'Don't you want to . . . ?' But she doesn't hear me, hurrying away out into the rain, her hair flying out in a golden sheet behind her.

CHAPTER 8

Rather than return home, I stay out to help staple laminated posters of Laurel to trees and telegraph poles all around the village, rain streaming down my hair and soaking through my coat and jumper to my skin. Staying out to put up posters makes me feel as though I am doing some good, but I also feel the eyes of others on me all the time, judging me, whispering the same questions I ask myself over and over. *Why didn't she keep an eye on her? Why didn't she keep her with her? Would you really let a little tot like that run off into a crowd?* But is it worse than going back to a house that isn't a home — even less so now that Laurel isn't there — to rattle around, trying to keep busy even though there isn't anything to do but attempt to avoid Fran's blank stare, and Dominic's simmering anger at the police? So I staple, unfold, staple, unfold on repeat, doing my best to avoid looking at Laurel's face on the posters. Wishing I could tell her how sorry I am, how I wish I could turn back the clock to that night. I'd never take my eyes off her for a second.

As I pass Mr Snow's house at the end of the lane, the posters all gone and my hands crippled with cold, he opens the front door and calls out to me.

'Anna!'

I stop, fumbling with the gate latch to let myself into his garden, but he waves me away.

'Stay there – I'll come to you,' he calls, leaning behind the door to pull out an umbrella before ambling up the path towards me. 'Filthy weather,' he says as he reaches the gate, holding the umbrella so that it covers both of us. 'How are things?'

'Oh, you know.' I shrug, conscious of the rain that drips down my neck from the prongs of the umbrella. 'No sign of Laurel yet. It's only been four days but it feels like a long time since Saturday.'

'Oh dear. Oh, dear me, that poor girl,' Mr Snow sighs, his mouth turned down. 'I watched the appeal earlier today. Her poor parents. I wish I could do more to help, but . . . I'm not as young as I was.' He gives a half-hearted laugh, and I nod sympathetically, even though he doesn't seem that old, not really.

'Everyone is being more than helpful. But thank you.'

'I remember my daughter being Laurel's age, you know. Precious, they are, when they're young – so inquisitive. Now she spends most of her time worrying about me.' His eyes light up, and he fumbles in his pocket, and I worry for a moment that he's going to pull out a photograph or something that he'll expect me to pore over, but it's only a hanky that he presses to his mouth. 'These days . . .' he coughs into the hanky and my stomach turns slightly, 'you can never be too careful, Anna. You never know who's out there. Never take your eyes off them for a second.'

I am drenched by the time I arrive back at the house almost three hours later, but at least I feel as though I have done something useful today, even if nothing comes of it. It's getting dark and cold and there is a hint of bonfire smoke on the air – a smell that I think now will forever make my stomach flip over and nausea rise in my throat. As I slide my key into the lock and take off my soggy trainers in the hallway, I can feel the row in the air. Something thick and dark and close enough to touch, and although there is no sign of Fran and Dominic, it's clear they are home and things aren't good.

If I was asked before any of this happened if Fran and Dominic had a good relationship I don't know how I would respond. On the surface, everything is perfect – when they do go out as a couple, everyone comments on how good they look together, how wonderful they are as parents – Jess frequently tells me how Claire says her husband Tom should be more like Dominic. They are the envy of everyone in Oxbury. They have it all – the beautiful daughter, nice house, fabulous careers, the occasional mention in the society pages.

Fran is often out in the evenings, working late in shows, then when she is home, she tries to spend a reasonable amount of time with Laurel, but things often get in the way. Things that she could ignore if she really wanted to. But if Fran is out a lot then Dominic is ten times worse – always working, always at the hospital, prioritising sick patients over his own wife and child, something that comes up time and again in arguments.

At first I used to think Fran was being a bitch, begrudging Dominic time with his patients, but I've since learned that it's not the hospital that she has a problem with. Fran is never one hundred per cent convinced that Dominic is where he says he is (namely at work), her jealousy rising to the surface over any little thing, and she is *so* obsessed by money sometimes, it's unreal. They don't want for anything and she has more than enough, but she is still frugal, bollocking me if I buy the more expensive brands of cereal for Laurel, as if I'm going to waste all their money and leave her destitute.

That said, Laurel never goes without. She gets everything she needs – materially, anyway – Fran loves nothing more than to dress her up in designer clothes that I then have to make sure stay clean. Not easy when Laurel would rather be outside playing in the garden in a pair of old jogging bottoms. It would just be nice if the three of them could spend more quality time together, without the threat of a row about to start, or the bitter aftertaste of one that has been resolved. But I suppose that's where I come in – it's my job to give Laurel a bit of stability, a routine. To reassure her that there is someone who will always be there.

I am the one who reads to Laurel before bed, baths her, sings songs to her in an attempt to drown out the angry, bitter words that float up the stairs. I am the one that teaches her to tie her shoelaces and encourages her to try new foods, all while Fran and Dominic are at work or having half whispered arguments in the kitchen about where he has been. Of the pair of them, Fran is the high maintenance one and I would say Dominic is more relaxed, less inclined to lose his temper – up until Sunday morning anyway, I haven't forgotten the way his fingers dug into my arms – but they rub along well together most of the time. So, on the surface, yes, they have a wonderful relationship, but sometimes, looking deeper, it's not all as rosy as it seems and there are times, more than usual recently, when Laurel and I come home to a house thick with spite and bitter words. Today it seems, even after the events of the past few days, things are still the same.

I creep up the stairs, not wanting Fran to hear me and call me into whichever room they've argued in. I just want to get changed into dry clothes and try to sleep for an hour or two, exhaustion having caught up with me. Managing to get into my room unseen, I pull on clean sweatpants and a hoody, a pair of thick socks to warm my feet, when my mobile alerts me to someone wanting to FaceTime me. I pause, head half in, half out of the hoody, before pulling it over my head and snatching up the phone before the ringtone alerts Fran to my presence.

'Hello?' I swipe to answer, hurriedly smoothing my hair back into place.

'Hello? Is that you, love?' My mother's face appears on the screen and my heart speeds up in my chest. Why is she calling me now?

'Errr . . . yes, it's me. How are you?' Sitting on the edge of the bed I angle the screen so that the blank magnolia wall is behind me. None of the press on the doorstep managed to catch me, did they? I've tried so hard to keep a low profile.

'Oh, you know. The usual.' She gives a little sniff and there is a pause while she waits for me to ask what the problem is. I don't ask. 'What have you been up to?'

'Not a lot,' I say, glancing at my watch. Let's hope she's not in for the long haul. 'Just working mostly.'

'Have you seen what's happened?' A note of sadness creeps into her voice. 'That little girl in Surrey . . . she's gone missing, you know. Out with her mother, she takes her eye off her for one minute and that's it, she's gone.' My heart bangs in my chest, and I have to take a deep breath before I can speak.

'I haven't seen it, Mum,' I lie, convinced that lightning will strike me at any minute. 'It hasn't reached up here yet.'

'Oh, well, good,' she says, 'It's not a nice story, but we'll simply have to hope for a happy ending. Anyway . . .' She pauses, and I close my eyes for a brief moment, seeing the house in Scotland, the blood on the flagstone floor, the way it had soaked into my hands, embedding the skin around my nails, and how I'd had to scrub until my hands were sore to get it out.

'You still there? I said, how's the weather up with you?'

Pulling myself back to the present I let out a silent whoosh of relief. 'Getting cold now. They think maybe it might snow next week.' I cross my fingers and hope she doesn't check the weather forecast. 'But it's OK. We're not so busy now the holiday season is over.'

'Will you be coming home for Christmas?' she asks, and I can still hear it, that little rise in her voice that tells me she doesn't really want me there, not after what happened. I'm not the daughter she can boast about to the neighbours, not any more.

'I doubt it, Mum. I'm sorry – Ewan has already invited me to spend Christmas with him and his family. He is the boss so I kind of had to say yes . . .' I trail off, trying to inject at least a tiny bit of disappointment into my voice.

'Don't worry, love. Of course, you should stay there! Who wouldn't prefer a white Christmas up north, over cold and grey Brighton? Ring me on the day, when you get up.'

I make reassuring noises and hang up before she does, and flop back onto the bed, puffing my hair out of my eyes. It's all OK – for now. She still thinks I'm in Scotland. I just have to keep it that way.

I wake with a jolt a short while later, the words, *it's your fault,* ringing in my ears, as though some unseen person had leaned over me in my sleep, whispering them into my ear. Thirst scratches at the back of my throat and my mouth is furred and dry, sweat coating my skin. I fell asleep without meaning to, my dreams full of Scotland and of Laurel, me chasing her along the slippery, wet rocks alongside Dochart Falls, trying to catch up to her before I lost her. There is salt on my lips when I run my tongue over them, and I realise I must have cried in my sleep, my eyes feeling heavy and sore. I tug off the hot, woolly socks that itch at my ankles, and after rinsing my face with cold water, I head downstairs, desperate for a tall glass of water – and to see if Kelly has any news following the appeal. Voices reach me before I manage to get to the kitchen and I pause in the dimly lit hallway, the wooden floor cool against my bare feet.

'Why though, Dominic?' Fran is saying, and as I peep through a crack in the doorway I can see her pacing backwards and forwards across the kitchen floor, a glass of white wine in her hand. She seems agitated as she takes a furious sip.

'Jesus, Fran . . .' Dominic pushes a hand through his hair in a well-worn gesture, 'why can't you just drop it? It's not important in the scheme of things . . . you do realise our daughter is missing?'

'Do *I* realise?' There is an ugly sneering tone in Fran's voice. 'Of course I bloody realise, Dominic. This is why this is important! Why can't you just tell the truth?'

82

I stand stock still.

'I told you, I am telling the truth. Why would I lie? Do you think I don't want Laurel to be found? Seriously, Fran, you're even more fucked up than I thought you were.' I hear the fridge door slam shut, and the glug as it sounds as though more wine is poured.

'I know you weren't at the hospital on Saturday night, Dominic.' Pure hate fills Fran's voice. 'Maybe I should call Pamela, and see where she was? Eh? Maybe *that* is closer to the truth.'

'For fuck's sake, Fran, will you *shut up*.' Through the crack in the door I see him stride towards Fran and grab her by the upper arms, causing her glass to fall and smash on the kitchen tiles. He thrusts his face close to hers, his cheeks flushing a violent red, spittle flying from his mouth as he shouts into her shocked face.

I am frozen by what I see, appalled by this ugly, violent side to Dominic, one that jars with the Dominic I thought I knew. I hover, one hand pressed to my mouth, unsure whether to burst into the kitchen and put a stop to it when the slam of the front door makes me jump and I turn to see Kelly struggling through the doorway, her arms full of plastic bags that are full, if the smell is anything to go by, of takeaway curry. I move towards her and grab a bag from her.

'Hey, Kelly,' I say in a voice loud enough to alert Fran and Dominic to her presence, 'this smells lovely!' I push through into the kitchen where Fran and Dominic stand on either side of the table, barely looking at each other. Fran's face is white and pinched, her nostrils flaring as she breathes deeply, her hands rubbing absently at the tops of her arms. 'Kelly brought some food home,' I say, stupidly.

'Lovely.' Dominic shoves his hands into his pockets, as Fran moves to the cupboard under the sink to get out a dustpan and brush.

'Here, I'll do that,' I say, gently nudging her to one side.

'Thank you.' She gives me a wan smile and turns to Kelly. 'I'm not terribly hungry, Kelly. Thank you, though. I might . . .' She waves a hand towards the kitchen door and Kelly nods.

'Of course, Fran. I'll save you something for later.' Kelly starts to bustle around the kitchen, pulling out plates and serving out dollops of rice as I finish sweeping the floor. I don't know how she hasn't picked up on the tense atmosphere that fills the kitchen; Dominic's violence still seems to reverberate around the room.

There is a muted buzz as Fran's phone on the counter lights up with the glow of an incoming text message, and I lean over and pick it up. I catch the first line of the text, under an unknown number, words of sympathy from someone.

'I might go and check on her,' I say, holding up the phone and avoiding Dominic's gaze as he looks up at me from the table, a poppadom crumbled into a thousand tiny pieces between his fingers. He looks tired and drained, and despite what I just witnessed, I can't help but feel a twinge of sympathy for him.

Upstairs, Fran sits on the edge of Laurel's bed, Bom gripped tightly in one hand. I go to sit next to her, a waft of Laurel's scent rising up as I perch on the duvet.

'You left your phone downstairs,' I say, passing it to her.

She takes the phone, swiping up and running her eyes over the text message. 'Another do-gooder, wanting to wish us well,' she sighs, 'some woman keeps messaging me, asking what she can do to help. How about *get my daughter back for me*?' She throws the phone down on to the bed and sniffs, blinking hard.

'You OK?' I say, tucking my fingers in a loose curl of fabric in the duvet.

'Just fucking dandy,' Fran says, her cut-glass accent slipping slightly. There is an edge to her voice, and who can blame her? 'I can't wait for this to be over.'

I look at her in horror, not sure if she realises what she's said, the way it could be interpreted.

'I mean, I just want her back,' she rephrases it, makes it easier to hear. 'I don't want her out there, without me. Without everything that she knows. I want her in her own bed at night, where I can go in and watch her sleeping any time I like. I want to be able to go to her when she calls me. I want our lives back to normal. And I want that *fucking* woman out of my house!' Her voice rises, filling the tiny room, bouncing off the mural-covered walls.

'Woman?' I say, not quite understanding. I heard her refer to Pamela, Dominic's ex, but she hasn't been here, has she?

'Kelly,' she spits out, her face contorting with venom. 'The so-called FLO. Who seems to not have a clue about anything except how to spy on people. I mean, what has she actually done? Nothing. Just snooped around listening in on people's conversations and going through our things. I found her in here earlier, looking through Laurel's chest of drawers.'

'She's only trying to help,' I say gently, still unsure of how to deal with this new, different Fran. 'It's her job, you know that.'

'Yes. Yes, I do, and I am grateful really, I just can't help thinking that things like this . . . they don't happen to people like us.' Fran looks up at me, blinking as her eyes fill with tears. 'I ask myself, what if I hadn't gone to the loo? To get drinks? What if I'd held her hand the whole night? She wouldn't have disappeared then.'

I consider how best to respond when all I can think is, *Me too! I feel exactly the same – why didn't I keep my eyes on her instead of just assuming she caught you up?* Before I can speak, a light tap comes at the door and it swings open to reveal Kelly, holding a cup of tea.

'I brought you this,' she holds it out to Fran, her expression neutral, and I realise that Fran is probably right, she must have heard everything Fran just said from the other side of the door. Fran takes the mug without a word, as I sit there, dumb.

'DS Wright is here,' Kelly turns back as she reaches the door. 'She wants to see you.'

Fran and I file downstairs in Kelly's wake, and I'm guessing that Fran feels as anxious as I do. Have they found something? More importantly, have they found Laurel? I find my hands are shaking as I follow Fran into the sitting room and perch awkwardly on the edge of the armchair.

'What is it?' Fran's voice is urgent, her hands folding together over and over in a wringing motion. Despite their row, Dominic moves closer to her, putting his arm around her shoulder.

'We don't have any further information for you – we haven't found Laurel yet. I should make that clear before we start. I'd like to request your permission to remove some of Laurel's belongings from the house, only for a short while,' DS Wright says in a low voice, before dabbing at her forehead with the back of her hand. It is abnormally warm in here. 'We need a toothbrush, hairbrush, something that contains Laurel's DNA – do you have something like that?'

'Yes,' Dominic says, after Fran just stares at her for a moment, seemingly unable to speak. 'Yes, her hairbrush is upstairs, but why? If you're telling us that you haven't found Laurel yet, why do you need her DNA?'

DS Wright is silent for a moment as if gathering her thoughts together, and I realise that she doesn't want to convey what she has to tell us. She's awkward, uncomfortable, a tense vibe filling the air and all of a sudden, I remember that feeling from before – that cold, sick sense of dread that fingered its way up my spine, as I heard the thud, then the deafening silence, punctuated with all that blood, a deep crimson stain spreading out across the cold, grey floor. I take a deep breath, willing the dizziness to leave me before I need to put my head between my knees.

'There are a number of footprints in the mud surrounding the lake area at the back of the field where the event was held last Saturday. These might be old – I have someone out there casting whatever prints they can – but it does seem as though there has been some activity in that area. So, with that in mind . . .' she trails off for a second and I tuck my shaking hands under my thighs out of sight, 'we're going to dredge the lake.'

CHAPTER 9

Two days later, a bitter wind bites into my cheeks as I stand alongside Fran and Dominic, behind the blue police tape that keeps us clear of the lake edge. I see Jessika behind the cordon at the edge of the woods, just as my phone flashes with a message from her – '*Behind police tape if you need me* ☺' – and as I raise my eyes to her face, she lifts a hand in a tiny wave. I slide my phone back into my pocket without responding, the smiley face emoji grating on my nerves even though I know she only means to give her support.

The press are lined up further along, and I pull my hat down low over my face, but they aren't interested in me. They're not even interested in Fran and Dominic right now – all eyes are on the lake and what might come out of it. DI Dove didn't want us here – in fact, he told us in no uncertain terms to stay at home – but as the dredging dragged into a second day, Dominic wouldn't have it, despite Fran begging him to stay with her. In the end, we all filed out of the house together this morning, and now we've been standing here in the freezing, damp November air for hours, waiting, waiting, waiting.

A movement out of the corner of my eye distracts me from the grey, flat water of the lake and I turn my head to see the mousy woman from the school step off the path and cross the churned-up, muddy grass towards us. I glance at Fran, who stands a few feet away, her arms folded across her body, eyes scanning the water, and step away, wanting to stop the woman before she reaches them. The Jessops don't need a stranger hassling them, not right now.

'How are they?' Without a word of greeting, the woman nods towards the Jessops.

'How do you think?' I say, frowning at her. She wears a headscarf over her mousy brown hair, a bulky black jacket, and paint-flecked jeans tucked into filthy black wellies. 'Was there something I could help you with?'

'I just wanted to show some support,' she says, 'it's a difficult time for them.'

I nod my head. 'Yes, it is. I'm sure they'll be very grateful. I've seen you at the school before, haven't I?' I'm curious about this woman – I'm sure I've seen her many times when I've collected Laurel, but I simply can't picture which child is hers.

'Yes, my . . .' her voice is croaky, and she stops to clear her throat, 'my daughter went there. I still help out on the PTA sometimes.'

That explains why I can't place her as a mother – her daughter must be at least eleven if she's already left the school. She must be dedicated to Oxbury Primary if she's still willing to be on the PTA.

'I'm Anna,' I say, 'Laurel's nanny.'

'I know who you are.' Her tone is short, and I look at her in surprise. 'I mean . . . I've seen you with Laurel before. I didn't introduce myself properly. I'm Ruth.' She holds out a hand, with short, slightly grubby fingernails and I have to force myself to take it. I give it a brief shake and then drop it, resisting the urge to wipe my hands on my trousers. 'This is so heartbreaking, isn't it? I went to drama school with Fran briefly, years ago, not that I'm sure she'll remember me.' I have to force myself not to raise my eyebrows at this news – compared to Fran, Ruth doesn't seem the drama school type at all. I realise she is still speaking. 'Is there anything I can do for them?' Ruth nods again in Fran and Dominic's direction.

'I don't think there's anything any of us can do,' I say, sadly, fighting back the knot in my throat as I turn back to look at the lake. The police team are crowded at the water's edge, while the Jessops are still held back by the crime tape. Fran's face seems oddly calm and I wonder if she took something. I know she keeps sleeping tablets in her bathroom cabinet, and I'm pretty sure I saw a Valium bottle in there once when I was looking for a spare bottle of Calpol.

'Well, let me know if I can help in any way. I have texted Fran but she hasn't replied. Maybe I'll drop off a casserole or something. I can't imagine any of you feel like cooking.' Ruth lays her grubby hand on my arm and I give her a small nod, even though I doubt we'll touch any food she brings over – none of us have an appetite. She's a little strange, but she seems harmless enough, and of course she's interested in what's happening, especially if she really does know Fran from years ago. It makes it all seem a little closer to home when something like this happens to someone you know. Laurel's disappearance has rocked the whole community. Peering past her, I catch sight of a mane of honey-blonde hair, as the woman from the school hall I met on the day of the appeal is being held back by Kelly.

'Of course, that would be . . . great. I have to go, I'm sorry.' I flash her a quick smile before hurrying over to where Kelly holds up a hand, clearly telling Ella she can't go any further. Lord knows how Ruth made it past her.

'It's OK, Kelly,' I say, 'I know her.' Kelly reluctantly stands to one side, telling me that I can speak to her here, but she's to go no further.

'Hi,' I say, pleased to see her, despite the circumstances. 'What are you doing here?'

'God, I look like I'm snooping again, don't I?' she says, pulling a face. 'I heard what was happening . . . it's . . . well, everyone seems to know what's going on.' She looks down at her shoes, and as I peer past her shoulder I see she's right – word has got out that the police are dredging the lake and there are people starting to congregate on the edge of the woods, the closest they can get without being moved on. I think I catch a glimpse of Mr Snow standing at the edge of the cordon, his black umbrella still in hand.

'I just wanted to see how Dom was holding up.'

I look over my shoulder to where he paces along the restricted tape line, one hand raised to run through his hair, before he scrubs his hands over his face. Fran stands apart from him, as if frozen, still staring into the water, her face a blank mask. 'We need to get this part over. I can't bear to think of Laurel being in that water.' Just the very thought of it makes my blood turn to ice in my veins.

'She won't be in there, she can't be,' my new friend says positively, one hand shooting out to grip mine, squeezing my fingers tightly in hers.

'How can you be so sure?' I ask, feeling the familiar hot burn that signals tears behind my eyes again. I wish,

91

for the millionth time, that I'd kept Laurel in my eyeline that night.

'I can't be. But if we can all hope . . .' she says simply, before she freezes at something over my shoulder. I turn to see Fran clinging to Dominic as DI Dove approaches them. Without thinking I turn and run across the thick mud, almost falling in my haste to hear what has been found. If Laurel is in that dark, silty water.

'What is it?' I gasp. 'Did you find something?'

'She's not in there,' Fran says, tears in her eyes, her whole body shaking. 'Oh, Anna, they've looked and she's not in the water.'

'Thank God.' I put my hands over my eyes, sucking in air to try and calm my racing heart. *Thank God*. I look over to the trees to where Ella stands, but no one is there.

We head back to the house in silence, me walking a little way behind in an attempt to avoid any cameras, as the press take some final snaps of Fran and Dominic. As we leave, Jessika comes over and offers to walk back with me, but I shake my head, not feeling able to make conversation with her even though I know she won't be expecting anything from me. Although relief floods through all of us, there is still the thought that now we are back at square one – no one knows where Laurel is, and no one knows who has taken her.

The mood is heavy and sombre, and I scuttle away into the kitchen on the pretence of making a pot of tea, but really, I just want to be alone to process how I feel about things. Of course I didn't want them to find anything in the lake, but where do we go from here? What happens next?

With Laurel gone for six days already, we are well outside the so-called crucial twenty-four hours. All the police have to go on so far is a witness saying they saw Laurel getting into a dark-coloured car. We don't even know for definite that it was Laurel. I feel a little as though there is only dead end after dead end and every minute that passes means a minute longer without Laurel. *How must Fran be feeling?* If I'm feeling like this, it must be ten times worse for Fran, even though she seems to be holding up OK.

My stomach gives a painful lurch as I remember Laurel slipping past me, running after Fran that night, and I let out a long exhale, trying and failing to squash the guilt that twists in my gut. In addition to the worry about Laurel, I also have the burden of the secret from my past that weighs heavy on my shoulders and I battle for control for a moment as shame and self-loathing swamps me. I snatch up Fran's £200 Arne Jacobsen teapot from Harrods and turn on the tap, pouring the boiling water over the tea leaves in the bottom of the pot.

I should never have taken the job with the Jessops. I never should have let that old boyfriend persuade me that things would be OK – although even he doesn't know the full story of why I came back from Scotland. Rephrase that – why I slinked home from Scotland without telling anyone, not even my own mother. Would it look suspicious if I were to leave them now? To say thanks but no thanks, the job isn't for me, I can't do this anymore? But then what about Laurel? I blink back hot tears. Could I really leave without knowing what has happened to her?

I look around the stark, almost clinically clean kitchen, with the stupid boiling water tap, and over-priced teapot, and think how if I left, I wouldn't miss a single thing. The Jo Malone candles that line the shelves above the dining table, because Fran doesn't like cooking smells to linger; the flooring that Fran delights in telling people cost over five thousand pounds, because the stone is travertine. The elegant Harvey Nichols chandeliers that hang, one at the bottom and one at the top of the stairs, thousands of pounds worth of extravagance, that no one even seems to notice in this house anymore. All these things, all this expense and decadence and what for? It doesn't make a difference – it doesn't stop bad things from happening. It didn't keep Laurel safe.

'Are you all right?' Kelly appears next to me, and I swipe at my eyes with the back of my hand. 'It's hard isn't it? The not knowing.'

It's like she's a psychic or something. I nod and let her take the ridiculously expensive teapot from me.

'So, who was that lady, the one you were speaking to at the lake earlier?' Kelly asks, her eyes on the counter in front of her as she wipes away the tea leaves I spilt.

'Ella? I met her at the school. She was one of the volunteers.' As I say it I realise that's not strictly true. She might have been at the hall, but I didn't see her join the search. 'I think she knows Dominic, from when they were at school.' I amend.

'Oh, right.' Kelly's voice is bright, and she smiles as she hands me a mug. 'You two looked quite friendly, that's all. I thought maybe you knew her from before . . . all of this.'

'No, I'd never met her,' I say, frowning as I think hard to myself. I have seen her though, I'm sure of it. There was something familiar about her when she slid into the seat

94

next to me that day. I shake my head, throwing the thought away – I would remember, that striking blonde hair would be difficult to forget.

'I was just wondering . . . seeing as you're from not far from here originally. I spoke to your old employers . . .' Kelly says casually, her eyes watching my face and I think for a moment I might be sick. '. . . they said you left to get married, and that you moved back to Surrey, so I thought maybe you knew her from school, or something. You're not married though, are you?' She frowns.

'Oh . . . no.' I give her a weak smile, trying to let my breath out in a controlled stream rather than a huge whoosh of relief. 'Things didn't work out. And I don't know her.' This time when my eyes fill with hot tears I don't blink them back.

'Are you sure you're holding up OK? Everyone is concentrating on Fran and Dominic, and quite rightly too, but you're the one who takes care of Laurel all day every day.' Kelly reaches out a hand and squeezes my fingers tightly.

Am I holding up OK? I don't really know. On the outside, yes, but on the inside is that constant dark hand of fear that grips my heart in its icy fist.

'It's difficult. It feels like everything seems to be grinding to a halt – that there are no clues at all to what might have happened to Laurel. I wonder if I'm best getting out of the way?' Relieved to change the subject, I turn the words into a question as I finally meet Kelly's eyes.

'I know that feels like the easiest option, but I promise you it won't help. Fran and Dominic need you – especially now . . .' she trails off and bites her lip.

'What do you mean, especially now?' I say.

'DI Dove is planning on holding a reconstruction,' Kelly says, glancing quickly towards the door. I guess that DS Wright is in the living room now, telling Fran and Dominic his plans.

'A reconstruction?' Bile rises in the back of my throat and I swallow hastily. The idea of reliving that night is unbearable. 'Like *Crimewatch*?'

'Exactly that.' Kelly gives me a small smile. 'Look, I know the idea of it is scary, but it's worked so many times before. All it takes is one person to remember something that they didn't realise was significant, and it could lead to a massive breakthrough.'

'Well, I suppose . . . if it can help, then it has to happen. I'm sure Fran and Dominic will want anything and everything done to find Laurel.'

'DS Wright wanted me to ask you something.' Kelly's eyes slide away from mine and I get the distinct impression that I'm not going to like whatever she says next. 'She wants to know if you'll play yourself? All you'll have to do is stand there behind the little girl who will play Laurel, and then look for her when you realise she isn't there. Oh . . . look, Anna, I know it's hard . . .'

'No. Absolutely not.' I'm already shaking my head before she even finishes speaking. 'I'm not doing it, OK?'

'She just thought that it might be helpful – people will remember your face, and that might lead . . .'

'I said, *no*.' I shove my chair back. 'I'm not doing it, Kelly. Let them get someone in who looks a bit like me, it's Laurel who is the main focus, not me.'

'OK.' She holds her hands up in a gesture of surrender. 'If you're definitely sure that you don't want to do it, I'll let her know and she can get one of the PCs to play you. It's fine. Honestly.' She gives a little shrug and picks up the tray of tea things to carry through into the living room. I settle back on to the chair, my heart rate returning to normal. There's no way I can appear on national television, not after all the lengths I've gone to, to make sure that no one knows I'm here. Not even if it means it'll help to find Laurel.

CHAPTER 10

'How are you feeling?' Jessika appears beside me as I stand shivering on the edge of the field, waiting for the reconstruction to start. She snakes her arm through mine, giving it a little reassuring squeeze, and I feel guilty for blanking her at the lake that day. My breath comes out in smoky plumes, drifting up and away to join the bitter bonfire smoke that rises up into the clear evening sky, like it did that Saturday evening, a little over a week ago. People bustle about, making sure everyone is placed exactly so, right down to the BBQ area and the PTA stand at the entrance to the field.

I see Ruth standing by the gate, taking direction from someone with an earpiece, and remembering what she said about being at drama school with Fran, I realise with a tiny twinge of distaste that she must be playing herself in the reconstruction. My stomach flips as the first firework bursts overhead and I see the woman playing me turn to 'Laurel' and usher her off towards where 'Fran' walks toward the portaloos, the cameras trained on her tiny frame.

'I don't know,' I say, wrapping my arms across my body. 'It feels weird, you know? Seeing her. Watching it all happen again.' The little girl they have chosen to play Laurel is a perfect match, and they've even managed to find the exact bobble hat I thrust on to her head that night to keep her warm.

'This will help, though, you know that?' Jess eyes me closely, her brows knitted together with concern.

'Let's hope so,' I say, glancing over to where Fran and Dominic stand stony-faced together, with Kelly in between them. I wasn't sure that any of us would be allowed to be there – having not had any experience with this kind of thing before, I didn't know what to expect – and at first Fran was adamant that she wasn't coming.

'Why would I want to see it?' she cried, pacing the living room floor at home, Bom discarded on the sofa as she marched backwards and forwards. 'Why would I want to relive that?' Dominic had also not been keen at first, before changing his mind abruptly, with no explanation. And that was how I find myself, shivering despite the layers of clothes I wear, watching one of the worst nights of my life being re-enacted. Jess inches closer to me and links her fingers in mine, giving my hand a tight squeeze as we watch the woman portraying me walk towards the BBQ stand, fake fear etched on to her features.

'Does Claire know you're here?' I whisper to her, conscious of the cameras around the field. I am anxious that I will do something, say something that will put the actors off and we'll have to start this whole painful process over again.

'I got the night off,' Jess says, 'she thinks I've gone for a drink with Mike.' Jess's on/off boyfriend.

'What does she think about everything?' I have to ask.

People have been very careful not to say anything to any of us, nothing that gives away what they really think or feel as they stand on the doorstep handing over Pyrex dishes of pre-cooked food and empty platitudes. I am intrigued to know what Claire's views are, given that she is a 'friend' of Fran's but we haven't heard from her at all, except to see her at the search hub in the school hall. The only person who has called at the house regularly is Ruth, and I have been accepting her offerings on the doorstep in an attempt to protect Fran from having to see people she doesn't know. It's as though people are too frightened to get too close, in case something about Laurel's disappearance rubs off on them. And I can't shake off the image of that woman behind me in the hall, whispering to her friend about how Fran still managed to put on make-up.

'Well, she's devastated for Fran, obviously,' Jess says, cautiously. 'I mean, we all are. She's keeping a tight hold on Daisy at the moment too. The whole thing has shaken the entire community up. The very idea that something this awful could happen here, of all places, has got people frightened.'

'Are people blaming me?' Finally, I pluck up the courage to ask the question, that nervous, sick feeling bubbling up again in my stomach. I was ostracised in Killin, in Scotland, following what happened, fingers pointing at me wherever I went. I couldn't bear it if it happened again, here, not after all I've done to try and put the past behind me.

'You?' Jess lets out a tiny huff. 'No. Don't be silly. This wasn't your fault.' She squeezes my fingers lightly again, but she doesn't meet my eyes.

The reconstruction airs later in the week, and we all huddle in the living room to watch it. The air is thick with tension as the opening credits roll, and as Dove appears on the screen with the presenter, saliva spurts into my mouth.

I jump to my feet, rushing to the downstairs loo, convinced I am about to be sick, but nothing comes up. My stomach just heaves and rolls, as I spit into the toilet. Rocking back on to my heels, I wipe my mouth with a shaking hand, before rising to my feet. I splash cold water over my face, rinse my mouth out and wipe away the mascara that has bled beneath my eyes, before heading back into the living room.

'Are you all right?' Kelly whispers to me as I slide onto the sofa next to her.

'Yes.' I nod, wiping at my mouth again. 'I'm nervous, I don't know why. Reliving the whole thing . . .' I whisper, shaking my head. 'I'm sorry.'

She gives me a reassuring smile, and I glance across the room at the Jessops. They occupy two separate armchairs, Fran curled into one, while Dominic sits, straight-backed and grim-faced, in the other, both of them with eyes trained on the television screen. Dove finishes speaking and the scene changes to the field and the bonfire. My heart starts to thunder in my chest.

We see Laurel, skipping into the field ahead of 'me', the pair of us meeting up with Fran. Tears spring to my eyes as we watch Laurel bounce away across the mud, running after Fran who keeps walking, not even realising that Laurel is chasing along after her. The camera cuts back to 'me', a woman who looks a little like me – close enough to jog people's memories, but not close enough to remind people from the past, I hope – as she turns back to watch the fireworks overhead, thinking that everything is OK.

We cut back to the studio, where Dove still sits, manspreading across the couch, leaning on his knees as the presenter starts to question him.

'Someone knows where Laurel is,' he states firmly, 'someone saw what happened to that little girl that night, and it is incredibly important that if you saw something, or if you even think that you might have seen something, you need to come forward.'

Fran gives a strangled sob, and before anyone can stop her she rushes from the room. Dominic gets to his feet and switches off the television.

'I'll go and make sure she's OK.' Kelly gets up, and then I hear her feet as she turns down the hallway, the clunk of the back door as it closes behind her. Dominic turns to me.

'Do you think that did any good?' he asks, his face pale and waxy, his forehead sweaty. I avert my eyes.

'I think it's better than doing nothing,' I say, knotting my hands together.

'But do you think it'll jog anyone's memory?' he persists. 'Do you think seeing a kid who looks slightly like Laurel will lead anyone to actually remembering something important? Something that could get her back?'

'I . . . don't know,' I stutter, unnerved by the intensity of his cold, blue eyes as he stares at me. Does he think I had something to do with this? A chill runs down my spine at the thought. I can't go through it all again – I can't be held responsible for something I didn't do. 'Possibly. I don't know, Dominic, because I don't know what happened to Laurel.'

'For fuck's sake.' He snatches up a glass that sits on the mantelpiece, rolling it in one palm before he flings it onto the marble hearth, shards shattering across the floor. I flinch, fear making my pulse race in my chest.

'Dominic . . .' I hold up my hands, trying to stop my fingers from shaking, 'please, calm down.' Kelly appears in the doorway and I give her a frantic look. I won't know what to do if he loses it completely and starts smashing the room up. Kelly takes him by the arm and gently guides him to the armchair, as he scrubs his hands over his face, apologising for losing his temper, muttering under his breath. While Kelly murmurs to him, I sneak out to the garden where I can see Fran's outline illuminated through the glass of the back door by the outside light. Hissing as the chilly night air hits my bare arms, I step out on to the patio and Fran turns.

'Anna. I thought it was going to be that bloody spy, Kelly. I've told her I don't want to speak to her,' she says, a lit cigarette in one hand. She catches my gaze and wafts it towards me. 'Do you want one?'

I take one from the pack, the smoke tickling the back of my throat and making me want to cough as soon as I inhale. I haven't smoked since Scotland. Since that night. The taste of the ashy nicotine on my tongue makes my head swim and my stomach roll. I don't puff again, but hold the cigarette loosely between my fingers.

'She's only here to help,' I say, defending Kelly. 'She's in there with Dominic now. He . . . he lost his temper a little bit.'

'I heard him shout,' Fran says, before drawing in another deep drag of her cigarette, filling her lungs with smoke. She exhales and lets out a long, steady stream of white before she speaks again. Her eyes water, but I'm unsure if she is crying, or if it's the smoke. 'No one ever believes me when I tell them what a temper he has.'

'He's under a lot of pressure,' I say, quietly, secretly a little dizzy at my bravery. I would never have dared say anything to Fran before. 'You both are.'

'Oh, you too?' She huffs out a tiny spiteful laugh, crushing her cigarette under one foot. 'Got you under his special little surgeon's spell, has he?'

'No,' I say, copying her and squashing my cigarette butt beneath my shoe. 'It's not like that. I'm here for both of you.' I stumble over the words. 'You're both going through a terrible, terrible time.'

'Yes,' Fran says softly, her eyes filling with tears. 'We are, aren't we? What are we going to do, Anna?' She blinks, and a tear rolls down each cheek.

'The reconstruction will help,' I say, trying to inject some positivity into the air. I ignore the comment she made about Dominic – she's hurting too, after all. She just wants to offload some pain onto others. 'Something will come of it.'

'That's what I'm afraid of,' she says, staring past me into the black, inky darkness of the garden behind me, before she turns her gaze back to me. 'What if we don't like what it throws up? And what if . . . what if it's someone we know?'

Fran's words haunt me for the rest of the evening and well into the next day. Kelly is in the kitchen when I come down in the morning, and there is a lighter feel to the air for the first time in days.

'Did something happen?' I ask, reaching past her for a banana from the fruit bowl. Fran and Dominic both perch at the breakfast bar, a plate bearing toast crumbs in front of Dominic, while a full bowl of granola and yoghurt sits in front of Fran.

'Last night, the reconstruction threw up some more information, stuff that might help,' Kelly says, with a smile.

'Really?' I look at Fran, who gives a thin smile. She looks a little better this morning, and I hope that she managed at least a couple of hours of sleep. 'What kind of information?'

Dominic, on the other hand, looks terrible this morning, his face lined and haggard. I'm guessing he didn't sleep, and there is the faint whiff of brandy on his breath. I'm not entirely sure that it's from last night, either. 'Someone else called into the television show and said they also saw Laurel getting into a car.'

'The same car?' I ask, pausing with the banana halfway to my mouth. 'This is good, isn't it?' I look to Kelly for confirmation.

'Yes, in a way,' she nods, 'we now have two separate sightings of Laurel getting into a car, both witnesses saying it was an SUV, although we don't yet know for definite which make. We'll be looking into this further, obviously. We also have had a witness call in to say they saw a woman.'

'A woman?'

'Yes – someone saw a woman hanging around outside the entrance shortly before Laurel was last seen. She was alone and didn't enter the field. The caller said it was almost as though she was waiting for someone. DS Wright will be chasing that up too.'

'It still might be nothing,' Dominic says, before pushing his stool back and getting to his feet. We watch in silence as he leaves us, and as the tension thickens again, that thick, stifling aura filling the room, I slide away, shoving my feet into trainers and escaping out to the fresh air, away from all of them.

*

The volunteer hub has been moved from the school hall to the community centre next door, to allow the children to get back into a normal routine. Part of me feels as though the school has acknowledged that there's a chance that Laurel won't be found anytime soon by moving the search hub, but equally I get that they need to think of the other children – it's been ten days now since Laurel was last seen.

Pushing the door open, I hear voices and realise the hub is still buzzing, only slightly less so than at the start of the search. While many of the original volunteers have had to go back to work and their everyday lives, a few dedicated members of the community are still here, still working hard. Posters are still piled up waiting to be given out, and a new stack of T-shirts bearing Laurel's face wait to be worn by new volunteers. I see Ruth as I enter, still in her familiar outfit of worn out, filthy jeans and headscarf. I raise a hand to her, but I don't stop when she looks as though she wants to speak to me, instead hurrying past her to where Ella stands by the toilets.

'Ella?' I was sure she would have been busy at work, doing whatever it is that she does, by now. 'You're still here.'

'Just checking in to see if there's anything I can do,' she says. She holds her phone in one hand, and her eyes keep drifting down towards it as though waiting for a call or a text.

'Well, I'm sure Cheryl will find you something.' I nod towards the front of the hall where Cheryl is busy handing out leaflets.

'How did the reconstruction go? I watched it,' Ella says, dragging her eyes away from her phone screen as she tucks the device into her pocket.

'Great.' I wince as I say it. 'You know what I mean. There's been a few leads from it. Someone said they saw Laurel getting into a car, and another witness said they saw a woman hanging around outside shortly before Laurel disappeared. Shit. I don't know if I should have said anything.'

Ella's face is pale, and she pulls out her phone again, checking the screen and fiddling with the ringer the way you do when you want someone to call and you're terrified you might have missed it. 'Don't worry,' she says, pushing her hand through hair that looks a little greasy. She looks as tired as I feel. 'I won't mention it. A woman, you say? Could they describe her?'

'I don't know . . . I didn't get the full details, but you know DI Dove, he's like a dog with a bone.' I think of the way his face seemed to come to life every time he discussed the case. 'I doubt he'll let it go, not until he finds out who she is and why she was there.'

'Excellent.' Ella says, giving me an awkward smile. 'You know, Anna, I need to get on. Catch up with you later?'

'Oh. Yes. Of course.'

There is a sudden rush of commotion as someone flies into the school hall, and I hear my name being shouted.

'Anna? Anna!'

Pushing my way past Ella, who stands frozen in front of me, I see Jess coming running into the hall, Daisy holding tight to one hand as she desperately tries to keep up with her nanny. Jess slides to a halt in front of me, pulling Daisy tight towards her as she tries to get her breath back, her cheeks pink and her hair standing out in a halo around her head.

'Anna . . .' Jess gasps, 'I've just seen Mr Snow. He was getting into a police car. Anna, they were taking him away.'

CHAPTER 11

The buzz of chatter in the hall dies away completely as Jess's words ring through the air and the world tilts on its axis briefly. There is a rumbling in my ears, as though I am under water and I feel for a minute as though I might faint.

'Anna? Anna, are you OK?' I look down to see Jess grasping my elbow tightly. She guides me towards a small, plastic chair, the kind children sit on to eat their school dinners. 'Here.' She passes me a cup of water. 'I'm sorry, I didn't mean to shock you.'

I take a tiny sip of water. 'Are you sure they were arresting him? What did you actually see?'

'Not much. Just him coming out of his house. There were a couple of police officers either side of him, and they bundled him into a car that was waiting outside his gate. I don't know if they actually *arrested* him, or if he's merely "helping them with their enquiries".' She crooks her fingers in quote marks.

'Do you think this is something to do with the reconstruction?' I ask, my mind racing. How could frail, innocent-looking Mr Snow have anything to do with Laurel going missing? He's . . . well, he's *nice*.

'I don't know. Seems a bit suspicious though, doesn't it?'

'But he's always so . . . friendly. So normal. I can't believe . . .' I trail off, not sure how to continue, as a horrific thought strikes me. *What if this really is all my fault?* What if Mr Snow is somehow responsible, and my encouraging Laurel to be friendly to him is what started it all? It all began because each day we would see him at his gate, on our way to school. I told Laurel to say 'good morning', and after a few weeks we went from a brief hello as we passed to a full-on chat every morning before we hurried up the lane to get to school before the bell rang. He gave her that tiny little doll. *Oh God.* I get to my feet, pushing my hair away from my face. 'I have to go.'

'Go? But Anna . . .' Jess shakes her head, 'you need to calm down – look, just sit for a moment before you go rushing off.'

'I can't, Jess. This is huge news – everyone overheard you, and I have to get home and see whether Fran and Dominic know what's happened. They can't hear it from someone else. They're . . . things are fragile at the moment.'

'Anna, at least let me walk you home, you've had a shock.' Ella appears beside me and I look at her in confusion. I had forgotten she was even still here.

'What? No, thank you. Honestly. I need to go.' I want to get home, and I'm sure the last thing Fran and Dominic need is an old school friend landing on the doorstep. A look I can't quite place crosses Ella's face before she gives me a quick smile.

'Of course. And I have a meeting to get to, so . . . I'll catch up with you soon.' Without saying goodbye, she turns on her heel and heads back towards the main table at the front of the hall. I hurry out and along the lane, averting my eyes as I pass the Snow house, but not before I catch sight of a police car parked outside and a flicker of movement at the window that tells me someone is inside, searching.

I let myself back in, my feet aching and my chest hitching as the dash from school to home catches up with me. The house is quiet as I make my way towards the kitchen, and I feel Laurel's absence acutely. No sound of her singing floating down the stairs from her bedroom, no tangle of shoes to be hurriedly tidied away before Fran gets home, no demands for snacks before tea.

As I reach the patio doors to the garden, I see Kelly is outside in the wintry sunshine, somewhat futilely hanging out washing that won't dry in these temperatures. Seeing as the cleaner hasn't been back since Laurel went missing (I'm unsure if Fran told her not to come, or whether she is avoiding us, in case it's catching), Kelly seems to have absorbed all of the chores that the cleaner used to do. Maybe it's a bid to make herself seem less like a police officer, and more like a friend of the family. I'm guessing then, that no one has been told yet. I walk along the hallway back towards the stairs, intending to head up and see if Fran is in her room, when I see that the door to Dominic's study is half open. A noise stops me in my tracks, as I realise someone is in there, and then Fran's voice floats out to me.

'. . . no, it's OK. I'm OK. I promise.' There is a noise that sounds like drawers being pulled open. 'Just stay there. I don't want you to come, all right?'

I hold my breath as Fran's voice rises and there is the thunk of another drawer slamming closed. I know I should move away, but I can't.

'. . . yes, it's fine. I mean, he's no better than he usually is, but no worse either.' A squeak as Fran sits in Dominic's office chair. 'Hang on . . . I thought I heard something.' Her footsteps tap lightly across the wooden floor of the office and I scuttle around the corner and put one foot on the stairs as if just coming down, but she doesn't appear. 'No, it's fine, must be my imagination. I thought he was back for a moment.' I let myself breathe again, and tiptoe back round to the office door. 'He's so . . . you know, he grabbed me again the other day, in the kitchen. Was screaming in my face. And I know that no one believes me when I tell them that he has this . . . *side* to him. I've got to hang in there, for Laurel, you know? Once I get her home then maybe . . . maybe I can see a way out. But I need her back first.' Fran gives a dramatic sniff, and I decide enough is enough. She's clearly on the phone to her mother again, so I am intruding on what is a private and personal conversation.

Fran's words run round in my head as I return to the kitchen to wait for her to finish her conversation. *He grabbed me again* . . . she must be referring to the day I saw them together in the kitchen. A shudder runs down my spine, as I remember the look on his face as he hurled the glass into the fireplace, the way his eyes narrowed, and his cheeks flushed an angry, ugly red. I have never, ever seen Dominic like that before. He simply isn't the man that I know.

I think back to the tail end of summer, when it was my birthday. I had come downstairs in the morning to find a home-made card next to a plate of toast and a mug of tea.

'A little bird tells me it's your birthday,' Dominic had said, as Laurel giggled on the stool next to him. I had kissed her, and thanked him, a little bit tearful at the thought that had gone into it, when Fran entered the room.

'It's your birthday?' she'd said, frowning at the card before turning to Dominic. 'Well, Dominic, I'm sure Anna is delighted to be reminded she's another year older. Why didn't you buy her some eye cream and be done with it?' Before flouncing out of the house to yet another audition.

I simply can't reconcile the man who would be that thoughtful – that *nice* – with the man I saw in the kitchen the other night.

Fran is right – I would never have believed her if she had said anything to me before – not that she ever did. My relationship with Fran has always had clear boundaries. We are employer and employee, not friends, which is perhaps why I am finding it so difficult to comfort her now. Dominic is usually the one who smooths things over when Fran has lost her temper about something. So, if Dominic has been violent towards her all this time, I would never have known about it, not unless she had said something. Once Laurel is in bed, I am off the clock, and spend most evenings holed up on my own in my room, watching Netflix with my headphones on. But now I've seen it with my own eyes, now that I've seen the way his face changes when anger consumes him, then yes . . . now I can believe it, and I feel slightly sick at the thought of the things that Fran may have had to hide from me.

Fran drifts into the kitchen, her eyes slightly tinged with pink, a thin floaty kimono-style dressing gown that is totally inappropriate for the outside temperatures wrapped around her skinny frame. As she enters, Kelly bustles in to the kitchen, empty laundry basket in her hand.

'Oh, you're both back,' Kelly says, and I wonder for a moment where Fran has been while I've been gone.

'I have something to tell you,' I blurt out before I can stop myself, before I can think through how I'm going to say it. 'It's Mr Snow.'

'Who is Mr Snow?' Fran asks, her eyes darting in Kelly's direction before coming to rest on my face.

'He's . . . he's a man who lives by the school,' I stammer, feeling flustered under her gaze, even though I am pretty sure I haven't done anything wrong. *Have I?* 'Jessika Lewis saw him being taken away by a police car this morning.'

'And you think this has something to do with Laurel?' There is a slight tremble to her tone, but her words are like chips of ice, and I recognise it as her professional-but-angry mode. It rears its head when I haven't done something I said I would, or if she disapproves of something I've said or done with Laurel. I knew I should have let Kelly or DS Wright tell her.

'I'm not sure. It just seems like a coincidence that . . . after the reconstruction . . .' I tail off, pathetically, looking away so I don't have to meet her eyes.

'And how does this Snow man know Laurel?' Fran asks. One hand comes up to brush a stray hair away from her lip, and I see her fingers shake slightly.

'I . . . I started talking to him. On the way to school. We pass by his house every day, and it was the polite thing to say hello. And then we got talking a few times. He was nice.'

'*Nice!*' Fran's voice rises to a screech and as she slams her hands down on the table in front of me I resist the urge to clamp my hands over my ears. 'He might have taken my daughter! What the *fuck* were you thinking, Anna? Encouraging a four-year-old to talk to a stranger? After everything I tried to teach her!' She shoves her hands through her hair and starts pacing the floor. 'I need to speak to Dove. Get me the phone.'

But Kelly has already beaten her to it, and is muttering into the phone, herself pacing backwards and forwards in much the same fashion as Fran.

'I can't believe you would be so stupid,' Fran hisses at me, out of Kelly's earshot, 'after all the things I did to try and drum it into her that she shouldn't speak to people she doesn't know, and you go and do this. No wonder there's a chance she got into someone's car.'

'I'm sorry,' I gulp back tears, forcing the words out through the lump in my throat. 'I didn't think . . .'

Kelly turns to us, hanging up the phone, a grave look on her face. 'Your information was right, Anna. George Snow is helping us with our enquiries, but at this moment in time that's all I can tell you.'

'What? Are you kidding?'

The shrill ring of the doorbell stops all of us in our tracks.

'I'll go,' I say, eager to get away from Fran before she turns on me again. I don't even care if it's the press, I want to get out of this room. There is a single silhouette in the glass of the front door when I reach it though, and I heave a sigh of relief that there is only one person outside, not a press mob.

'Oh, it's you.' Opening the door, I stare in surprise as Ruth stands on the doorstep, yet another foil-covered dish in her hands.

'I brought a casserole,' she says, shoving it towards me. The dish is lukewarm and a vague meaty smell wafts out from under the foil, making my stomach turn.

'Thanks.' I don't know what else to say.

'Can I come in?' Ruth has one foot on the doorstep, one grubby, denim-clad leg already poised to push her way inside.

'It's not really a good time,' I say, thinking of Fran in the kitchen, her hair standing on end, kimono slipping off one porcelain-white shoulder as she shrieks at me.

'I thought Fran might want to talk to somebody,' she says, her dirty trainer still wedged on the doorframe. I don't think I'll be able to get rid of her, and I don't have the energy to fight with anyone else today. I sigh and pull the door open a fraction.

'It's really not a good time. Things are . . . fraught at the moment.'

'There's never a good time, not when something like this has happened.' Ruth gives me a sympathetic smile and steps past me into the hallway before I can react. She follows me through into the kitchen, and I can feel her eyes running over everything, peering into the living room before we reach the kitchen door.

'Who . . .?' Fran looks startled when she sees Ruth standing beside me.

'This is Ruth,' I say cautiously, not sure if Fran is about to launch herself at me again. 'She brought you a casserole.' I lift the heavy dish slightly in Fran's direction before placing it on the counter.

'Oh, isn't that lovely of you?' Kelly flashes a quick smile at Ruth. 'Are you a friend of Anna's?' She looks between the two of us, a slight frown creasing her brow, probably wondering why Ruth hasn't appeared on her radar yet.

'My daughter was at Oxbury Primary – Laurel's school,' Ruth says, 'I'm on the PTA. How are you, Fran?' She turns her pale, limpid gaze to Fran.

'How do you think?' Fran says, before dabbing at her nose with a tissue. I don't see any sign that she recognises Ruth at all. 'I'm sorry, it's a terribly difficult time for us.'

'I understand.' Ruth's eyes fill with tears, and I think that maybe she knew Laurel better than I realised. Or maybe she's thinking that it could have been her daughter instead. 'I just want you to know, I'm here if you need me, Fran. OK?' She grasps Fran's hand earnestly, pulling it towards her.

'Yes. Of course.' Fran frowns as she gently tugs her hand free. 'Thank you.'

'Anything at all, you know? This is my number.' Ruth pulls a ragged piece of paper from her back pocket. 'I'll come by tomorrow and bring you another dinner. Lasagne, OK?'

'Thank you,' Kelly comes round and gently guides Ruth towards the door, 'it's so very much appreciated, but we're waiting for a phone call. We'll see you tomorrow?' I hear her still murmuring to Ruth as they head towards the front door.

'That was nice of her,' I say to Fran, anxiously waiting to see her response, to see if she is still terribly angry with me.

'Yes,' she says, her face blank. She dabs at her eyes with a tissue, and sighs. It's as though she's run out of steam, no energy left to even be cross with me anymore. 'I'm not too sure what she really wanted though. Is she the one who has been texting me?'

'I think so,' I say, 'she used to go to drama school with you apparently. Years ago, she said.'

Fran gives a tiny shrug of her shoulders, a barely there movement. 'I don't remember her. But yes, nice of her I suppose.'

That gives me an idea. I run upstairs and grab my laptop, setting it up on the kitchen table in front of Fran.

'Ruth was only being supportive,' I say, quickly typing in my password and opening up Facebook. 'The whole town is being supportive and doing everything they can to help. You don't have to deal with everything alone.' I search for the 'FIND LAUREL' page and twist the screen round so Fran can see.

'Look,' I say, 'everyone is hoping Laurel will be home soon.' I scroll down slowly, until Fran pushes my hand away and starts scrolling herself.

'Oh,' she breathes, 'look at all these lovely, lovely comments. This one look – *I hope you get your beautiful angel back home safely soon* – isn't that so kind?' She looks up at me, tears making her eyes shine brightly, George Snow seemingly forgotten for a moment. 'And this one . . . and, oh.' She stops, her hand going to her mouth.

'What?' I say, peering over her shoulder. 'What is it?' Running my eyes down the screen I see what has made

Fran so upset. A message, from someone calling themselves Lois Burns, whoever that may be – there is no profile picture.

'*Did anybody look into the parents yet? The girl's mother says she took her eyes off her for a second and she was gone. Maybe if she'd looked after her properly this wouldn't have happened. She doesn't deserve to have children.*'

Clearly, not everybody in our small community feels the same way.

CHAPTER 12

Dominic walks back through the door an hour later to a silent, dry-eyed Fran, and an atmosphere that you could cut with a knife. Kelly and Fran sit at the breakfast bar, while I lean against the counter, itching to get away, to head upstairs to my room at the very least. The room is suffocating me, Fran's distress coating everything in something heavy and sticky, and I am desperate to get out of the house completely. Dominic throws his jacket over a chair and stops to survey the room, clearly feeling the tension.

'What's happened?' he asks, looking from Fran to Kelly and back again. 'Fran? What's going on?'

Fran sniffs, pulling the thin silk kimono she still wears more tightly around her neck. 'Where have you been, Dominic? Why didn't you answer your phone?' She raises her eyes to his and he rubs the back of his neck before he answers, pulling at his collar as if it irritates him.

'I had to go to the hospital, for a meeting,' he finally answers. 'You were asleep when I left, Fran. I didn't think you'd . . .'

'Didn't think I'd what? Notice? Mind?' Fran's nostrils flare and she presses her lips together tightly before she speaks again. 'I do mind, Dominic. You should have been here this morning, not at the bloody hospital.'

'I . . . sorry. I had to get out of the house, just for a short while.' I can totally relate to that, but I say nothing. 'There was an important meeting that I was committed to . . . before. I thought I might as well go.' Dominic turns to Kelly, who sits watching their exchange silently, taking it all in no doubt. 'Kelly – did something happen today?'

'They *arrested* someone, Dominic,' Fran snaps, before Kelly gets a chance to speak. 'They arrested someone *right after* they did the reconstruction. Not that anyone will tell us what's going on or what it has to do with Laurel.' She glares at Kelly, who doesn't flinch.

'Fran, to clarify, he hasn't actually been arrested, but they have brought someone in, Dominic,' Kelly says, 'and I believe it is off the back of a lead brought about by the reconstruction but at the moment the gentleman in question is simply helping with our enquiries. As soon as I have more information I can tell you exactly what is happening.'

'Who?' Dominic asks. 'Who is it? Someone we know? Someone who lives round here?' Questions fire from him, but there is something in his tone – something that almost sounds like relief. I look away, busying myself at the sink as I wait for the onslaught to begin again from Fran.

'Tell him, Anna.' Fran's voice is bitter, her lip twisted into a curl of disgust as she directs her glare in my direction now. Still, I say nothing. 'Some *man* that Anna introduced Laurel to. That's who.'

'It wasn't like that,' I say, finally turning to meet Dominic's gaze. He takes two long strides across the kitchen to stand in front of me, his hands reaching up to grip my shoulders so that I can't turn away. My heart starts to thump in my chest, the memory of how he grabbed Fran rising to the surface as fear of what he might do makes my hands shake, but he merely holds me in one position.

'Anna – who . . . can you please tell me?' His eyes bore into mine and I can't blink for a moment, held in his gaze.

'He was just a man . . . he lives on the way to school. I never . . . I didn't know . . .' I stammer, and Kelly steps in, gently tugging Dominic away from me. 'I wouldn't have ever let Laurel speak to him if I had known something like this would happen.'

Dominic bows his head, scrubbing his hands over his face before pushing them through his hair. I sag against the sink slightly, fear and adrenaline draining away to leave me feeling exhausted, my nerves ragged.

'Maybe if you'd been here more often, Laurel wouldn't have felt that she needed attention from this Snow man,' Fran says, her tone filled with bitter hate, like a poison seeping out into the air. 'Maybe if you'd spent more time here, instead of at that bloody hospital.'

'And maybe,' Dominic says cautiously, a quiet rage sparking to life behind his eyes, 'if you hadn't been such a bitch I would have spent more time here.' Without another word he turns on his heel and marches from the room, the slam of the front door sounding behind him.

Fran shoves her stool away from the breakfast bar and hurries out, her footsteps thudding on the stairs, leaving Kelly and me alone in the kitchen. I sink into the chair Dominic threw his jacket over, the harsh taste of the Jessops' bitter words tainting the air around us.

'Not your fault,' Kelly says, quietly. 'This is putting a strain on the whole family. They're not usually as bad as this, are they?'

I shrug, 'No. Sometimes. Who knows anymore?' Guilt makes me snappy and abrupt.

'This really isn't your fault, Anna – you weren't to know what was going to happen.' She reaches over and squeezes my hand, and I won't lie, I'm grateful for this tiny gesture designed to make me feel better.

'Do you think he has got something to do with it?' I bite down hard on my bottom lip, a wave of nausea making my stomach roll at the thought of Mr Snow grabbing Laurel, dragging her away to God only knows where. 'They wouldn't have gone to his house and picked him up for nothing, would they?'

'No . . .' Kelly pauses, 'they'll just be asking him some questions at the moment. As soon as we know anything more they'll let us know.'

My phone buzzes in my pocket, and I pull it out to see Jessika's name on the screen. 'Do you mind if I take this?'

Kelly shakes her head, getting to her feet and heading out into the garden, pulling the door gently closed behind her. I push my chair back, swiping to answer as I do so.

'Hi, Jess.'

'Anna. How are you?' It's a bad line – I can barely hear her, and I wonder where she is. 'Listen, I'm at the park with Daisy. Do you think you could come and meet me? I've got some stuff to tell you. Things I heard after you left. I think you'll want to hear them.'

I'm already on my feet, telling Jess to wait for me, I'll be there, struggling back into my jacket with the phone clamped to my ear. As I stand, something catches my eye, the light reflecting off something on Dominic's jacket. I peer closer, pinching my finger and thumb together to remove the offending item from the shoulder, swallowing hard as I realise what it is. *A long, thin strand of bright blonde hair.* The exact shade of Laurel's hair.

Heart thumping in my chest, I glance out of the kitchen window to where Kelly paces the patio, phone clamped to her ear. *It doesn't mean anything*, I tell myself, *that hair might not be Laurel's. And even if it is, it could have been there since . . . any time.* I inspect it closely, holding it vertically between my fingers. I'm not even sure it looks long enough to be Laurel's hair – could it belong to someone else? Is Fran right, is Dominic seeing another woman? Or is it simply nothing, and I am being stupid, trying to read something into a single hair? This whole horrific event has me jumping at ghosts, seeing things that might not even be there. Even so, I pinch the hair between finger and thumb, and wrap it in a piece of kitchen roll before tucking it into the back pocket of my jeans, my fingers snagging on something small and hard in the pocket of denim. *The doll.* I pull it out, careful not to dislodge the tissue with the hair in it, running my fingers over the doll's face before I tuck it safely away again.

Yanking a dark blue beanie hat over my hair – although the sun is out, it's windy and there is a deep, winter chill in the air – I sneak out the front door, silently latching it behind me. I tell myself I'm not sneaking out, but I don't want to have to explain to Kelly, or to Fran, why I need to get out for a while, and I hurry up the path eager to get to Jess and whatever it is that she's discovered.

I arrive at the park ten minutes later, my cheeks flushed and my armpits prickling with sweat, no longer feeling the chill in the air. Jess is at the slide, watching as Daisy launches herself down it over and over again. She turns as she hears me approach, a concerned frown on her face before she forces it away, pasting on a smile that would look fake to anyone who knows her as well as I do.

'OK,' I say, impatient to hear what she has to tell me. 'What did you hear? Is it about Mr Snow?'

Jess is quiet for a moment as she watches Daisy climb the steps to the slide one more time, awkward in the thick-lined wellies she wears. Laurel has a pair exactly the same, and my heart turns over at the thought of them lined up underneath the radiator, waiting for her to slide her feet into them.

'Don't freak out, OK?' Jess finally says, pushing her thick hair back as the wind whips it across her face. 'I'm not even sure how true this is, it's basically something I overheard someone saying back at the school hall after . . . well, after I saw him being taken away.'

'What? Jess, please just tell me.'

'The thing is . . . what they're saying is that this isn't the first time. They're saying that he did it before. He abducted another little girl.'

It takes me a moment to fully process what Jessika has just said, my brain playing catch up. Surely, *surely*, this can't be true?

'What do you mean?' I whisper, knotting my fingers together so tightly my knuckles turn white. 'Another girl? But how? How come he's walking around out there, living next to a school if this is true?'

'I don't know, Anna.' Jess looks over at Daisy, supposedly keeping an eye on her charge, but really it's so she doesn't have to make eye contact with me. 'It's exactly what they said at the school. Listen, the police will know about it. They'll investigate him properly and it'll be OK. If it's him, then they'll find her, won't they?' She hoists her bag onto her shoulder and calls to Daisy. 'I have to get her back home. Do you want to come with us?'

I shake my head. 'No, thank you. I have some things I need to do.'

'OK.' Jess runs her eyes over my face one more time but doesn't make a move to hug me goodbye. 'Be careful, Anna.'

I wait until Jess and Daisy have left the park before I find a bench and pull out my phone, bringing up the Safari page. My fingers are itching I'm so eager to start my search, but before I can type in Mr Snow's name, I find my fingers typing my own name into the Google search bar.

The screen fills with links, underneath tiny thumbnails of my own face, the same picture used over and over. The one they used at the time, of me sitting on a rock at the beach, the sea in the background. My hair, much darker and longer than it is now, is whipped across half of my face, as I laugh up into the camera. Not a care in the world. A picture taken before everything changed. Before my dreams were haunted by that sickening crack, the blood that spread quicker than I ever thought possible, that pale, white face, eyes closed. I don't read the articles, simply scan over the headlines, picking out my own name, the words *nanny* and *disgrace*. Feeling sick – it seems it still hasn't gone away, not even after five years – I shut the browser, before reopening it and giving myself a mental slap in the face.

125

I type in *George Snow.* All this brings up is a list of Wikipedia pages, one for a film-maker, one for a researcher, and one for a park in Boca Raton. I should have known it would never have been that easy – it's not like it's an unusual name, after all. I think about my own situation, about why I am so terrified that they will find out about the secret I have been keeping, and what they would think if they knew. What if that was the same for Mr Snow? I start typing again, trying different combinations of key search words. *George Snow, Manchester, crime. George Snow, Manchester, Surrey, arrest. George Snow, Manchester, kidnapping.* Bingo.

Hand to my mouth, I click on the first link, the one from 1995, an article from a newspaper – not a tabloid, but not far off – the headline proclaiming, 'MAN ARRESTED OVER KIDNAPPING OF LITTLE KATRINA.' *Kidnap?* Even though Jess told me herself, I didn't really think that Mr Snow would be capable of something like that – I thought, *hoped*, that it was merely idle gossip. Quickly, I start to scan the article, getting the main gist of things. There isn't a lot of information, but it seems as though Mr Snow really did kidnap a little girl, named Katrina. Who was five years old at the time, close enough to Laurel's age. Armed with a fraction more information, I delve deeper into the internet, piecing together facts – or alleged facts – from different sources, trying to make up the main picture. It seems that on a damp, chilly October evening in 1995, Mr Snow picked up little Katrina, and never took her home again. He was married at the time to Emira, Katrina's mother. They were separated and according to her, she had allowed him to spend time with Katrina over the first weekend of the October half term, with the condition that he returned her to her home early on Monday morning. Monday morning came and went, and Katrina never arrived. What came after was a nationwide manhunt, searching for little Katrina, who, according to her mother, was in the hands of an unstable man, intent on destroying the last tiny vestiges of the relationship they had had together.

I read in horror, one hand pressed to my mouth, about the search, the way he had just vanished and Katrina along with him, pictures of Emira appealing to him to return Katrina filling my screen. She is dark, pretty, Arabic . . . Turkish, maybe? She is less held together than Fran, her eyes red and swollen, her distress evident in every photograph, in every paper, her clothes rumpled as though she has slept in them. Finally, I reach the end. A picture of George Snow being led away in handcuffs, a jacket thrown over his head to shield his face from the lens of the paparazzi, as in another, Emira clutches Katrina, her face screwed up with relief, tears of joy streaming down her cheeks. I zoom in on the picture, examining every detail. Snow's head is bowed, and I can't make out his features clearly, but I recognise something about him, the way he holds himself, maybe. It's definitely him, the Mr Snow that I encouraged Laurel to speak to because it was *polite*.

A damp chill seeps into my bones from the wooden bench beneath me, and I have to take a deep breath, filling my lungs with cold, crisp air, before I go back to the picture. Katrina looks bewildered by the events, her face smudged with dirt and her long, dark hair tangled down her back, but she looks OK. She doesn't look hurt. *Maybe I could speak to her?* The idea makes a spark pop low down in my belly. If Snow does have form for this (which it appears he does), and if he does have something to do with Laurel disappearing, maybe Katrina can help? I'm sure the police will have already spoken to her, but maybe she'll talk to me. I just want her to tell me that he didn't hurt her, that he wouldn't have hurt Laurel. That Laurel will be OK.

CHAPTER 13

Scrolling, scrolling, scrolling, I scour the internet for information about where Katrina Snow might be now, ignoring the curious glances from dog walkers and passers-by. She might have married and be using a different name . . . she might not even be in Manchester any more . . . what if she's gone abroad? All these thoughts cross my mind as I try and figure out where to start searching for her. All I can do is start with what I already know.

I type in *Katrina Snow, kidnapped, father, Manchester*. This brings up another lengthy list of articles, newspaper reports and some downright weird websites, all about what happened, but with no further information on where Katrina might be now. I rub my hands over my face, my eyes feeling dry and tired from staring at the screen for so long, my body stiff and cold from being hunched over the phone screen. She must be here somewhere, I just have to know where to look. I, for one, know how hard it is to try and disappear completely – after all, I've never quite managed it, no matter how hard I've tried – the articles from Killin prove that.

Wearily, I type her name in again, only her name, nothing else and yawn as I wait for the search results to load. If nothing new comes up then I'll go home, get warm, and try again later. But maybe . . . if something does show up, I can track down a telephone number . . . Manchester will be difficult for me to get to, but maybe if she'll speak to me . . . I start to scroll through the links again, not really believing that I'll find anything, when all of a sudden, I see it. *Of course.* Excitement starting to fizz in my veins, my heart rate speeding up, I glance furtively around before I click on the link, anxious that someone will approach me before I get a chance to read it. No one is around.

Letting out a slow breath to steady my nerves, I click, and get my first glimpse of Katrina Snow as an adult. She's dark, like her mother, her skin a deep olive, cheeks flushed red with exertion, her hair sticking to her forehead as she holds out her arms in triumph, her feet flying as she crosses the finish line. Her eyes are closed in the photo, but there is no mistaking the look of elation on her face. Her bib reads KATRINA with a race number underneath pinned to her vest, and I scroll down to read the information beneath the picture. It reads: *KATRINA SNOW – 2798 – time: 2:27:15 – Surrey Half Marathon – March 2014.*

Surrey Half Marathon. All this time, Katrina Snow hasn't been in Manchester at all. She's been in Surrey, close to her father. Now I know where she is, or at least where she was in 2014, it makes it easier for me to carry on searching, and before too long I have found her Facebook profile (mostly private, but there's access to profile pictures) and finally, an address. It's on the other side of Oxbury, over towards Chertsey, and I glance at my watch, already knowing what I'm going to do, regardless of whether it's the right thing or not. I screenshot the information and stretch out my stiff limbs, a buzz of excitement rippling through me, before I hurry away towards the bus station. It's a sign, I tell myself, as I wait at the bus stop for the next bus towards Chertsey. If she'd still been in Manchester, then maybe . . . but she isn't. According to the electoral roll she lives near Chertsey, with a man that I am assuming is her partner. So surely, the fact that she is in Surrey is a sign that I should go and see her, speak to her, see if she can tell me anything at all about Mr Snow and what he might have done to Laurel. That's what I'm telling myself, anyway.

When I get off the bus Google Maps tells me it's only a three-minute walk to Katrina's house. As I turn into her road, the clouds that have gathered throughout the morning start to empty and rain begins to splatter the pavement with thick, heavy drops. I hurry my stride a little, not wanting to appear like a bedraggled hobo when I eventually reach her place. Checking the numbers as I walk, I reach number twelve. Katrina's house.

I pause for a moment before I start to walk down the path to the front door which is covered in flaking red paint, a dirty brass knocker in the middle. The front garden is in stark contrast to Mr Snow's. In contrast to his carefully tended lawn, stripes mowed into it religiously every Sunday afternoon, the shrubs and bushes he keeps neat and trimmed, and the tulips, lobelia, roses that spring up throughout the spring and summer much to Laurel's delight, this garden is slightly shabby. The grass hasn't been cut since the end of the summer, and dead leaves litter the path from a cherry tree in the corner. A child's trike lies upturned on the lawn, and there is a faint whiff of rubbish from the large black refuse bin at the end of the path, a bulge of black sack peeping out from where the lid doesn't quite close properly.

I tuck the rain-soaked ends of my hair back under my hat and lift the battered knocker, letting it fall three times. It's only a matter of seconds before the door is pulled open, and Katrina stands in front of me.

'Yes?' Her face is creased into a scowl, but it is unmistakably her. She looks slightly different to the photo I found, her body plump and curvy as opposed to the skinny runner's frame in the picture, but I recognise her olive skin, the wide curve of her mouth, even if it is downturned now.

Nerves make my mouth freeze for a moment before her name tumbles out. 'Katrina?'

'Yes?' she says again, the frown on her forehead deepening. 'Oh – no. I'm not speaking to any journalists.' Her voice is soft, a faint hint of a northern accent peeping through. Quickly, I raise my hand to push against the door as she starts to close it.

'I'm not a journalist,' I say, 'I know your dad.'

'You know my father?' she says, and the pressure of the door lessens slightly against the flat of my palm. She still looks uncertain, so I plough on.

'Look, can I come in? It's pouring out here.' I give a little laugh. 'I just want to talk to you if that's OK? I swear I'm not a journalist, or police or some weird vigilante type.'

'No, you're not coming in. Jesus, I don't even know who you are – you say you know my dad but how do I know you're telling the truth? You could be anyone.' She folds her arms across her chest, a barrier against me, but she doesn't close the door.

132

'Look, I know you don't know me, that I could be anybody, but please, Katrina . . . I wouldn't be here if it wasn't important. I know that he loves his garden, and his grandchildren.' I think for a moment, picturing him coughing into his hanky. 'I know that he's not well at the moment, and that you're worried about him.'

Katrina frowns and I think, *maybe I shouldn't have said that*, but then the door is pulled open and she reluctantly nods behind her, her eyes still narrowed with suspicion. 'Come in then. Only for five minutes mind, and only because it's raining so hard.'

I follow her through into a cramped sitting room, toys littered across the floor. A small boy sits amongst them driving a car round and round in circles. He looks up at me and smiles, his face a tiny replica of his mother's.

'So,' Katrina says, throwing herself in to an armchair, 'if you know my dad as well as you say you do, then you know what's happened to him.'

'Yes,' I say, unsure whether to sit or not. In the end I settle for perching on the end of the couch, where the small boy immediately starts driving the toy car up and over my leg. 'That's what I wanted to ask you about . . . see, I know the little girl who is missing.'

'Right.' She sits up straighter in the chair and I think maybe she's changed her mind about letting me in.

'I . . . I'm her nanny. I look after her.'

'I know what a nanny does, thanks,' she snaps at me and I realise I'm going to have to speak fast before she throws me out.

'I was the one who got Laurel speaking to your dad. We'd pass him every morning, and we got chatting. He's . . .

I thought he was a nice man, but then the police took him in and said he was "helping with enquiries" and . . . well, I did some research and I read about what he did to you.'

'He *is* a nice man,' Katrina says, quietly. Her voice is low, but I can see a tiny spark of anger flicker in her dark eyes. 'What you read – it didn't happen the way they said it did.'

I lick my lips nervously, before I speak again. 'Katrina . . . do you think your dad has anything to do with Laurel's disappearance? If there was anything, anything at all, that you think could help me . . . I have to get her back – this is all my fault. If I hadn't . . .'

'Are you kidding me?' Katrina's eyes widen in disbelief, as she shakes her head. 'I thought you said you knew him?'

'Well, as an acquaintance,' I say, trailing off, my eyes drawn down to the little boy at my feet.

'If you knew him, you'd know that he would never do something like this.' She catches herself, as she realises that that technically isn't true. 'Take a kid he doesn't know, I mean. You don't have any idea about what really happened, do you?'

'So, tell me. Please,' I say. I haven't come all this way to leave with nothing, even if it doesn't lead me to Laurel.

Katrina is quiet for a moment, as if wrestling with something internally, before she begins to speak. 'I'm only telling you this because I don't want you to think badly of him, OK? I don't owe you anything.' She glares at me, and I nod to show her I understand. 'He was getting divorced from my mum. She said I could stay with him over the weekend. I missed him, you know?' Her dark eyes are sad as she watches the boy playing on the floor in front of us. 'We had the best weekend. Then, on the Sunday night he said I didn't have to go back, not if I didn't want to. And I didn't want to. I wanted to stay with him.'

'Surely he knew your mum would call the police?'

'I don't think he cared.' Katrina fiddles with the tassel on a pink cushion next to her, avoiding my eyes. 'She was going to take me away, you know. She had it all planned. He'd left because she was so unbearable to live with, so . . . volatile. She's high maintenance, my mum. He was unhappy, and he left, and then she wanted to punish him. So, she was planning on flying us both to Turkey on the Tuesday after I came home, and she wasn't going to come back. He found out, and he wasn't going to let that happen, even if it meant getting arrested.'

I let out a long breath and lean back against the couch. 'Wow. It really didn't happen like they said it did. I thought . . . God, I'm sorry. I don't know what I thought. I literally jumped to conclusions.'

'Yeah,' Katrina gives a sad half smile, 'the same way whoever called into that crime show did. And now the police are all over him, and he's got to go through it all over again. He's an old man – he doesn't deserve this.'

'But . . .' I don't want to say it, but I have to. 'Surely, they must have had something other than this, to be able to bring him in? I mean . . . if it happened like you say, surely the police . . . ?' I rub my hands over my face. I am confused, tired and nothing seems to be making any sense any more.

'He's got the same sort of car that they're looking for. A dark SUV?' Katrina says. 'Someone knows his history, and what car he's driving and put two and two together. But they got five, Anna. He didn't do it. I know he didn't take Laurel.'

'How?' I say quietly, my eyes on Katrina's son. 'How can you be so sure that he didn't have something to do with Laurel going missing? And don't just say it's because he's your father.'

Katrina gets to her feet, scooping the boy up from the floor into her arms. He wails as he drops the toy car, and I stoop to pick it up for him.

'He gave Laurel this.' I pull the little toy doll from my back pocket. Katrina plucks it from my hand, turning it over, inspecting it.

'That belongs to Maryiam. My daughter. The fact that he gave it to Laurel doesn't mean anything. He's kind. That's all.'

'But ...'

'It's time you left,' Katrina says, her voice like steel as she ushers me towards the front door, angling herself so that I have no option but to leave. As we reach the door, Katrina giving me a gentle shove over the threshold, she speaks again.

'I know he didn't do it, Anna, because he was with me.' Her voice is low and serious, as she hefts the boy higher up on her hip. 'It was Oskar's birthday on Saturday. Dad came over in the afternoon, to help me with his party. He had his nursery friends over. Dad stayed here till probably ten o'clock, and then he left. Long after Laurel went missing. That's how I know. And that's what I've told the police. Don't come here again.' And she slams the door firmly closed in my face.

Ruth is in the kitchen when I arrive home, my head filled with my conversation with Katrina, which I replay over and over again. I look to Fran in confusion.

'She brought food. Again.' She sits at the table, her fingers playing with a single cigarette, as Ruth bustles about the kitchen reheating something from yet another foil-covered dish. The fact that she is here again makes me feel slightly uncomfortable – after all, she barely knows any of us and surely, she should be at home with her own family?

'Fran, can I talk to you?' I say.

'Yes. Of course.' Fran starts to stand as I gesture with my head towards the back door.

'Oh, you can speak freely in front of me,' Ruth says, as she loads a tray into the oven.

'It's family stuff,' Fran says, snatching up the cigarette from the table, and we step out into the damp, drizzly rain.

'Mr Snow didn't do it,' I say, straight away, the feeling of relief that comes with the words making me feel lighter than air. *This wasn't my fault.*

'Oh, Anna. Is that where you've been all afternoon?' Fran says gently. 'The police called not long before you arrived home. They told us he has a rock-solid alibi. Some family party or something. He's off the hook.' She fumbles in her pocket for a lighter, shielding her cigarette from the rain as she lights it.

'Oh.' I thought I had been so clever this afternoon, using my initiative, but it turns out I needn't have bothered after all. *Although what else would I have done?* There's nothing for me to do at home now that Laurel isn't here. 'Does Dominic know?'

'Who knows?' Fran's face hardens as she blows out a stream of grey-blue smoke. 'I haven't seen him all day. Perhaps you know where he is? After all, you seem to have

137

had quite the investigative day.' All at once the tension returns, the air thickening and I struggle to find the right words to say, knowing by Fran's tone that whatever I say will be wrong, as it so often is.

'No. No I don't know where he is.'

She must catch something in my voice because an unreadable expression crosses her face and she reaches out to gently touch my arm. 'Sorry, Anna. This is hard for you too, isn't it? I know I'm a prickly old bitch.'

'No, no of course you're not,' I say automatically. Fran raises an eyebrow and gives a small laugh, one that is crammed full of sadness.

'You're a good girl, Anna. I'm sorry you've had to go through all of this. I forget that you love Laurel too, that you miss her probably just as much as I . . . as *we* do. I really am so dreadfully sorry.' She stubs out her cigarette and turns on her heel, leaving me alone outside in the rain. *So, Dominic is gone again.* I recall his words from earlier today. *Perhaps if you hadn't been such a bitch . . .* I push away the thought of the long, blonde hair that I plucked from his jacket from my mind. Where are you, Laurel? Please, come home.

CHAPTER 14

Dominic is in the kitchen when I come down from my room the next morning, and he's clearly not happy by the way he is slamming things around. Kelly sits quietly in the corner, a cup of coffee to her lips as she just sits observing. Dominic throws his empty mug into the sink and marches out, slamming the door behind him.

'Jesus,' I breathe, helping myself to a slice of toast. I've barely eaten since Laurel went missing, and now I have to force myself to butter the bread, bring it to my lips, bite and then actually swallow. 'Did something happen?' Every day seems to feel like it stretches into weeks, time passes so slowly, all the time that Laurel isn't here.

'You could say that.' Kelly raises her eyebrows at me. 'Fran . . .'

'Good morning!' Fran slips into the room, an anxious smile on her face and I look to Kelly in alarm. Something isn't right. Fran hasn't smiled at all, I don't think, not since Laurel went missing. 'Anna, did Kelly tell you?'

'Tell me what?' I look between the two of them – Fran's eyes shining, a healthy glow back in her cheeks, and Kelly, sitting there quietly, her face pale – I'm not sure what to make of it.

'Oh, Kelly.' Fran rolls her eyes, but I see the flash of irritation there before it disappears. 'So, Anna. Something exciting is happening today – something that could give us a real breakthrough in finding Laurel.' She pauses, as if to ramp up the tension and I have to bite back a mild feeling of disgust that she is turning this into a dramatic announcement, almost like one of her shows. 'I have a psychic coming to the house!'

I stare at her, open-mouthed. *A psychic?* This goes against everything I know about Fran, in all the time I have been working for her. She is the biggest sceptic going – she doesn't even bother to read her own horoscope. This is the last thing I thought she was going to say, and it also explains why Dominic is in such a foul mood.

'Obviously, Dominic isn't keen,' Fran says, 'but we need to do anything and everything that might help Laurel, don't you think?' She looks pointedly at Kelly.

'Look, Fran, you know my feelings on this,' Kelly says, a little awkwardly. 'I'm not sure this is the right decision. I mean, you are vulnerable at the moment, and we don't know this woman – she could simply be trying to take advantage of your situation.'

'And she *might* tell us where Laurel is.' Fran's teeth are gritted, and I watch her fingers wander to her pocket, to the outline of her cigarette packet. 'She'll be here soon. I need to go and get ready.'

My heart leaps in my chest as the piercing ring of the doorbell cuts through the silence of the house, and I dash to the front door, only to open it to find Ruth standing there.

'Ruth.' I am reluctant to let her in, knowing the plans Fran has for this morning.

'Can I come in?' She peers past me, smiling. 'I have some cookies for you all – I baked them fresh this morning – and I designed a new poster for the search volunteers to hand out, I wondered if Fran could have a look at them, make sure it's OK.' She rests a hand against the front door as if she's going to push it open.

'Ruth! How kind of you.' Fran glides up behind me, her slippered feet silent on the tiled floor, and I worry for a moment that she's going to invite Ruth in to sit in with the psychic, another ally against Dominic's refusal to support her. 'I'm terribly sorry, now really isn't a good time. Here, let me take those.' She reaches out and takes the plate of cookies, leaving me to take the rolled-up posters from Ruth. 'Thank you though, darling.' And with a brief, sad smile she closes the door gently in Ruth's face. Despite how uncomfortable Ruth's attention makes me, I can't help but feel relieved that she isn't here to see Fran go straight into the kitchen and slide her plate of cookies directly into the bin.

Dominic is back by the time the doorbell rings for a second time, announcing the arrival of the so-called psychic. Part of me still feels sceptical, convinced that this is someone just out to take advantage of Fran and Dominic. The other part of me is slightly terrified, half hopeful that she will tell us something that will lead us to Laurel, half frightened that she'll reveal something about me. About before. As the bell rings, Fran jumps and then gets to her feet. Some of her excitement seems to have worn off a little now and I hear her clearing her throat before she answers the door, a sure sign of her nervousness. Kelly slopes over to the armchair in the corner, out of sight, but still present, balancing her small notebook and pen on the mantelpiece.

Fran enters, leading a woman in behind her. 'Everyone. This is Margaret.' When I catch a glimpse of the woman, I almost have to hold in a snort of laughter. The psychic is definitely not what I was expecting. I thought she would be colourful, adorned with scarves – if I'm honest, I pictured the tiny psychic woman from the *Poltergeist* movie – but this woman is the opposite. Pale, mousy, in her late fifties, and so completely nondescript she could almost be related to Ruth. They have that same aura of appearing invisible unless they want to be noticed.

'Hello.' Margaret nods to everyone, before Fran guides her over to the sofa. Dominic says nothing, just nods back, his face devoid of any emotion. I perch on the edge of Kelly's armchair, in the furthest corner of the room. I'm still not sure how I feel about all of this and want to fade into the background a little.

'Before we begin,' Margaret's voice is soft and low, almost soothing, 'do you have something of Laurel's? Something that is special to her, that I could just hold on to? It would give me a better sense of her, that's all.'

'I'll go.' Dominic leaves the room, returning a few moments later with Bom, Laurel's stuffed tiger teddy in his hands. I notice his fingers shake as he passes it to Margaret. Margaret takes it from him, bringing it briefly to her nose before she holds it tight against her chest. Fran is seated on the edge of the Chesterfield armchair opposite the sofa, and now Dominic comes to stand behind it, one hand on Fran's shoulder. Margaret closes her eyes and exhales slowly, and I feel the air around us thicken with something I can't quite put my finger on. Anticipation, maybe?

'Oh, she's pretty,' Margaret says, her eyes still closed, Bom tight to her chest. I glance at Kelly, who gives a tiny shrug and I realise we are both thinking the same thing. *Laurel's face has been all over the news – everyone has seen her, of course you know she's pretty.*

'She's a little monkey,' Margaret smiles a little, and Fran twists round to look at Dominic.

'Yes, she is,' Fran says, her voice thick with tears. 'A proper little madam.'

'She loves it outside . . . playing. She likes the woods, the trees. Getting mucky.'

I find myself nodding along with Dominic and Fran, despite my scepticism. She does love getting dirty – Lord knows the amount of times I've had to throw her clothes in the machine before Fran sees them and freaks out.

'There are woods where she is now.' Margaret's voice has taken on a different tone, but still her eyes are closed, her breathing coming slightly faster in her chest. Fran's face has paled, and I look at Kelly, but her eyes are fixed on the psychic. 'There are woods, and stone. It's not close by. There are lots of fields around. Very flat.'

Kelly reaches for the notebook on the mantelpiece and starts to scribble things down and I find my heart is beating faster in my chest. Maybe there is something in this? Dominic's forehead shines and he wipes the sweat with the back of his hand.

'Is she OK?' Fran is leaning so far forward on her chair it looks as though she might fall at any minute.

'She's not hurt.' Margaret frowns. 'Someone close to you is lying. Someone isn't who they say they are.'

I pinch the back of my hand, to keep myself in the here and now, ignoring Kelly's curious glance in my direction.

'She's . . . she knows the person who did this. Who took her.' Margaret squeezes the tiger once more before she drops it to the floor, her eyes springing open and fixing on Dominic, where he stands behind Fran. 'You know where she is.'

Fran gasps, tears spilling over as she presses one hand to her mouth. Dominic, however, springs into action.

'Right, that's it. Out.' He grabs Margaret by her arm and hauls her to her feet, marching her towards the front door.

'Dominic, wait!' Kelly runs after him, presumably to stop him from physically throwing Margaret out on to the pavement. Fran sits, stock still, tears running down her cheeks.

'Fran?' I approach her tentatively, like you would a wild animal that has been hurt, unsure of the response I will get. 'Are you OK?'

'I didn't think it would work,' Fran says, 'I didn't think she would be able . . . Oh.' She rubs a hand across her eyes. 'She knows who did this to her . . . and we know where she is?' She raises her red-rimmed eyes to mine. A pulse beats in her temple, a twitch under her pale skin. 'Why would she say that? Oh, Anna, I feel sick.' She holds her hand tight against her flat stomach.

'I don't know.' I feel helpless, like I should know the right things to say, but I don't. I didn't last time either and look how that turned out. 'Maybe she means you know the area where she is being kept? I'm sorry, Fran, I simply have no idea.'

Dominic comes crashing in then, his face a white mask of rage.

'Are you happy, Fran? Now you've let some . . . charlatan in? She'll probably go straight to the papers, telling them how we know something we're not letting on.' He shoves his hand through his hair, pacing the floor, anger coming off him in hot waves.

'She's not a charlatan, Dom, she could be telling the truth! Maybe . . .' Fran's voice breaks and she starts to sob, hiding her face in her hands as her shoulders hitch up and down dramatically.

'And if she's not? If she's just used it to get inside the house so that she can sell a story to the papers? How is that going to help Laurel then? Turning the focus on to us instead of the person who really took Laurel? I can't believe you did this.' He keeps pacing, his footsteps heavy on the oak flooring. 'Where did you even get her from?'

'She called the house.' It is almost a whisper, coming from behind Fran's hands. She lowers them to her lap, her cheeks blazing red as she gets to her feet to stand in front of Dominic. The fire in her eyes is back. 'She called here, and she said she could help. I just wanted to see what she said. Surely that's better than doing nothing?'

'Oh, Jesus,' Dominic scrubs his hands over his face, 'how could you be so stupid, Fran? She was probably from the fucking *Daily Mail*! I have to get out of here.' He snatches up his car keys from the coffee table and slams his way out of the house. I hear the sound of his engine revving, and then a squeal as he peels out of the driveway. Fran rushes from the room with a sob, and I step forward to go after her, but Kelly lays a hand on my arm.

'Leave her for a second,' she says, 'let her go upstairs and cry for a bit. She's hurting.'

I nod, in two minds about things. Half of me wants to go and comfort Fran, the other half is relieved that I don't have to.

'What do you make of all this?' Kelly asks, looking down at the squiggles she's made in her notebook. 'All that, "you know where she is" business.'

'I don't know.' I am reluctant to say anything much in case I accidentally incriminate myself. 'Maybe that wherever Laurel is, when we find her, it'll be somewhere that is familiar to one of them? I've never really believed in this sort of stuff if I'm honest.'

'Hmmm.' Kelly doodles in the corner of the notepad, an intricate swirl that fills one section. 'You can talk to me you know, Anna. As a friend. Not a police officer. If you wanted to, I mean.'

'Thanks. But I really don't know what that could have meant.'

'You don't think it was weird? Her saying that Laurel knows who took her, and that they know where she is?'

'That's if she was even telling the truth. You know half the time these people make things up, just to extort money from desperate people.' Kelly's words give my skin a tight, itchy feel as if they have burrowed into my bones. I push the thought of the shiny blonde hair, still wrapped in a tissue and hidden in my drawer, to the back of my mind. 'Dominic is probably right.' *Someone isn't who they say they are.* I shake the thought away and get to my feet. 'She probably was from the *Daily Mail*. I hope you people are prepared to deal with the fallout if she is.'

Drawing a line firmly between us and them, between me and Kelly, I leave the room, not waiting to hear her response.

As I reach the landing, I hear the buzz of a mobile phone on silent. Pausing, I listen for a moment trying to figure out where it is coming from. *Laurel's room.* Quietly, so as not to disturb Fran, I push open the door to see a silver iPhone X lying on Laurel's bed. Dominic's phone. He must have been in here earlier. We all seem to have found our way into Laurel's room at one point or another since she went missing, although I felt I didn't really have the right to be there, sneaking in when Fran and Dominic were elsewhere, trying to soak up a little bit of Laurel's aura, to find a little bit of comfort. There isn't any though, not without her here.

The buzzing stops, and it's almost eerily silent in here. I'm used to Laurel filling the room with chatter and laughter, not this dead, thick silence. I stoop to pick up some Lego bricks that lie tumbled in a corner, left in a half-constructed version of a square house that Laurel was building on Saturday afternoon. Pausing, my hand hovering over the jumble of bright plastic, I don't know whether to pack them away or not, before deciding that Lego will be the last thing on Laurel's mind when – if – she comes home, and I throw them gently into the plastic tub they live in.

Turning my attention to the pile of clean laundry that sits on the rocking chair, still waiting to be put away from that fateful Saturday two weeks ago, I open drawers and start to pack away her clothes, pausing at her favourite sweatshirt. I lift it surreptitiously to my nose, hoping to inhale some small fragment of her scent, but all I can smell is soap powder and fabric softener, tears thickening at the back of my throat. There is nothing left of Laurel in her clothes, it has all been washed away.

The buzzing of the iPhone starts up again, making me jump. I shove the sweatshirt into the drawer and hurry across the bedroom to answer it before Fran hears it. The screen shows a number not stored in Dominic's phone, so I pick it up and answer it, thinking that maybe it's something to do with a patient, an emergency perhaps.

'Hello?'

'Dominic?' The voice on the other end of the line is breathy and low, but unmistakably female. 'Is that you?'

'No. Dominic isn't here at the moment. Can I take a message for him?' I ask, my mind already starting to work over time.

'Ah . . . no. Thank you.' The phone beeps three times in my ear and the line goes dead.

Not a work-related emergency then. Not work-related at all by the sounds of it, her voice had that flirty, throaty tone to it. I frown, turning the phone over in my hand. Is Fran right after all? Is Dominic seeing someone else, or have I just got caught up in Fran's paranoia? And does that mean Dominic had something to do with Laurel disappearing that night? After all, he wasn't where he said he would be, and although he told me he'd told the police where he was I don't know for definite that he did. And he asked me not to tell Fran. And what about the hair on the jacket? Does it belong to this mystery woman, or is it Laurel's? And does that mean the psychic isn't a fraud – Dominic really does know something?

I lay the phone back down on Laurel's bed where Dominic can find it and pull the door to Laurel's room gently closed. All this time, all these days have passed and all I have are questions, and yet more questions. No answers.

CHAPTER 15

The following day, I text Jessika and arrange to meet her and Daisy at the park, needing a bit of space to clear my head after the psychic's visit. I slip quietly out of the back gate and along the alley behind the houses – there are still a few press lurking at the bottom of the cul-de-sac, having moved on slightly after Kelly threatened to arrest them, but they won't leave completely, not until something breaks.

'Hey.' Jess smiles at me, bundled up against the cold in a thick puffa jacket and bobble hat. 'How are things?' She pushes Daisy on the swing, the little girl squealing and laughing as her feet fly over the soft, spongy safety mat underneath.

'Well, she's still not home.' Aware that I am snippy, I try and smile. 'It's awful. The atmosphere is just . . .' I puff my fringe away from my face. 'Fran got a psychic in, you know.'

'Yeah, I know.' Jess slows the swing to a stop and Daisy jumps off, running towards the slide. 'Everyone has been talking about it.'

'Really?' I frown in confusion. 'How did they know? I mean, I expected everyone to be talking about George Snow, that was in the paper. But not this. Who told you?'

'It was in the paper, though,' Jess says, quietly. 'Front page of *The Oxbury Echo*. "PARENTS CALL IN ACCLAIMED PSYCHIC." That kind of thing.'

'Shit.' I sink down on to the damp, mossy bench on the edge of the playground. 'Dominic will go crazy. He didn't want her to come in in the first place. What did the article say?'

'Just that the Jessops called in Margaret Lawler. She's well-known, you know. Me and my mum went to see some stage show thing she did years ago. I suppose in psychic terms you could call her quite famous. She's written books and stuff.'

'I had no idea.' I wonder whether Fran knew all of this when she took the phone call from Margaret Lawler. I'm certain Dominic didn't – he never would have agreed to her visit in the first place and certainly not if he knew she was well-known.

'People are starting to talk,' Jess says suddenly, her cheeks flushing scarlet as she toes the mulchy leaves that surround the bench.

'What do you mean, people are starting to talk?' I feel my pulse flutter in my throat, heat making the back of my neck prickle.

'Just . . . you know. Gossip.' Jess looks over to where Daisy spins on the roundabout, making sure her charge is safe and in her eye line. 'It's like the McCanns . . . Fran and Dominic are successful, wealthy . . . they're going to be judged. Dominic wasn't where he said he would be that night . . . things like that. People like to have someone to blame, someone to pin things on. It makes life feel safer for themselves . . . like, if they have someone to blame, then bad things can't happen to them.'

'I'm not sure that Fran and Dominic would see it that way.' I get to my feet, pushing away the thoughts that jostle at the back of my mind. *Dominic, not where he promised to be, with no explanation. Dominic, violent and aggressive, not the man I thought I knew.* 'I should probably head back.'

'I didn't mean to upset you – I just thought you should know. About the psychic. And, you know . . .' Jess gives a little shrug, her brow creasing in distress.

'It's fine. I guess we should have expected it, but I think we all thought Laurel would be home by now, or that someone would have been arrested and charged for it at the very least.' I don't want to think about what would happen if someone was arrested and charged but Laurel didn't come home safely. 'It's been over two weeks.' My throat closes over, and I swallow back the painful lump that rises. 'I really do have to go.'

I hurry away from the park without looking back. Three weeks ago, I would have been meeting Jess with Laurel by my side, giving Fran a precious few hours to go over her lines. It feels strange to be here without her. I mull over Jess's words as I walk along the damp streets, stepping over puddles left by yesterday's rain, so lost in my own thoughts that I don't even realise there is anyone else nearby until I crash into them.

'Oh, gosh . . . I'm so sorry!' I reach out a hand to steady the man I have walked into, lowering it as I realise who it is. 'Oh.'

'My apologies, too. It seems neither of us were watching where we were going.' Mr Snow stands in front of me, a hat pulled low over his head, which explains why he also didn't see me. 'How are you, Anna?'

'Um . . . OK.' I feel flustered, not sure what to say to him. I know it's not my fault he was brought in over Laurel's disappearance, but what *do* you say? 'You?'

He gives only a ghost of a smile. 'Not bad. I hear you met my daughter.'

'Yes. I . . . yes, I did. She was very helpful.' I pause for a moment, feeling the heat of a blush rising up my cheeks. 'I'm very sorry, Mr Snow. For what happened to you, for jumping to conclusions. You didn't deserve it.'

'Thank you, Anna.' He is far more calm than I would be in this situation, if I'd been arrested for something I hadn't done – I know that from experience. 'Please tell the Jessops that I understand. And if they need to talk, well, you know where I am. I'm sure it won't be long before the speculation turns toward them, unfortunately.'

'Right.' There is an awkward silence and I know that even if Laurel comes home today, things between us will never go back to how they were before. No more easy chats in the afternoons on the way home, no more lollies for Laurel. 'I'll let them know. I'm really sorry but . . . I must go.'

Eager to put some distance between us, I don't wait for him to reply, I just head in the opposite direction towards home, his words ricocheting around my brain.

I thought that maybe before too long, some people would take a dim view of the Jessops – I heard that woman at the school comment on Fran's make-up the day of the appeal, and there was that message left on the Facebook page – but I thought the Jessops were well-liked in Oxbury, and that they would have most people's support. If anything, in the beginning, there was a constant stream of people all wanting to help, all wanting to be involved with this terrible tragedy that had befallen the glamorous Jessop family, but from what Jess says, things may be starting to change.

Lost in my own thoughts, I don't notice the graffiti until I am almost on top of it. My feet slow and a swirling, nauseous feeling rises in my stomach. It looks as though Mr Snow is right, people are starting to take against the Jessops. There, scrawled in red spray paint across the back fence is the word, *MURDERER*.

'It's coming off, see.' Kelly pauses to look over her shoulder at Fran, as she stands silently behind us, her thumb pressed against her lips as she bites at the skin around the nail. Kelly and I are crouched next to a bucket of hot, soapy water, scrubbing at the offensive stain on the fence. I feel sick every time I look at it, the idea that someone in our community felt it was OK to do this.

'It was probably kids,' Kelly says, catching the look on my face as I scrub hard, soap suds drifting down my wrist and soaking my sleeve. 'Try not to read too much into it.'

'Try not to read too much into it?' Dominic snarls, as he paces behind us, his face pale, his breath coming in angry gasps. 'This is your fault, you know that?'

I flinch at his words, thinking they are aimed at me, but Kelly rises to her feet, her knees clicking awkwardly as she stands.

'Dominic, please.' She splays her hands in a gesture designed to calm him. 'This is purely . . .'

'Purely your bloody fault!' Dominic halts in front of her, pointing a shaking finger in her face, 'If you hadn't made us do that TV appeal maybe this wouldn't have happened. I told you a TV appeal would make people point the finger at us – didn't I say that, Fran? And you could have stopped that bloody psychic coming to the house – don't think

154

I didn't see the front page of the papers, telling the world she was here! Now look – you should be out there searching for whoever took our daughter, not here scrubbing that shit off the fence.' He shoves his way back through the gate and marches up the path towards the house.

'And there he goes, storming off again,' Fran sighs, her arms wrapped around her skinny frame as if trying to keep warm. 'We won't see him for hours again now. Have you noticed that?' Her voice is almost dreamy, her eyes blank. 'He storms off and goes to God knows where for hours, leaving me to deal with everything on my own. He should be here, with me, waiting for Laurel to come home.' She blinks, and a tear rolls down one cheek. I get to my feet, my thighs protesting.

'Come inside. It's freezing out here.' I guide her towards the gate, glancing back at Kelly who nods. 'I'll make you a cup of tea.'

Fran is right – Dominic's car is gone, and when we re-enter the house, it's empty. I set about making the tea, Fran sitting silently at the table, any animation from Margaret's visit has been washed away by the offensive graffiti on the fence. The shrill ring of the telephone makes me jump, and Fran pushes herself to her feet, but I wave her back down.

'Sit down, I'll get it.' The landline rarely rings. I head out to the hallway and lift the receiver.

'Hello?' There is no response, merely the hiss of static on the line. 'Hello? Can you hear me?' My heart starts to bang in my chest, my ears straining for any little noise. 'Is someone there?' Nothing. The line goes dead in my hand. Fran looks up as I walk back into the kitchen.

155

'Who was it?'

'No one. There was no one there. Maybe a wrong number?' I say, even though I don't think it was. And there was someone at the end of the line, I thought I could make out their breathing. 'Maybe we could check the Facebook page, while we wait for Kelly to finish with the fence?' Perhaps reading some of the supportive messages will reassure Fran that people do love Laurel, and that they aren't all against the Jessops.

'OK.' Fran logs into the laptop and pulls up Facebook just as the telephone begins to ring again.

'I'll go.' I hurry out to the hallway and snatch the phone up again, pressing it hard to my ear. 'Hello?' Static again, the faint whistle of breath going in and out. 'Hello? Who is this? Seriously, what do you want?' *Ransom*. The word floats across my mind and my stomach flips. What if it's the person who has Laurel? What if they're calling to demand money? There is no response on the end of the line, and a few short seconds later the dial tone sounds in my ear. I walk slowly back into the kitchen and Fran looks at me closely.

'Well? Who was it this time?'

'The same again. No one there. But I could hear them breathing.' I take a seat next to her and pretend that the dead calls haven't unnerved me. 'Let's check the page, shall we?'

'Do you think it has something to do with Laurel, the dead calls?' Fran asks, leaning forward on her elbows, frowning hard. 'Ransom, maybe? Kelly should be able to trace the calls, right?'

It's as if she's read my thoughts. 'I guess. I don't know.' The Facebook log-in screen loads and I swivel the screen towards Fran, so she can log in. As she types in her password, the telephone starts to ring again and my stomach lurches.

'I'll answer it this time.' Fran shoves her chair back, the feet scraping across the tiled floor and making me wince. I follow her out to the hallway, waiting anxiously as she snatches up the receiver.

'Hello?' Her voice is surprisingly firm. 'Who is this?' She waits for a second and I hear the muffled tones of the person on the other end of the line. 'How . . . you utter bitch.' Her face crumples as she slams the receiver back into the cradle, her hands flying up to cover her eyes.

'Fran?' I go to her, but she shakes her head, waving a hand at me. 'Who was it? What did they say?'

'I don't know who it was . . . it was a woman's voice though. Not one I think I know, but I'm not sure. There *was* something familiar about it maybe?' She pulls her hands away from her face and I see she is crying again.

'But what did they say?' I ask, a cold finger running its way down my spine.

'They said . . .' Fran hiccups, 'they said that Laurel going missing was all my fault.'

Kelly comes in from the garden, and straight away I tell her about the phone call, despite Fran's feeble protestations.

'We can try and trace it if they call again,' Kelly says, 'but if it leads back to a pay-as-you-go phone we won't have much luck finding the caller ID.'

'It's probably just a prank,' I say, trying to make Fran feel better. 'No one honestly thinks that you had anything to do with Laurel going missing. How could you have done? I was right there with you the whole time.' I deliberately don't mention Dominic, and the persistent nagging feeling in my belly that I get every time I think about his absence that night, the way he asked me to not mention it to Fran.

'Yes. OK.' I can almost see Fran pulling her big girl pants on to get on with things. 'I'm going to reply to some of these messages of support that have been left on the "FIND LAUREL" page.' She pulls up the page and starts scrolling. 'Oh, there are some lovely ones.' She smiles as she reads, and Kelly pulls up a chair next to her. It doesn't take long though for the smile to slide off her face, and for a frown to appear on Kelly's brow.

'What is it?' I ask, scooching round to their side of the table so I can see the screen. To top off everything else that has happened today, there is another message from Lois Burns. Just as vicious and vitriolic as the last.

'*Where were you, Dominic? You should have been there, looking after your kid.*'

'*Well done on the acting, Fran. Acting like you could give a shit.*'

And then, again, the same as before:

'*Maybe if you'd looked after her properly this wouldn't have happened. You don't deserve to have children. Maybe now she's with someone who does.*'

'Jesus,' I breathe out, bile scorching the back of my throat. I swallow hastily, before I risk a glance at Fran. 'That's just . . .'

'Horrible.' Fran's hand goes to the necklace around her throat. She looks ill, is the only way to describe her, as though the life has been sucked out of her. 'How could someone say such horrible things?'

'I'm going to make a call, get DS Wright to start looking into this,' Kelly says, closing the lid of the laptop and walking away, fumbling for her mobile phone. Fran pushes her chair back, gets to her feet.

'I'd like to be alone for a while,' she says as I also stand. 'I'll be in my room.' And she hurries from the kitchen, leaving me alone, the bitter taste of hatred lying thick on my tongue.

Later, the house quiet, I sneak along to the bathroom for a shower, Dominic having come home earlier and gone straight to Laurel's room where he sat, with the door closed, for over an hour. Dinner was a half-hearted, stilted affair, Kelly rustling up soup and cheese sandwiches that ended up laying dried and curling at the edges when nobody could face eating them. *How does she do it?* I wonder, as the hot water thunders over my head, *how does she spend day after day in the thick of events like these?* As I rub shampoo into my hair, a thick clump falls out in my hand, washing away down the drain, and I blink back tears.

A sure sign of stress, my hair came out in clumps in Scotland once the accusations were made. And now it's happening again. I carefully rinse the soap from my hair, trying not to touch it too much. How long before this nightmare is over? There are so many pieces, it's like a jigsaw that I can't quite fit together – today, the graffiti and the abusive messages added another element to it all, another part of the picture that I can't make fit. Does the person who did this have information about Laurel? Or are they just out to be vindictive? The blonde hair on Dominic's jacket, the psychic raising her eyes to his – *you know where she is* – the phone call from the woman who quite clearly wasn't a work colleague. Is it all related? Or am I simply clutching at straws?

CHAPTER 16

Shouting rouses me from my dozy state of almost-sleep, and I blink, my eyes feeling dry and sore. Twisting my head round to look out of the window, I can see that I must have been asleep for at least a couple of hours – the sun has set behind the houses, and while it isn't quite fully dark yet, the sky is a deep indigo colour, the last dying rays of the sun scorching the horizon a deep orange-y red. The moon is already out, and I can see the beginnings of a glittery frost on the cars parked across the street. I haven't slept properly since the night before Laurel disappeared, and I find myself sleeping when I don't expect to. Muffled voices float up through the floorboards again, and I swing my legs round and tiptoe to the door, inching it open just a crack.

'Fran, please . . . you're being a little bit unreasonable, don't you think?' Dominic's voice is low, as if he doesn't want to be overheard.

'Unreasonable?' Fran's voice is considerably louder, 'you're talking about going back to work – *full-time* – when Laurel isn't home. How can you even think about it?' Her voice breaks on the last word, and I hold my breath, waiting to hear Dominic's response.

'The hospital needs me, Fran. They've covered my list for two weeks, but they can't cover it any longer. People have had their operations put off already – and for some of them this is life-saving stuff. I have to go back. But I've told them that if anything – any tiny little thing – comes to light about Laurel, I'm coming straight home.'

'Oh, Dominic,' Fran gives a soft laugh, full of bitterness, 'we both know that isn't true. Maybe if you'd been there that night, maybe if you'd kept your promise to Laurel, instead of putting the hospital first, then she would be here tonight.' *He still hasn't told her he wasn't at the hospital.* I bite back the gasp that springs to my lips. There is a thick, heavy silence from downstairs before Dominic speaks again.

'Is this how it will be now? Even if . . . when . . . she comes home? You'll blame me, forever?' I hear the jangle of keys as he scoops them up. 'You've always been happy to spend the money, Fran. And you haven't exactly been there for her yourself – always at that bloody theatre, rehearsing lines for auditions that you never win. How many school plays, parents' evenings, fêtes, have you missed because you just *had* to be in London, so Anna had to take her? We've both made mistakes, Fran.'

I peer over the bannister to see him slide his keys into his pocket and pull open the front door.

'I'm going out for a while,' he says, not looking back at Fran.

'That's your answer to everything, isn't it?' Fran's voice rises, and there is a screechy tone to it. 'Just run off? Leave me here, on my own, to deal with everything. Well, go on then. Off you go. I only hope she's worth it, whoever she is.'

Dominic shakes his head, and I step back quickly into my room as Fran turns and starts thundering her way up

162

the stairs. I sit back on my bed, watching Dominic out of the window as he strides away up the street, his head down, not looking back. The door to Laurel's room clicks open, and then closed again as I hear Fran heading in there. I'll let her calm down – if I go in there now, she'll only turn on me. It wouldn't be the first time I got it in the neck for something someone else has done to upset her.

The thought of leaving floats across my mind again and I have to force it away. *What if Laurel comes home and you're not here? How can you leave her to these two, warring and fighting, always in a constant battle?* the devil on one shoulder asks me; *What if she never comes home? Will you just stay here forever?* the one on the other side asks. I sigh and scrub my hands over my face.

If I'm honest, I'd thought about leaving a few times, long before Laurel disappeared, but couldn't bring myself to leave her with Fran and Dominic. Both of them busy with their careers, I was often, as Dominic just threw back in Fran's face, the only one available to take her to school plays and go to parents' evenings. And I was attached to her – the way her eyes lit up when she saw me in the playground at the end of the school day, the way she snuggled down under the duvet while I was reading her a story. We have a connection, the two of us, one that I can't bring myself to break even though she isn't here. *You've been more of a mother to her than Fran ever has,* a voice whispers way back in the dark corners of my mind. No, I can't leave. Not without knowing that she's home and safe. The click of the door breaks into my thoughts and I see Fran coming out of Laurel's room through the gap in my door. She hurries down the stairs, and I wait a few minutes before I follow her down.

'Fran? Everything OK?' She is closing the door to the garage as she steps into the kitchen, and she jumps, placing her free hand to her chest.

'Oh. Anna. You made me jump. I was only grabbing this.' She waves a bottle of wine in my direction. 'One of Dominic's "good" ones from the cellar.' She says *cellar*, she means *garage*. But I don't pick her up on it, I wouldn't dare. 'Actually. Shall we save it for later?' Her eyes darken, and I shrug. I don't drink. I don't know how many times I've told her that, although I suppose she can be excused for forgetting lately. I haven't touched a drop since I left Scotland. 'I think I might take a walk down to the church.' She looks at me, and I can feel her desperation leaching off her in waves. 'Come with me? I'm not sure I want to be alone right now.'

'I'm sure Kelly would . . .' I start.

'No, not Kelly. I want you to come, Anna. Kelly doesn't even know Laurel.' Fran lifts her chin as if daring me to say no.

'I'll get my coat,' I say.

We walk in silence along the narrow lane that leads to the church, the sun completely set by the time we reach the top of the slight hill that the church sits on. It's almost eerily quiet, the moon casts a pale, white glow across the pavement and our breath comes in smoky clouds as the temperature drops. Again, there is that faint tinge of bonfire smoke on the air, that makes my stomach flip. In the houses further along from the church one brave soul already has Christmas lights in the window, despite the fact that we still have another week before November fades into

December, and they twinkle brightly, a puff of colour in the dark, chilly evening. We follow the short gravel path to the heavy church doors, pausing when we reach them. The dark oak doors are pulled tightly shut.

'Is it even open?' I ask, in a low voice, as though if I speak too loudly I'll wake the ghosts in the graveyard.

'A church is never closed,' Fran says in a solemn voice, shaking her hair back from her eyes before she reaches for the handle, turning it stiffly and shouldering the heavy door open. Inside, the church is dimly lit, and the temperature is not much above what it is outside. Fran makes her way in confidently, and I get the feeling that despite the Jessops' not being a particularly religious household, she has been here before.

She heads straight to the front of the church and fumbles in her pocket, pulling out a pound coin that she throws into a tin before helping herself to a candle. I stand there silently as she lights it, her head slightly bowed, the lights from above reflecting on her hair. She presses her hands together in front of her mouth and closes her eyes, whispering to herself (or to God) fervently. Awkwardly, I glance around the church while I wait for Fran to finish, the musty aroma that seems to fill every church I've ever been in making me want to sneeze. Finally, Fran opens her eyes and turns, making her way to the empty pew behind us. She slides in and then taps the seat next to her for me to sit.

'It's so peaceful, isn't it?' she says, her eyes fixed on the lit candle ahead of us. 'I find it easier to think here.' So, I was right – she has been here before.

'I didn't think you and Dominic were especially religious,' I say, cautiously.

'Oh no, we're not, not really. Can you see Dominic putting God before his patients? That's why we never go on a Sunday.' Fran gives a small smile, casting her eyes down and clasping her hands in front of her, almost as if she's playing a part. I can practically see her on the screen, portraying the devout, religious mother. 'I've just found it gives me some peace, to come here and think about Laurel. The vicar has offered to hold a service to pray for her safe return.'

I say nothing, unsure of what to think. In Scotland, church was a big part of family life. Today is the first day I have set foot in a church since I left the village, and it doesn't feel peaceful, or calming to me. It feels claustrophobic and stifling.

'Anna . . .' Fran speaks, but keeps her eyes straight ahead on the flame of the candle. 'You would tell me, wouldn't you, if you thought Dominic was keeping a secret from me?'

Shit. I shuffle my feet slightly, if only to reassure myself the ground hasn't fallen away beneath me.

'What do you mean?' I stall.

'I . . . I think he's hiding something from me, but I don't know what. I thought maybe . . . no, I am pretty sure he's having an affair, but I think there's more to it than that.'

I bite down on my lower lip, frantically thinking how best to respond, but Fran doesn't wait for me to speak.

'I mean, why would he be so desperate to go back to work? I know his job is important, and life-saving and everything he constantly rams down my throat about it, but Laurel is his daughter! How can he think about work at a time like this?' She turns to me, eyes shining with unshed tears.

'I don't . . .' I stutter for a moment, 'I don't think he knows what else to do.'

'I'm sure he's having an affair. The way he storms out at any little chance. Have you seen or heard anything, Anna?'

I think about the phone call I answered, the breathy, flirty voice at the other end of it, but it's not enough, it's not proof. 'I don't think so.'

'There was a woman before me, you know?' Fran gives me a conspiratorial look, as if sharing a secret. 'I honestly think that she and Dominic would have got back together if it hadn't been for me.'

'Really?' I'm not sure what to think. The Jessops have a volatile relationship – Fran is high maintenance and they argue about ridiculous things sometimes – but it always seemed, before, anyway, that the volatility was what kept them coming back for more.

'Oh, yes. I got pregnant within a few weeks of Dominic and I meeting each other. Of course, he wanted to do the right thing, so we got married. But I sometimes think that he and Pamela would have got back together and lived happily ever after if I hadn't had Laurel.' Fran pauses for a moment. 'I think maybe he was with Pamela that night . . . or maybe he was somewhere else. The night Laurel went missing.'

I freeze for a moment, ice trickling through my veins, before I try and hide it by reaching down to scratch at my ankle, hiding my face from Fran. 'Why would you think that?' I say, eventually, when I can't keep up the fake scratch any longer without looking weird.

'He said he was at the hospital. That's what he told me and the police anyway. But I overheard you, Anna, on the phone.' Fran's eyes meet mine and my breath sticks in my throat. 'You rang the hospital that night, didn't you?'

'Yes,' I say, quietly. She knows – there's no point in lying to her about it.

'And they told you he wasn't there?' I nod, and she closes her eyes for a moment. 'I suppose he told you not to say anything, didn't he? Don't look so sheepish, Anna, I'm not cross with you. Dominic is your boss as well – he put you in an awkward situation.'

'He did ask me not to say anything to you, not until he had a chance to speak to you himself. And he told me that he'd already spoken to the police and told them his whereabouts.'

'I don't think he did that, Anna.' Fran gets to her feet and I follow suit, relieved that we are finally leaving. Fran puffs out the candle, crosses herself, and we walk back up the aisle to the heavy oak doors where she stops for a moment. 'I don't just think he's having an affair, Anna. I think there's something else. I think he's hiding something worse.'

As we walk back to the house, through the damp fog that has descended whilst we sat in the church, I toss Fran's words over and over in my mind. Does she really think that Dominic is hiding something? It makes my stomach hurt to think about what she's really saying. *Does she think Dominic had something to do with Laurel's disappearance?* The hair on his jacket springs into my mind, my own suspicions rising to the surface, and my stomach does a somersault. Maybe I should tell Fran about it? But it could be from weeks ago. And if I'm really honest with myself – *Dominic?* He has his faults, but could he really do something this . . .

awful? My mind bounces from one thought to the next and back again, my thoughts conflicting. I jump when Fran lays a hand on my arm at the bottom of the hill.

'You won't say anything to Dominic, will you? About what we've talked about this evening?' she says, her eyes wide with something like fear.

'No. Of course not. But maybe you should speak to Kelly . . .'

'Maybe.' Fran starts walking again, slowly this time, the fog leaving fine droplets in her hair. 'When Laurel comes home, things will be better. With Laurel at home we can talk about things, I can make a decision about how we're going to carry on.' It's almost as though she's talking to herself. I stay silent, letting her speak. 'I've missed her so much. I never realised how much it would hurt, how difficult it would be, until she wasn't there every day. I hate myself for all the time I could have spent with her, instead of at the theatre, or all those auditions. Things will be very different when she's back.'

'I'm sure they will be.' I don't know what else to say – clearly Fran is clinging on tightly to the idea that Laurel will return. We reach the front path, and I step to one side to let Fran in first, catching a glimpse of someone loitering a little further down the street, watching us.

'What is it? Anna?' Fran turns back to me, a frown creasing her brow.

'Nothing. I thought I saw something.' I peer back down the path, and there is a long shadow where someone stands, tucked behind the hedges further down. 'You go in. I'm going to have a quick look.' Grumbling, Fran goes into the house, warning me not to speak if it turns out to be yet another journalist, and I walk silently down the path to the bank of hedges.

'God, you scared me.' Ella steps out of the hedges, and I press my hand to my racing heart. 'What the hell are you doing, lurking about in the bushes?'

'I had to walk this way home, so I thought I'd see if you were OK. Things were . . . tense, when I saw you last. When George Snow was arrested.'

'That still doesn't explain why you were in the hedge?' I force out a laugh, but with the dark, the fog, and Fran's words about Dominic I am feeling on edge.

'I'm sorry,' Ella raises her hands in a gesture of surrender, 'I saw you walking with Fran, and it looked like an intense conversation. I didn't want to disturb you – I know Fran is going through enough right now, without strangers ambushing her on her doorstep. But, as long as you're OK?'

'Fine. Thank you – I appreciate the gesture, even if it was a little bit weird.' We both laugh, and after we say our goodbyes I head back towards the house, trying to throw off any feelings of unease but no matter what, I just can't shake the idea that Ella wasn't walking past as she claimed. She was watching the house.

CHAPTER 17

Fran is already in the kitchen when I make my way downstairs early the next morning, her laptop in front of her. Today marks three weeks and two days since we last saw Laurel, and I barely managed an hour or two of sleep, my mind fizzing with Fran's words the previous evening. Every time I closed my eyes, I saw Laurel getting into a car, Dominic behind the wheel, spiriting her away never to be seen again. As a result, I feel sick with exhaustion this morning, my stomach churning and my face clammy and pale. Fran would look the same, if she hadn't taken the time to smooth on some foundation and a lick of mascara. She holds out the coffee pot to me and I shake my head, acid already burning at my stomach lining at the thought of it. There is no sign of either Dominic or Kelly.

'Where is everyone?' I pour myself a glass of water and sip at it slowly, relishing the icy feel as it slides down my dry, sore throat.

'Kelly will be over later, apparently. She had to go to the station for a briefing or something. God knows.' Fran sighs, and as she types I see she's bitten her nails down to the quick. She still hates Kelly, still thinks her a nosy snoop and no support for the family. 'Dominic is upstairs. Asleep.' Bitterness seeps into her voice and I can see the dark rings under her eyes showing through her make-up. She punches a key on the laptop and I see the screen come to life.

'Are you working?' The words tumble out before I can stop them.

'Huh. No. I'm not Dominic. I'm not ready to start working again, not yet.' She types rapidly, the screen giving her face an eerie blue glow. I feel like a bit of a spare part this morning, with no Kelly to talk to, no updates to hash over . . . no Laurel to take care of. Things feel like they are slowing down, almost to a stop, and I know that before long Laurel will fade from everyone's memories and something else, something bigger will take over the news. I don't want that to happen. I finish my water and get to my feet.

'I might go over to the community centre. I haven't been for a few days and I'd like to see how they're getting on over there.' Fran is silent, her eyes still fixed on the screen. She hasn't been over to the community centre once to meet the volunteers and see what a brilliant job they've been doing. I overheard Kelly asking her if she'd like to, a few days after Laurel went missing, and Fran had simply shaken her head, saying that if she saw all of those people searching then it really would feel like Laurel was lost.

'OK, I think I'll stay here. It's still a little . . . Oh.' Fran sucks in a deep breath and a look of hurt crosses her face.

'Fran? Are you OK?' I come around behind her, peering over her shoulder at what is on her screen. 'Hey! That's Ella – do you know her?'

'Ella?' Fran twists round in her chair to face me. 'Do you know this woman?'

'Well, yes,' I say, a bit unnerved by the strange look on Fran's face. As I say it I know immediately that I've said

172

the wrong thing. Fran pats the chair next to her and I obediently slide into it, my bare feet cold on the floor.

'How do you know her?' Fran's voice is like the cold blade of a knife against the frayed edges of my nerves.

'She was at the school the first morning that they were searching for Laurel,' I say. 'I got talking to her. Her name is Ella, and she moved back to the area a short while ago. She went to school with Dominic. She was quite concerned when she heard about Laurel, said she wanted to help look for her.'

'Ella?' Fran lets out a screech of laughter. 'Is that what she's calling herself?' She scrolls up the Facebook page to show the profile picture and name, and my heart sinks in my chest.

'Pamela?' I whisper. Unable to believe what I'm seeing, I yank the laptop towards me, peering closely at the screen.

'Yes,' Fran bites back, 'Pamela. Bloody, bloody Pamela. Popping up exactly where you least expect her.'

'Is this . . . ? Is she Dominic's Pamela?' I already know the answer, as I scroll down to see a picture of a younger Ella, her face squashed against Dominic's as they both grin wildly at the camera. It's the same picture I once found tucked inside an old copy of *Rebecca* I had borrowed from Dominic. A picture I hadn't given any thought to at the time, aside from a passing curiosity. No wonder I thought her face looked vaguely familiar. I feel the sharp bite of betrayal as I think about the way she struck up a conversation with me that first day, telling me she knew Dominic from before. The way she lurked in the hedges last night, all under the pretence that she was my friend, that she was looking out for me, when really, she was only spying on the Jessops.

173

'Of course, she's Dominic's Pamela. And she's been hanging around, getting friendly with you?' Fran stares at me. 'What did you tell her, Anna? Have you been reporting back to her? Does she know something about what happened to Laurel?' A note of hysteria has crept into her voice, and I rush to reassure her.

'No, Fran, I swear, I had no idea.' I look back at the photo on the screen. It is unmistakably her. Thank goodness I never confided anything in her. 'She just . . .'

'You don't know the full story, Anna.' Fran's voice thickens even though her eyes are still dry. 'You do know they were together before? Pamela and Dominic?'

'Yes, you told me that. But honestly, Fran, I don't think she's had anything to do with Laurel's disappearance.'

'Just listen.' Fran is impatient, keen to tell me the story. 'They were childhood sweethearts, engaged to be married, but Dominic kept putting it off. You know Dom, the hospital comes first.' She takes a sip of her coffee, her eyes never leaving mine. 'So, one day they have a row and Dominic tells her that it's over. He doesn't want to get married. He throws her out of the house . . .'

'Wait – *this* house? They lived here together?' That's how she knew where I lived – it never crossed my mind until I went to bed last night, and I wondered how she knew where to find me.

'Well, yes. Of course, they lived here. Anyway,' Fran rattles on, the words clear and concise as if she is performing a monologue on stage. 'Not long after they split, Dominic and I met and ended up having this wonderful whirlwind romance. Only, then I found out I was pregnant with Laurel. For whatever reason, Dominic

174

decided to do the right thing and marry me, so that's what we did. Pamela turned up here three days after we got home from our honeymoon in tears, telling Dominic that she didn't care if they didn't get married, she just wanted him back. Obviously, Dominic had to tell her that we were married. She was a bit deranged, if you ask me.'

Jesus. I have no idea what to think. Poor Pamela. Knowing Fran as I do, knowing how Fran always gets what she wants, I can't help but feel a tiny bit sorry for Pamela/Ella. Until I remember how she lied to me.

'I think Pamela is in contact with Dominic,' Fran says, quietly. 'What if she had something to do with Laurel going missing? Remember someone saw a blonde woman lurking around by the gates that night? What if that was Pamela and she took Laurel for revenge? To get back at Dominic and me?' She looks at me in horror. 'What if they've planned this together? What if Dominic planned to take Laurel and start again with Pamela?' She presses her hand to her mouth, as a low moan seeps out from between her lips.

'We have to tell Kelly.' I get to my feet, reaching for my mobile with shaking hands.

'Wait.' Fran lays out a hand to stop me from dialling. 'What about Dominic? Shouldn't we speak to him first? Maybe I can get him to tell me the truth, if I have something to back it up.'

'OK,' I say slowly, 'but do you really think he'll be truthful with you? I mean, to be honest, Fran, you don't even know that he and Pamela are in contact . . . and there's nothing to suggest that Pamela had anything to do with Laurel's disappearance.' I want to say there's nothing to suggest Dominic did either, but there is still that heavy, dark suspicion that makes my stomach turn over when I let myself think of how Dominic has proved himself to not be who I thought he was these past few weeks.

'His phone,' Fran says.

'What – you think you . . .' I stop, seeing the frown settle in on Fran's forehead. '*We* should check his phone?'

'Yes . . . well done, Anna. That's a brilliant idea.' Fran nods, frown easing away, and I hurry away to the stairs, horror and betrayal leaving a bitter, metallic taste on my tongue.

I knock on their bedroom door, but there is no answer and I hear the faint rush of the shower running in the en suite. Tentatively I push the door open and slide in, spying his mobile phone left on the bedside table, exactly as Fran suspected it would be.

I cautiously pick it up, my ears straining to hear the moment the shower goes off. Fran told me his passcode – turns out it's the same as the alarm code for the house – and with shaking fingers I tap in the code waiting for the screen to come to life. His background picture is a photo of Laurel taken last summer, on a rare day when they went to a theme park as a family, leaving me at home, and my heart twists at the sight of her blonde hair, her gappy grin. Swiping into his messages I scroll down, scanning over them until I see the one I was really hoping I wouldn't. It's a number, not a stored name, and as I open it I swear I can hear my heart thundering in my chest so loudly it drowns out the sound of the shower. It says:

'I KNEW YOU'D SEE SENSE IN THE END. THIS WILL ALL BE OVER SOON. P xxx'

What? I can't even begin to make sense of the message. What will all be over soon? Dominic and Fran's marriage? Or the fact that Laurel is missing? And it's signed P, so surely it can only be from Pamela? The abrupt sound of the shower turning off startles me and I jump, throwing the phone back on to the bedside table, scurrying downstairs to the kitchen before Dominic returns.

'Well?' Fran looks as though she's been pacing since I left the room. 'Did you find anything?'

I nod, urgently. 'Yes, there's a text message on his phone from P . . . I think it must be Pamela. It didn't really make much sense, but they're definitely in contact. But that doesn't mean she had anything to do with Laurel's disappearance.'

'I'll have to speak to DS Wright about it though. Any lead helps, doesn't it? And if Pamela had something to do with Laurel disappearing I have to say something. She's already trying to steal my husband, why not take my child? She's trying to steal my whole life.' Fran's face crumples, and she puts her head in her hands as she starts to sob.

'You speak to DS Wright,' I say, already pulling on my jacket, 'I'm going to go and find Pamela and ask her exactly what is going on. I can confront her – she lied to me, remember? Oh Fran, please don't cry.'

I stand there awkwardly unsure of what to do, how to comfort her, the ghost of the old, spiky, prickly Fran still standing between us. The ring of the doorbell saves me from my indecision and I hurry to open the door, thinking it will be Kelly only to see Ruth on the doorstep.

'Ruth. Hello.' My hearts sinks a little at the sight of her on the doorstep, once again. At least she doesn't have a casserole with her this time.

'Nice to see you, Anna. Is Fran home? Only I wondered if she'd had a chance to look at those posters I made, or if she needed any cleaning doing, any errands running or . . .' She peers past me, looking over my shoulder into the hallway.

'She's . . .' I pause for a moment, thinking that if Ruth is so insistent on being here then maybe I can use her for my own means, just this once. 'Listen, can you stay for a minute?' I pull her inside quickly before anyone sees and push her through into the kitchen.

'Well, of course I can stay. I've been telling you since the day Laurel disappeared that I'm happy to help in any way I can, any way at all . . . Oh, no. What's happened?' Ruth trails off, her hand to her mouth as she looks at Fran slumped crying over the kitchen table. 'Oh, is it Laurel? Did they . . . did they find her?'

'No,' I say, shortly. 'Look, can you look after her for a bit?' I gesture to Fran who still sniffs and snuffles into her arms. 'I have to go out for a little while. I need someone to keep an eye on Fran, until Kelly arrives.' I jump as the front door slams and Dominic's outline passes the front window before I hear the beep of his car unlocking.

'Was that . . .?' Ruth points to the window, her coat sleeve falling back along her wrist.

'Yes. He's back to work,' I say, frowning. Something has caught in the back of my mind, something that doesn't feel right, but I can't put my finger on it. 'Look, can you stay for a bit until the FLO gets here or not?'

'Of course I can,' Ruth says, leaning down and rubbing Fran's back. I see Fran's shoulders tense and take a step backwards towards the front door. 'I'll make us a nice cup of tea, Fran, shall I?'

'I won't be long, OK?' I almost sprint out of the front door, turning left towards the library. I'm going to get to Pamela before she gets a chance to arrange her story for DS Wright.

CHAPTER 18

I remember Pamela/Ella, whatever she wants to call herself, telling me she worked in the library, that first day we met, so I hurry over there but she isn't anywhere to be seen, and when I ask someone they tell me it's her day off. I ask for a telephone number, kicking myself at not thinking to jot down the number from Dominic's phone, but understandably they refuse to give it to me.

Outside the library I pause for a moment, thinking what to do. I am still stunned by the revelation that Ella is Dominic's Pamela, and my gut twists as I think of all the things I confided in her about Laurel's disappearance, things that I never would have mentioned if I had known who she really was. *What does she want? Is she here for Dominic — are they having an affair? Or is she hanging around for more sinister reasons?*

I start to walk back along the road, taking the turning that will lead me down the narrow country lane that ends up at the community centre. There's no point in going home quite yet, and although I may not have found Pamela at the library, I can at least make myself useful by seeing if there is anything I can do to help the search team — and there's every chance she might pop up there, as she has so many times before.

As I pass the school gates, I can't help but peer into the playground, wishing Laurel would come running out of the hall to meet me, lunchbox in one hand, big, beaming smile on her face, eager to tell me all about her day. Instead, I look round to see Mr Abbott walking towards the gate.

'Anna, hello.' He stands on the other side of the palisade fencing, making no move to let me in, or to come out to my side of the metal barrier. 'How are you?'

'I, err . . . I'm just on my way to the community centre to see if the search needed any help with anything. You know, looking for Laurel?'

'Ahhh, yes.' He looks a little uncomfortable, avoiding my gaze and staring intently at the tips of his shoes. 'I'm sorry we had to move the volunteer centre from the hall. I wish we could have kept it here but . . .' Finally, he raises his eyes to mine, an ugly red flush starting to creep up his neck. 'I'm really am sorry, Anna, we had to get things back into a normal routine for the rest of the children.'

'I understand. Really. It's fine.' It's not. It's the beginning of everything going back to normal, of life carrying on exactly as it did before. It won't be long before everyone forgets about Laurel and starts to move on. 'I'm sorry for disturbing you.' I walk away, towards the squat, cream building that is the community centre.

As I push open the door, I notice straight away that the number of volunteers has reduced by over half since the last time I was here. The quiet murmur of chatter lowers slightly as I step into the room, people glancing up, only to look away disinterestedly when they see it is only me, and not someone more exciting. Fran, maybe. I am halfway across the room, approaching the slightly bowed trestle table where Cheryl Smythe is still in full-on action, her arms laden with flyers, a biro clamped between her teeth, when I see the last person I was expecting to see – the one person I was hoping to see.

'Anna!' Ella steps forward, holding out her arms to me as she pulls me into a tight hug. I stand there rigidly, her hair tickling my nose, the smell of her perfume strangely familiar. 'Is everything all right?' She frowns as she pulls back, holding me at arm's length.

'I think we need to talk.' Pushing my hair back, I look behind me, seeing the volunteers milling about the room, all ears open to our conversation. 'Not here though.' I push past her and head for the door, hearing the low heels on her boots clacking across the lino floor.

'Anna, what is it?' Once outside, I march her round the corner, away from prying eyes. 'Did something happen?' Her blue eyes are wide.

'You could say that.' *Someone is lying. Someone is not who they say they are. Someone else.* The psychic's words float through my mind. 'Is there anything you want to tell me?'

She pauses for a moment, then blinks. 'Like what?'

'*Seriously?* Are you actually going to do this? I know, Ella. Or should I call you Pamela, like Dominic does?'

Her face goes white and her mouth opens and closes for a moment, but no sound comes out. She covers her face with her hands, and I wait, silently, for her to respond.

'I'm so sorry, Anna.' Eventually she speaks, her hands dropping to her sides. 'I wanted to tell you . . . I was going to tell you but then . . .'

'I think you need to tell me everything, Ella. Pamela. Ugh.' I scrub my hands over my face and let her follow me away from the community centre, towards the centre of town.

*

We are tucked away in Davey's diner, the only place I could think of where we could speak freely without being overheard. The diner is mostly frequented by groundworkers and lorry drivers, and we don't have to run the risk of bumping into the yummy mummies the way we would in the upmarket café in town. The smell of grease and bad coffee hangs heavy in the air, and what was welcoming warmth after the wintry air outside is now stifling. Pamela pushes a piece of toast around the plate in front of her, before sipping at the tea we ordered for appearance sake.

'So,' I push my mug away from me and lean forward onto my elbows, 'are you going to tell me what's going on?'

Pamela sighs, twisting a silver ring round on her right hand. 'It's not how you think, Anna, I promise. I know I lied to you, but I didn't want to . . . disrupt things any more than they already were. I can explain everything.'

'Go on then.' I lean back, snatching up a sugar packet from the bowl in front of me and fiddling with it, just for something to do with my hands.

'Look, you know I was . . . Dominic and I were together before he met Fran, right?' Pamela's voice is low, and I have to lean forward again to be able to hear her. 'We were together for a long time, and as far as I was aware everything was perfect. Until the baby.'

'Baby?' I hiss. 'What baby?'

'Fran didn't tell you?' Pamela frowns, her hand to her mouth. 'Maybe she doesn't know.'

Impatient, I nudge her into talking again.

'I found out I was pregnant. We weren't even trying, and then I felt sick, and tired, so I did a test and it was positive. Dom always said he never wanted children, but I thought – we'd been together for five or six years at this point, were engaged to be married – I thought once he got his head round it, it would be OK. We'd have the baby, get married and be a proper family.'

'Obviously that didn't happen.' My heart softens a little at the look on her face, devastated even five years after this all happened, before I remember that she lied to me. That she could know something about Laurel's disappearance, might even have something to do with it.

'No. Dominic was . . . not happy, to say the least when I told him I was pregnant. Furious would be more accurate.' Her eyes fill, and a single tear spills on to her cheek. 'He told me that he didn't want the baby, didn't want to be a father, and that he'd made that perfectly clear from the word go. In his own words, he told me I'd have to choose between him and the child, that he couldn't stay with me if I carried on with the pregnancy. I was devastated, and we rowed, ferociously. I told him I wouldn't have an abortion and he packed my bag and told me to leave.'

'Jesus.' I can't believe that Dominic could be that heartless. Then, I see in my mind's eye the image of him grabbing Fran by the arms, the fury that was written all over his face, the way he smashed his glass across the hearth, and I think, *maybe*.

Pamela reaches for her mug, taking a sip of the, by now, lukewarm tea. 'I had nowhere to go. My family disapproved of my relationship with Dominic, so I had cut all ties with them.' *That sounds familiar.* I think of Fran's face as she spoke about Polly, the way she hadn't spoken to her sister for years because Dominic didn't like her.

'So, what did you do? I mean . . .' I trail off, not wanting to say that I haven't seen Pamela with a child.

'I waited, to see if he would change his mind, but he didn't contact me. I lost the baby. Nothing sinister, he or she just didn't make it. I was sad, but in the end, I realised that I couldn't live without him. I didn't want to be alone, and now I knew that he would never change his mind I could make sure this never happened again. I didn't want to fall pregnant again – I couldn't stand the pain if I lost another baby. I went to the house to tell him that I had done what he wanted but I was too late.'

I say nothing, my brain whirring overtime trying to process everything that Pamela has told me.

'I went to the house and Fran answered the door. In the time it had taken me to lose our child and come to terms with what I wanted in life, he had found Fran, got her pregnant and married her. He'd moved on.' Her voice is bitter, laced with years of hurt and anger.

'So why are you here now? Coincidence?' I deliberately keep my face neutral, not letting her know all the things that are racing through my mind. The fact that he kept her from her family, just as he did to Fran. The idea that he never, ever wanted children.

'I still love him. Always have.' Pamela lets out a snort of rueful laughter. 'I know I'm an idiot, Anna, you don't need to look at me like that. Have you ever loved anyone so much that you feel like you'd die if you couldn't be near them?'

185

I shake my head. 'Have you been in contact with Dominic? Does he know you're here?'

'Of course, he does, Anna.' Pamela frowns at me. 'I was supposed to meet him that night.'

I have to take a moment to catch my breath, feeling as though the floor has given way slightly beneath my feet. No wonder Dominic didn't want Fran to know where he was the night Laurel went missing. What kind of man promises to take his child to a fireworks display, then scurries off to meet his mistress instead?

'Hang on . . . wait a minute,' I say, holding up a hand as a thought strikes me. 'You said you were *supposed* to meet him that night? Did he not show up?'

'No.' Pamela sighs, twisting the ring on her finger again. I realise this must be the ring Dominic gave her when he asked her to marry him. 'I waited for him, but he didn't show. He'd said that he was supposed to meet Fran and Laurel at the Oxbury Primary display, so I thought maybe he went straight there. I waited there too, by the front gate, but I left before the . . . before it happened.'

I remember the police saying there had been a call from a witness saying they'd seen a woman hanging out outside the front gate that night. It must have been Pamela. I look hard at her, at the lines at the corners of her blue eyes, the tiny streak of grey in the front of her blonde hair that you would never notice unless you were looking for it.

'So, you have been seeing Dominic? Has he been cheating on Fran with you?' Maybe Fran was right to be suspicious after all.

'No, not as such.' Pamela avoids my eyes, dabbing her finger into a pile of spilled sugar. 'I bumped into him in town a couple of months ago. We had a coffee and he mentioned that things weren't great between him and Fran. I thought . . . maybe this was my opportunity to have another chance with him. We've been in contact over the phone mostly, but we've had a drink once or twice. I know that if I simply wait, if I'm patient, then he'll see sense. He'll come back to me. I was his first love, Anna, we're meant to be together.'

The conviction with which she speaks is slightly shocking, and I realise that she genuinely believes Dominic will come back to her. I wonder what he's said to make her believe in him so wholeheartedly. 'You texted him, saying not to worry, that this would all be over soon. What did you mean? What will all be over soon?'

'I only meant . . . I meant that he and Fran would be over soon, that's all. He sent me that message asking me to meet him that night and I thought . . . I thought he meant that he'd had a change of heart – seen reason, if you like. I thought this was it – he was going to tell me he'd leave Fran and be with me.' Her hands shake as she reaches for a napkin and blows her nose. 'I called him the next morning, not realising Laurel had gone missing. He told me what had happened the night before, he was in pieces.' I realise that Pamela must have been who Dominic was on the phone to that first morning, when we were back at the field.

She goes on, 'I'm not an idiot, Anna, anyone can see that Dominic and Fran aren't right for each other. But it's OK. I've waited this long, I can wait a little while longer. I'm sorry I didn't tell you the truth, Anna, but I couldn't.' She pushes back her chair and snatches up her coat, thrusting her arms into the sleeves.

'Pamela, I have to ask you this. Have you got any idea what might have happened to Laurel? Did you have anything to do with her going missing?' My stomach flips as I make my accusation, my heart thudding in my throat.

'What?' Pamela looks at me in disgust. 'No, Anna, I had absolutely nothing to do with what happened to Laurel.' And as she stumbles out of the diner, tripping over the leg of a chair left thrust out into the walkway, I believe that she doesn't know anything about Laurel's disappearance. But I'm starting to think that maybe Dominic does.

Fran's face is white when I let myself back into the house, having walked the long way home from the diner, trying to process everything I have heard from Pamela. Some of what she said seems to confirm that I don't really know Dominic as well as I thought I did, and the thought makes my stomach swoop, as though I'm on the last leg of a giant rollercoaster. The idea of Dominic demanding that she abort their baby leaves a nasty, bitter taste in my mouth, and I wonder how he dealt with Laurel being born. *Maybe he never wanted her either?* The implications of that thought make my mouth go dry, and I lick anxiously at my lips.

'Anna, you're back.' Fran grasps me by the arm and pulls me into the living room, where Dominic sits, his face grey and exhausted, next to Kelly on the sofa. DS Wright stands in front of the window. 'DS Wright wants to speak to us . . . no, no, don't look like that! It's not Laurel.' Her voice cracks on Laurel's name. I follow her into the room, standing in the corner on shaky legs.

'OK,' Wright looks from Fran to Dominic, her eyes kind despite her tough exterior, 'we want to do a brief statement from you to the press.' Dominic goes to speak, but Fran presses the back of his hand, her fingers leaving a white mark. 'First, something from me to update them on where we are with the investigation – as you know, the reconstruction did throw up some new leads, so we'd like to appeal to the public to come forward if they have anything else to add to this new information, and then a brief sentence from the two of you, appealing to whoever has taken Laurel. I know this is very hard on you both, but it's something we need to do. If we can appeal to him or her, make them appear human, then there's every chance that we will get some response to that.'

It sounds like a load of rubbish to me – whoever has taken Laurel, whoever could steal a child away from their family has to be somewhat inhuman, don't they? I say nothing, just wait as Fran and Dominic obey orders and get to their feet, ready to step outside and face the press on their own territory this time.

As they step out on to the doorstep, my heart stutters in my chest and I feel my palms grow damp and clammy. The flashes from the cameras almost blind me, and I pull back into the living room, anxious not to be caught on film. It's been hard enough keeping out of sight of the press as it is, there is no way I want to appear on the front page of tomorrow's newspapers. Wiping my hands on my jeans, I peer through the living room blinds as DS Wright stands on the step, making her speech. Then, she steps aside, letting Fran and Dominic take centre stage as she steps around the press pack, taking up a position slightly behind and to the left of the them, her eyes trained on the Jessops as they stand there, Kelly beside them.

'Whoever has Laurel,' Fran starts haltingly, a small nervous smile on her face, 'whoever has our daughter, please bring her home. She belongs with me, with us.' She takes a deep breath, but seems unable to carry on, holding a tissue to her face as her shoulders begin to heave. Dominic takes over.

'Please, bring her home. We love her and miss her so much. Life isn't the same without her. We need her home, so please, please let her come back to us.' His voice is calm and steady, and he gently squeezes Fran's shoulder as they turn to come back indoors.

I turn my gaze back to Wright as they return to the house, her eyes never leaving them, a slight crease between her eyebrows showing that perhaps she isn't entirely happy with what she's just witnessed. Kelly catches my eye, before looking away and gently steering a weeping Fran towards the stairs. Something about this TV appeal feels different to the last one, and not only because I watched the last one from the safety of the screen. I look back at DS Wright, where she stands still looking at the house, her hands twisting the lid on a bottle of mineral water. It's almost as though the perspective has changed. I close the blinds on her, obscuring her from view, blocking out the camera flashes and baying calls of the press. It's almost as though Wright's eyes are now on us.

CHAPTER 19

It is early the next morning, so early the sun is barely over the horizon, when a thumping at the door rouses me from a restless sleep. The house is cold, the heating not yet kicked in, and I shiver as I pull on a dressing gown and head downstairs. Dominic is at the front door, his hair mussed on one side as he pulls the door open to reveal DS Wright and several police officers standing behind her. There is a clamour from the press that still congregate outside, flashbulbs popping as Dominic squints, one hand rising to shield his face. Drawing back, pressing myself against the wall of the staircase, I wonder if the press knew the police were coming, or whether they just didn't go home after the Jessops' statement yesterday. I hear a gasp behind me, and I turn to see Fran at the top of the stairs, her hand to her throat.

'Is it . . .' Her voice is shrill, sending a shiver down my spine as the chill wind blows in through the open front door, wrapping itself around my bare legs.

'No, no news on Laurel.' Wright steps into the entrance hall as Dominic stands to one side letting the officers file into the hallway. 'Sorry to wake you.'

'What exactly . . .?' Dominic says, as Fran asks, 'What the hell is going on?' She pushes past me on the stairs and comes to stand beside Dominic. She looks tiny next to his six-foot frame, in her pyjamas and bare feet. While Dominic's face is flushed, Fran's is deathly pale, any slight colour she might have had in her cheeks draining away to leave her white and pasty.

'Look, Fran, Dominic, I need your co-operation here, OK?' Wright says, her voice firm. 'We need to carry out a search of the property, and it would make things a hell of a lot easier all round if you could . . . well, be co-operative.'

'What?' Dominic raises his voice, and his cheeks flush an even darker red. I recognise the look on his face as anger, the same dark, stormy look I saw when he grabbed Fran by the arms in the kitchen. 'What the hell are you talking about? You've already searched the house once and you didn't find anything! You're supposed to be out there looking for my daughter, not buggering around in here.'

I watch in silence, as Wright glances towards the waiting officers, who I now realise are only here to search through the house, to turn over everything that the Jessops own. To find out if there are secrets hidden in this home. Fran's eyes are huge in her face, and dark circles stand out starkly against her white skin. Her hands shake as she pulls her flimsy dressing gown tightly around her.

'Dominic, please . . .' she says, with difficulty.

'Please? Please, what?' Dominic stands in front of Wright as though he is about to deny her access to the rest of the house. 'Let them ransack our house again? They didn't find anything last time, they won't this time. They should be out there looking for her.'

'Mr Jessop,' DS Wright raises her hands, trying to make peace, 'if you would please just let us do our job. We are doing everything we can to find Laurel, and this search is part of that. We have to make sure we haven't missed a single thing that might lead us to where she is.'

'Dom, please,' Fran says again, resting her small white hand against his chest. He looks down at her absently, before shaking his head, but stepping to one side to let Wright and her officers in.

'Fine. Do what you need to. I don't need to be here for it, do I?' Without waiting for a reply Dominic turns and starts back up the stairs. As I shrink back against the wall to let him past, DS Wright pushes past after him, telling him he'll have to wait downstairs. I catch Fran's eye and flick my head in the direction of the kitchen. It's going to be a long day.

Fran stands in the window, peering through the blinds at the mob of press outside. Every time she parts the blinds even slightly you can hear the excited murmurs of the journalists outside, the calls of 'Fran!', the snaps of photographs being taken, and I wish she would come away and sit down, keep the blinds closed and give us the chance to shut out the outside world. Every time she peers out and the noise from outside reaches my ears I feel the tension in the room ratchet up yet another notch. It's unbearable.

Finally, she comes to sit at the table, her face a ghostly shade of white, and I make her a coffee with extra sugar, in the hope that it might bring a bit of colour back into her cheeks. I've no idea if it works, but I remember the police officer in Scotland making me hot, sweet tea in the first moments after things went wrong. Before they decided I had something to do with it. Shaking away thoughts of before, I ask Kelly, who has now made an appearance, if it's OK for me to go up to my room and get dressed.

As I pass the study at the end of the hall the door is ajar, and I can't help but glance into the room, expecting to see a police officer rifling through the filing cabinet, or Dominic's desk drawers, but it's not a police officer in there. Glancing up from the screen of the computer, Dominic's forehead is beaded with sweat as he slams the lid of the laptop and marches towards me. I back away, my heart starting to thunder in my chest, feet all ready to rush along the corridor to the stairs when he pulls the door open, jumping slightly when he sees me.

'Oh! Anna, you startled me.' He glances down the hallway. 'I was only checking some emails. I'll be at the hospital if anyone needs me. I might as well go to work while all this is going on, not much use being here, is there?' He makes a show of glancing at his watch before snatching up his briefcase and heading out the front door.

I creep up the stairs, knocking on my own bedroom door before I enter the room, sweating slightly now that the radiators are warm. The police haven't reached my room yet, and I allow myself a quick moment of relief, knowing that my secret is safe, for a few more minutes anyway. I think I've hidden things well enough that they won't be found – and if I haven't . . . well, I'll have to cross that bridge when I come to it.

I sink down on to the rumpled bed, not sure what to think. In addition to the stress of keeping my own secrets, am I now in possession of Dominic's secrets? *Why was Dominic on his laptop just now? Surely, he would know that the police would want to look at it? What is it that he has to hide?*

The suspicions that were aroused by my conversation with Pamela yesterday bubble to the surface again. Everywhere I turn, something seems to crop up that makes me think that perhaps Dominic hasn't been entirely truthful about things since Laurel disappeared. He lied to Fran (and possibly to the police) about his whereabouts on the night that Laurel went missing. He was supposed to meet Pamela, but Pamela says he never showed, so, where was he? He's never explained himself, merely asked me not to tell Fran he wasn't at the hospital. He never wanted children – and was engaged to Pamela, although according to Fran marriage was never brought up. He cut Pamela off from her family, the same way Fran says he cut her off from her own sister. That on its own doesn't seem all that suspicious, but when you factor in his reaction to having to do a police appeal to find his own daughter . . .

I pause for a moment in my thinking, remembering the way his voice had risen, *they'll think we have something to do with it*. A cold finger runs down my spine as I face up to the fact that perhaps whoever took Laurel is closer to home than we first thought.

Kelly is alone when I re-enter the kitchen, the hanging copper lights bright overhead to counteract the dimness caused by the closed blinds. The kitchen drawer is open in front of her as she rifles through the old takeaway menus and school letters that fill the junk drawer.

'Sorry.' She stands upright, rubbing the bottom of her back with both hands. 'I was only tidying these things away. They just searched these drawers, I didn't think Fran would want to see the mess they made.'

'Where is Fran?' My skin prickles uncomfortably at the sight of Kelly rifling through the drawers. It's been easy to slip into thinking of her as an ally, when really Fran was right. Her job is to keep an eye on us.

'She's popped out for some fresh air – she didn't want to be here for the search. I think it's all a bit much for her today, she looked ever so pale.'

'She's struggling, I think,' I say, 'she's had a few nasty messages on the Facebook support page for Laurel. Really nasty, vile stuff. This isn't going to help today.' I wonder for a moment if I should mention my feelings about Dominic, but Kelly is talking again.

'. . . she's probably gone there.'

I look at her in confusion.

'To the church. I said, she's probably gone to the church. She gets a lot of comfort from being there these days. She said something about going there with Laurel for school harvest festivals and things. I think it makes her feel closer to Laurel.'

'Yes. Right. Of course. Maybe I'll go and catch up with her.'

Frowning, I snatch up my coat from the back of the kitchen chair and head towards the front door, not knowing what it was that Kelly did or said that made something itch away at the back of my brain, like a memory I can't quite grasp.

I see Fran before I reach the gate into the churchyard, her bright red coat visible through the fine mist that has descended over the town this morning, a damp, drizzly fog that soaks the sleeves of my jacket and sends the ends of my blonde hair into frizzy spirals. She paces in front of the heavy oak doors, her mobile phone clamped to her ear. I wait a short distance away, not wanting to intrude on her phone call. She looks up, noticing me, and gives a small smile before she hangs up, shoving the phone into her pocket as she walks towards me.

'You found me,' she says, rubbing her hands together as if cold. 'Sorry, but I had to get out for a while. That was my agent on the phone. He says he was calling to check up on me, but it was really to see if I wanted to go to an audition next week. It's the perfect role for me apparently, but I told him I'm not ready.' She smiles, but it doesn't reach her eyes. 'It's easier for Dominic, obviously. He's had no problem going back to the hospital.'

I don't speak for a moment, anxiety about my suspicions regarding Dominic making it difficult to find the words.

'Shall we go inside for a bit?' I lead Fran towards the church doors, not wanting to say what I need to outside where journalists could be lurking, waiting to overhear our conversation. We sit in the front pew, the wood hard and unforgiving under my thighs. Fran lights a candle, like she did before, and I wait for a moment as she bows her head, eyes closed, lips moving in a whispered prayer for Laurel. After a few seconds her eyes open and she lays her hands in her lap.

'Fran,' I mouth weakly. I realise I am terrified of telling her what I think, especially as I don't have anything concrete, no proof to back up my suspicions. *She might sack you if you tell her,* my brain blurts out, and I think for a moment, *maybe that's no bad thing.* 'Fran, can I talk to you about something? It's . . . I've been thinking . . .'

'Yes?' Fran turns to me, her eyes bright. 'Anna, what is it? You can tell me.' A hint of the old Fran peeps back through.

'I don't have anything to back up what I'm about to say, I should probably tell you that first.' My fingers knit together so tightly my knuckles go white.

'Anna, please, whatever it is it can't be worse than what's already happened to this family, can it?'

'I think Dominic might be lying.' I blurt the words out, in a rush of relief. 'I thought about things after we talked in here the last time and well . . . things simply aren't adding up for me. The more I think about it the more I think that he might . . . he might have something to do with Laurel's disappearance.' I close my eyes for a moment, waiting for Fran to shout, storm off, anything . . . but there is only silence. When I cautiously open my eyes, she is staring at me, one hand covering her mouth.

'Anna . . . what do you mean?'

'He wasn't at the hospital that night – you know that already. He asked me not to say anything to you, and he told me he spoke to the police, only I don't think he did, and if he did I don't think he told them the truth.'

'So where do you think he was?'

'I don't know. But Pamela – I saw her after I read the text message from her on his phone, I asked her what's been going on between the two of them – she said he was supposed to meet her that night, the night Laurel went missing, only he never showed up.'

'Really?' Fran is frowning, her neat brows drawn together in a deep V. 'So, do you think Pamela is involved?'

'Well, no, I don't think so. I don't know. But someone said they saw Laurel getting into a car, an SUV. Dominic has a Porsche Cayenne, couldn't it have been his car? I know they said it was a dark-coloured car, and Dominic's is silver, but what if they got it wrong? It was dark after all. And at the time, they weren't actively looking for something out of the ordinary – people remember things wrongly all the time.' I pause for a moment to take a breath, before I carry on. 'And I know I said that there was a chance Laurel could have got into a car with someone she didn't know . . . but if it was Dominic, then she knew him, didn't she? There would have been no reason for her to not get into the car, if she saw her dad.' I wait a second for her to digest what I have just said, her eyes fixed on the candle at the altar. 'I saw him this morning, coming out of his office. He was on his laptop – what if he was deleting something that he didn't want the police to find?' I find I am shaking and tuck my fingers under my thighs out of sight.

'And the TV appeal . . .' Fran says quietly. 'Remember how he responded to the idea? I remember thinking at the time why wouldn't he want to do it? Why wouldn't he want to do everything he possibly could to find Laurel? Oh God, Anna, do you really think that Dominic could have something to do with all of this?'

'I don't know. But whatever he's hiding, I think we need to speak to DS Wright ourselves.'

Sliding along the back alleyway to the house, we hear Dominic shouting before we reach the end of the garden path, and Fran gives me a worried glance before she forges ahead, hurrying up the path that runs along the side of the house to where Dominic stands in front of the open garage door.

'Dominic, what is it? Please, stop shouting.' Fran looks back over her shoulder to where a group of journalists still wait, enjoying the spectacle, a couple of them with their cameras raised, snapping pictures of Dominic's fury. My heart thunders in my chest, anxiety at being recognised making my breath come in short pants as I tug my hat lower over my face and turn away.

'They're taking my bloody car, that's what it is!' Dominic shouts again, shoving his hands through his hair. 'How am I supposed to do anything without a car?'

'It won't be for long,' DS Wright says calmly, 'as I said this morning, Mr Jessop, it's all part of the routine search. It's important we get this done, and with your co-operation.' I note the way she calls Dominic 'Mr Jessop', no longer using his first name in that easy way of that first day, three weeks ago. 'While you're all here, there is one other thing.'

We all stand in silence, eyes on Wright as Kelly shifts uncomfortably next to her, waiting to hear what she is about to say.

'We'd like to take you all in to the station, just to go over a few things. It shouldn't take too long.' She turns on her heel, leaving Kelly to walk us all to the waiting patrol cars. I feel sick, my stomach churning and my palms clammy. *What do they think they know?*

CHAPTER 20

I am left waiting for what feels like an interminable amount of time, but in reality, is probably no more than maybe half an hour or so before a police officer enters the room. It is more formal this time than when DS Wright last talked to us all about Laurel going missing – it's exactly as I imagined a police interview room to be, cold and stark, designed to make you uncomfortable in an effort to make you spill the beans. I shift in my seat, a hard, plastic chair reminiscent of school days, as she takes a seat opposite me, and I realise she is familiar to me – she is one of the officers called out on that first night.

'Hi, Anna. My name is DC Bishop, I've been working with DS Wright on Laurel's disappearance. I'm going to record this interview, OK?' As she runs through the official stuff, like my right to legal counsel, she leans forward, pressing a button on the tape recorder that sits on the desk between us. Her blouse is ever so slightly too small, and I see the fabric at her shoulders pull at the seams as she stretches over. There is a hard, cold lump in my stomach, and I swallow. I am scared, there is no other word for it.

'Would you like some water?' DC Bishop pushes a glass towards me and I take it, careful not to spill it as my hands shake. 'Anna . . . there are a few things we'd like to go over with you, with regards to Laurel's disappearance. Can you tell me again exactly what happened that night?'

I go over everything again, the way Laurel and I left the house earlier than Fran, Laurel keen to get to the field. The way I called out to her as she skipped after Fran, the silver threads in her bobble hat reflecting the light. The way I looked down and she simply wasn't there anymore. The words come slowly at first, my tongue feeling too big for my mouth, before I start to cry and then the words and the tears flow freely.

'And what about Fran? How was she that night?'

'She was fine . . . until Laurel disappeared, that is. Then she was frantic, obviously, we all were.'

'Even Dominic?' DC Bishop asks, her pen scratching over the paper in front of her, making notes that I can't decipher.

'Well, yes.' I pause, not sure even now what I should be saying. 'Once he knew she was missing.'

DC Bishop inhales, as if about to ask another question before she closes her mouth and scratches the side of her head. I wait, my heart thundering in my chest, the silence in the room feeling tangibly thick.

'Is there anything you want to tell us, Anna?' Her eyes meet mine, and I think for a moment that my heart will stop dead in my chest.

'What do you mean?' I slide my gaze away, focusing on the damp patch on a ceiling tile above her head, the brown stain in the shape of a boat, stark against the white of the other tiles.

'I mean, is there anything we should know? Anything at all?' She leans forward on the desk, steepling her hands under her chin as she stares at me.

'No,' I whisper, shaking my head slightly.

'Really? How about we start with the fact that we know you're not Anna Cox.'

I go hot, then cold, sweat drenching my body then leaving me chilled to the bone. The floor feels as if it is liquid under my feet, and I shuffle my toes under the table in order to ground myself, to feel as though I am still really here, that this isn't one long nightmare.

'We spoke to your previous employers – or should I say Anna's previous employers? I think you've probably realised now that things didn't quite stack up for us.'

'It doesn't have anything to do with Laurel, that's the only reason I didn't say anything, I swear.'

'We know who you are, Anna, or can I call you Charlie?'

'I can explain everything.'

'Yeah, I think you probably should.' DC Bishop leans back in her chair and flicks her fingers towards me. 'Fire away. I think you've got quite a bit of explaining to do, don't you?'

I scrub my hands over my face, buying a few seconds to calm myself before I begin to speak. I haven't talked about what happened before, not since I left Scotland, and I've spent even more time lately trying to block it from my thoughts entirely, but I suppose there had to come a point when I had to be honest. But I wish it wasn't under these circumstances.

'It was the summer of 2012. I had been in Scotland for a few weeks after finishing my training, staying with a boyfriend who lived there. To be honest, things didn't work out with him pretty quickly, but by then I'd already got the job with the Mackenzies. I was faced with a decision – either move back home to try and find a job in Brighton or try and make a go of things in Killin on my own. The Mackenzies offered to let me live in once they heard I'd broken up with my boyfriend, so I jumped at the chance to stay with them and carry on looking after Archie.'

I break for a moment, taking a sip of the lukewarm water. Just thinking about Archie, his huge dark eyes, those plump little baby thighs, brings stinging hot tears to my eyes.

'So, what went wrong?' DC Bishop asks. 'Presumably something happened there that meant you wanted to change your name, become someone else?'

'They were quite a prominent, well-known family in Killin, the Mackenzies. He did something in local politics, she was . . . I don't know; she'd done some modelling before they were married, she was Greek, and they'd met while he was out there on holiday. They had no problems with being out every night, leaving me to look after the baby. I didn't get a day off, rarely anyway. I was exhausted a lot of the time.' And I was – any new mother will tell you how exhausting it is to take care of a child all day and all night. 'I'm not making excuses about what happened, you know?'

DC Bishop nods, and I wonder if she has children, if there is someone at home, employed by her, putting her children to bed while she is searching for another lost child.

'That night, the Mackenzies had gone to a dinner. I'd been up since five o'clock in the morning with Archie . . .

204

I'd put him to bed and he'd kept getting up, wanting to see Gabby, his mother, before she left. He was almost two, and he could reach the door handle to the bedroom to let himself out – she refused to put a child gate up, said they looked untidy. She was angry with him, shouting at me to get him out so she could get ready. She had a temper.' I pause for a moment, seeing Gabby in my mind's eye, all dark hair and heaving bosom. She was never maternal, not cut out to be a mother. 'They left, and finally Archie fell asleep. I was so tired, too tired to even eat dinner, so instead I poured myself a glass of wine, and went out into the garden to have a cigarette. I forgot to pick up the baby monitor.'

For a moment, I am back there, in Killin, standing in the garden of the Mackenzies' huge stone house. The UK had been in the grip of a short heatwave, the day had been hot, and the evening was still stiflingly warm, rare for this far north. My feet dusty in my worn New Look sandals, the thin cotton of my summer dress brushing against my knees in the warm evening breeze, heavy with the scent of the roses that grow all along the path. I clamp the cigarette between my teeth, the rasp of the lighter and then that first trickle of smoke pouring into my lungs soothing away the stress and exhaustion of the day.

'I don't know how long I stood out there for. Long enough to finish my wine and smoke two cigarettes and watch the stars. When I came back in, Archie was at the bottom of the stairs. He'd let himself out of his bedroom and come looking for me. The staircase was polished oak . . . he must have lost his footing and fallen. He was unconscious.' I feel that familiar, sick, panicky feeling, and

I am frightened that if I open my mouth I will vomit all over the table. *The crimson stain spreading out across the flagstone floor, the weight of his head as I cradled his tiny skull in my hands, his blood seeping into the skin around my fingernails.* I clamp my teeth together, breathing in and out through my nose until I feel under control again.

'And then what happened?' DC Bishop's voice is soft now, her eyebrows creasing together slightly as she listens.

'I called the ambulance, the Mackenzies . . . I can't really remember, it was all such a blur. Archie was taken to hospital and put in a medically induced coma. He'd hit his head pretty badly. And then . . . they said I did it.' I remember the fear, the shock that rattled my bones as I was arrested and questioned for hours on end. 'He'd hit his head so badly that his skull was fractured, and he'd suffered such extensive damage that the doctors had no choice but to turn off his life support machine – and the police thought I was responsible. So did his parents.

'There were other bruises on him, all over his body, that they said couldn't have been caused by the fall. I was the one in the frame. I knew I hadn't hurt him – I loved that little boy so much – but I had seen Gabby grab him roughly when he wouldn't do as he was told. I tried to tell them that, but why would they believe me? The English nanny who would rather sit outside, drinking and smoking, leaving a tiny boy all alone inside?' I let out a huff of bitter laughter. 'The police couldn't make it stick – they could say that I had been negligent, but they couldn't definitively say that I had pushed Archie on purpose. It was the media, and the people who lived there who crucified me. I had no other option but to come back to England.'

'And that's when you changed your name?'

'I didn't feel I had a choice – who would employ me? Who would give me the time of day if they knew I was Charlie Seddon? I haven't even told my mum I'm home. She still thinks I'm in Scotland working in a bar, for Christ's sake. I didn't want her to know I was here, looking after a child again . . . I just wanted to protect her – I thought if she doesn't know I'm here, then she doesn't have to see me, she doesn't have to explain anything to anyone. She got terrible abuse when people found out I was her daughter.' I drain the last of the water, pushing the glass away from me, a single tear dropping onto the formica table in front of me. 'I thought the best thing to do was become someone else, so I bleached and cut my hair, dropped some weight and changed my name. Anna Cox was on my nannying course years ago. I knew via Facebook that she'd given it all up to get married, so why not use her name for some references? I never meant any harm, not to anyone.'

'That's quite a story,' DC Bishop says, her face devoid of any expression. I have no idea whether she believes me, or what she's thinking about it all.

'Am I in trouble? I mean, I only wanted to protect myself, to try and start over, you know?' I ignore the irony here – that in starting over I have inadvertently found myself in much the same position as I was in before. Caring for a child, something bad happening to said child, and me in the firing line, all lined up and ready to be accused of something I didn't do.

DC Bishop skips over my question, asking one of her own instead. 'So, Anna – I'm going to keep calling you

Anna, no point in adding to the confusion – let's go back to Laurel's disappearance.'

I feel a rush of what can only be relief, as I realise that, for now, we are done talking about what happened in Killin on that awful, terrible night.

'So, Dominic didn't turn up that night?'

'No,' I say firmly, 'he was supposed to meet us, but he never showed.'

'And did he explain to you where he was? Give you a reason as to why he didn't meet his daughter as planned?'

'No,' I say, cautiously. I am aware that whatever I say now could change the whole course of the investigation, but I owe it to Laurel to tell DC Bishop the truth – it doesn't matter anymore if I don't have anything to back it up, they'll be questioning him now anyway. 'He wasn't at the hospital, even though he told Fran that's where he was. He asked me not to say anything to Fran, and I . . . assumed that he was meeting someone. But then I spoke to his ex-girlfriend, Pamela, and she was waiting to meet him that night too. He never showed up for her either.'

'So, where do you think he was?'

'I have no idea.' *Driving Laurel away in the back of his car.*

'And do you think that Pamela knows where he was?'

I think for a moment. If she had asked before I knew who Pamela was, I would have known how to answer, but now I'm not so sure. 'I don't know. She says not, but Fran has been receiving abusive messages on the "FIND LAUREL" Facebook page, about how she doesn't deserve to have children. I wouldn't be surprised if Pamela had something to do with that.'

'And what about Dominic's car? Does everyone use the car, or just him?'

I frown. 'Just him, I guess. They might go out in it as a family, but that's very rare. Fran uses a car service when she can, and usually I use my car or walk with Laurel. There is one other thing . . . I maybe should have mentioned it earlier, but I didn't know . . .' I stop, not sure how to explain why I didn't tell Kelly or DS Wright about it in the first place. I reach into the pocket of my jeans and pull out the tissue-wrapped hair. 'I found this hair on Dominic's jacket right after Laurel went missing. It might be nothing, but . . .'

DC Bishop scribbles another unintelligible scrawl in her notebook, and carefully drops the tissue and hair into a clear plastic evidence bag. 'Leave this with me. Thanks, Anna, you've been very helpful. Interview terminated at 14.26.' She leans over, shirt straining at the seams again, and switches off the tape recorder, before showing me towards the door, telling me it's OK for me to go home, but not to discuss anything we've talked about with Fran or Dominic.

I walk home, my whole body aching with exhaustion as my mind runs over the questions that DC Bishop fired at me. It was exhausting reliving what happened to Archie in Scotland, but I am somewhat relieved that I finally got it off my chest – I finally told the truth. Now all that remains to be seen is whether I have spent the last three years sharing a house with a man who could abduct his own daughter.

CHAPTER 21

As I walk back towards the Jessops' house (I am losing the ability to refer to it as *home*, it no longer feels like home, not without Laurel there), I try not to notice the icy, cold air, the frost glittering on the pavement, more Christmas lights twinkling in the front windows of the houses I pass; a stark reminder that in a few weeks Christmas will be upon us and there is every chance that we will be waking up on Christmas morning without Laurel. Although I initially felt relieved to talk about what happened with Archie, to get the burden of the lie off my chest, now all I can think about is Laurel, where she is, if she is safe, if she is warm enough, and the burden returns, heavier than ever.

Shoulders hunched, exhaustion pulling at my core, I push the front door open, a deafening silence telling me that Fran and Dominic aren't back yet. Tugging my boots off, I pause as a noise from overhead filters downstairs. The sound of a floorboard creaking. I freeze, wondering if I imagined it, before it comes again, the soft creak of someone walking around upstairs. Slowly I lower the boot to the floor and step quietly onto the stairs, creeping my way up. *Maybe Fran is home?* But no, Fran wouldn't be creeping around, you can always hear Fran coming a mile off. At the top of the stairs I stop, holding my breath, listening hard, and see that Laurel's bedroom is partially open. Pushing it open, I see Ruth standing in front of Laurel's chest of drawers, a tiny T-shirt in her hands.

'What the hell are you doing in here?' I demand, a tiny thrill shooting through me at seeing her jump, a scarlet flush creeping up her neck. 'Does Fran know you're here?'

'Anna . . .' Ruth turns, laying the T-shirt back in the drawer. 'I didn't hear you come home.'

'And you didn't answer me. Why are you in Laurel's room? And where is Fran?' I thought she was a bit odd before, the way she's forced herself into our lives, offering her help even though we've told her we don't need it, but this is simply too weird.

'I was just . . . I came to help Fran.' Ruth steps past me into the hallway, leaving me no choice but to follow her downstairs.

'So, Fran knows you're here?' Now I am convinced something isn't quite right, Fran would never leave someone she barely knows alone in the house, no matter how many pre-cooked dinners they brought over.

Ruth walks into the kitchen and lifting an apron from the hook that hangs behind the door, she ties it round her waist and opens the oven. 'No, not exactly, but Fran needs me. I heard what happened today with you all having to go to the police station and I came straight over. I thought you'd be hungry.' There is the smell of garlic in the air and my stomach turns. So now she's taken to cooking in the house instead of just bringing food over, it seems.

'So . . .' I frown, the ease in which she moves around the kitchen as if it is her own making me feel quite uncomfortable. 'How did you get in?'

'Oh, I borrowed the spare key,' she says breezily, and I feel a chill snake down my spine. She's still wearing those horrible, grubby, paint-stained jeans, and as she reaches towards the tap for boiling water, I glance at her fingernails, shuddering at the black marks beneath the nails. I can only hope that it's paint. 'Will you have tea?'

'No,' I say shortly, 'Ruth, I don't mean to be rude, but we've all had kind of a stressful day, and coming home to find you in Laurel's room . . . well, it's a bit weird. I know all you want to do is help, but Fran isn't home now, and I think she'll probably be tired when she does get in. It might be best if you leave now, maybe come and see her tomorrow?' I cross my fingers behind my back, hoping against all hope that she'll take the hint and go.

'I'm sure Fran will be tired.' A dark look crosses Ruth's face, and she turns the tap off a little too forcefully. The air between us changes, and I'm not sure what is going on, my pulse picking up a little bit of speed as Ruth tugs at the strings of the apron around her waist, yanking it up over her head, muttering to herself as she does so.

'I don't mean to be rude . . .' I step to one side as she snatches up her bag from where it sits in a bulky, beige hessian puddle by the table.

'You people never do,' she snaps, freezing at the sound of the front door opening and then slamming shut reaches our ears. Slowly she places her bag back down on the floor, with a slightly triumphant glance towards me.

'Anna? Are you here?' Fran's voice calls out, and I can picture her in the hallway, throwing her boots under the radiator, shaking cold, frosty droplets from her sleek, dark hair, so different to Laurel's blonde ponytail.

'In the kitchen.' I call out, sliding into a chair at the table, hoping my voice doesn't wobble. My hands are cold, and I tuck them under my thighs to warm them, avoiding Ruth's gaze. Fran bursts in, closely followed by Kelly.

'Anna, you poor thing. How was it?' Fran crouches next to me, tugging my hand out and clutching it between both of hers. 'Was it dreadful? Did they ask you awful things?' Her face is pale, two spots of deep red dancing high up on her cheekbones. Her dark eyes glitter, and she looks hectic, almost manic. I dread to think how her interview went.

'It wasn't as bad as I first thought,' I say, 'but I don't think we're supposed to talk about it.'

'No, no, of course not.' Fran straightens, pressing her hands to her cheeks. 'I'm just so relieved it's over. Kelly, can you make us some tea?'

'I can do it.' Ruth jumps to attention, dishing out a quick smirk in my direction. 'Hello, Fran.'

Fran turns to her, a mild look of surprise on her face. 'Oh, it's you. I didn't realise you were here.' She frowns for a moment. 'Why are you here?'

'She was in Laurel's room when I came home,' I burst out, 'she said she had the spare key.'

Fran stares at Ruth, confusion clouding her features. 'You let yourself into my house? Into my daughter's bedroom?'

'Fran, I only wanted to . . .' Ruth says, her hands raised in surrender. She looks at me, furious. '*You* don't understand.'

'Actually,' Kelly breaks in, her hands going up to tug at her ponytail, pulling it so tight I wonder how she can be comfortable, 'I wondered if I could have a quick word with you, Ruth?'

213

'Of course.' Ruth wipes her hands on a tea towel, casually slinging it over the cupboard door handle as if she lives here.

'You might want to speak in private,' Kelly says, firmly.

'No,' Ruth says, raising her chin a little defiantly. She flicks her mousy hair away from her face, and I see a tiny crop of pimples on her make-up free forehead. 'Anything you want to say, you can say in front of Fran. And Anna, I suppose.' An ugly, dark flush starts to creep up her neck and for a moment, I don't want to hear anything that she has to say. I know that something bad is coming. I glance at Fran, who stands rigidly, her whole being vibrating with unspoken anger. She nods at Kelly. 'Go on then, if she wants to speak in front of us, let her. I'm interested in what she has to say, now that she thinks it's acceptable to break into my house.'

'Ruth,' Kelly says, 'I wanted to ask you about some abusive messages that have been left on the Facebook page set up to find Laurel.'

Ruth's face goes pale, but she still stands there, rigid, not moving a muscle. 'What about them?'

I think for a moment, not listening to Kelly's reply, as something tugs at the back of my mind. Something that bugged me on and off for days, but I couldn't quite put my finger on, has all of a sudden become clear.

'It was you,' I say, the smudge of red paint on the sleeve of her jumper as her coat slipped back on her wrist that day suddenly larger than life in my mind. 'All of that was you, the paint on the fence, the messages . . . I thought it was Pamela.'

'What?' Fran is looking between Ruth and me with an expression of horror on her face. 'Anna, what do you mean?'

'It was Ruth all along – she's the one who painted *MURDERER* on the fence, she's the one who sent all those abusive messages on the Facebook page. God, I feel like such an idiot.' I scrub my hands over my face. 'I saw the paint on your sleeve that day . . . but with everything that was going on, I just didn't put two and two together. Why? Was it because Fran didn't let you in that day, the day the psychic came?'

'The Facebook user name . . .' Fran says, clicking her fingers together, 'Lois Burns. But . . . your name isn't Lois? What is it – a middle name? Or did you pluck it out of thin air? And Burns . . . what's that? Your maiden name?' Her face changes as something clicks. 'Oh my God, it is, isn't it? You're Ruth Burns, that weird girl from my drama course. I'm right, aren't I?'

'You can't prove anything,' Ruth says, but she picks anxiously at the skin around her fingernails, a tiny bead of blood welling up by her cuticle and making me feel sick.

'I'm afraid we can.' Kelly has kept silent so far, simply absorbing everything that is being revealed. 'I've had someone tracing the IP address that the messages were sent from. I'm pretty sure we're going to get a match on your address, aren't we?'

'I thought it was Pamela,' I say, quietly. 'In the interview room earlier, I told them that I thought Pamela had done it. Why, Ruth? Why would you pretend to be Fran's friend, why would you come round here over and over? You kept on offering to help, pushing your way in even though you must have known you weren't particularly welcome. And why send the messages? I really don't understand.' I risk a glance at Fran, who sits silently, her fingers tapping lightly on the table top, a sure sign that she is close to losing her temper.

'I don't even know you,' Fran says tightly, 'I don't even know who your child is. We didn't want you here, you pushed your way in with your casseroles and sympathy! You took advantage of the fact that we were vulnerable, and you used it to do something horrible. Anna is right – why would you do this?'

'Exactly that reason,' Ruth says, her voice strong, but her shaking hands show her bravery is all an act. 'When I first heard you'd moved back here, I thought maybe I'd bump into you, but I never did. And then I heard that your daughter was starting at the primary school . . . I was still on the PTA even though Josephine had left a year before Laurel started.'

'Ruth, I think maybe you should come with me,' Kelly moves forward, but Fran holds up a hand to stop her.

'No, Kelly. I want to hear this.' Fran's voice is like steel. 'I want to hear what she has to say.' Kelly steps back, and Ruth continues.

'You say you don't even know me, but I know *you*. You ignored me all the way through drama school, you made sure I was always on the outside looking in while you were there, swanning around with all your precious actor friends. I thought when you moved back here, when you had a child, that it would be different, that we could be friends, finally.'

'Look, I'm sorry, Ruth,' Fran says, 'I didn't recognise you, drama school was a long time ago, a lot has happened since then . . .'

'All I ever wanted was to be a friend to you, do you know that?' Ruth's voice breaks a little, and I can't help but feel some small sense of pity for her. 'When Laurel went missing, I thought I could get involved, I could help look for her. I could be your *friend*, Fran.'

Fran opens her mouth to speak, but Ruth carries on, 'I offered to help you so many times and every time you just threw it back in my face – I *wanted* to get involved, Fran, I wanted to be part of it all, to be part of your circle, not like your so-called mummy friends who've steered well clear, in case they catch *abduction* from you.'

Fran lets out a gasp, as though Ruth has slapped her in the face. 'Ruth, that's not . . .'

'No, Fran, let me finish. That's why I sent the messages, that's why I painted that word on the fence . . .' Ruth scrubs her rough, paint-stained hands over her face. 'I thought it would make you need me. I thought that if you thought everyone was against you, you'd need me, you'd let me in.'

'Jesus.' Fran shakes her head, and I see that familiar set to her jaw that says she is utterly furious. 'You did all of this . . . you made my life even more of a living hell than it already was, because you wanted to *be a part of it all*? You actually thought this would make me be your friend? When my daughter . . . when Laurel . . .' Her voice thickens, and she has to stop.

Ruth lets out a bitter bark of laughter, and I can almost taste the toxic poison radiating out of her every pore. 'You didn't deserve to have Laurel. She was the most precious thing you had, and you lost her because you couldn't be bothered to look after her properly. You never bothered to turn up to watch her in school plays, you never took her to the park, or spent quality time with her – that's why you hired Anna. You're thoughtless when it comes to other people, Fran. I thought maybe you'd be different now, but you're not. Careless, that's what you are.'

I watch as Fran's face seems to crumple in on itself, pain etched into every feature. 'Ruth, please, that's enough.'

'I'm thoughtless?' Fran gets to her feet, stumbling slightly. 'Don't you understand what you've done? How could you ever think that I could let you in? Oh my God, the phone call . . . the dropped calls and then that call where I was told it was my fault . . . do you remember, Anna? That was you too, wasn't it?'

Ruth nods, but her bravado seems to have fled, as she stares shamefaced at her feet. 'I only wanted to help you, Fran. I don't know why you wouldn't let me help. I just wanted to be there for you . . . for Laurel.'

'Do you know where she is?' Fran demands, stepping towards Ruth, white-hot rage pouring off her in waves. 'Did you have something to do with this?'

'No, I . . .' Ruth steps back, hands raised as if to ward Fran off. 'I told you, all I ever wanted was to be your friend.'

'Come on, Ruth, time to leave.' Kelly has appeared beside Ruth, holding her elbow in a vice-like grip.

'Get her out of here,' Fran says.

As soon as Ruth leaves, guided by Kelly, the charged atmosphere dissipates, but I am shaking, my nerves feeling as though they are barely below the surface of my skin. Fran has shoved her chair back and is fumbling with the key to the back door with one hand, an unlit cigarette in the other. I follow her out to the back garden, shivering as the chill air meets my bare feet.

218

'Jesus.' My breath plumes out in great clouds of smoke in front of me. 'She is . . . crazy.'

'Yeah, well,' Fran takes a huge drag on her cigarette, coughing as the smoke hits her lungs, 'it looks as though I was right not to let her in. I mean, she said I shut her out years ago? I didn't even realise who she was, not until just now, when I twigged she was Ruth Burns. Christ. I don't know what to think.'

'Are you OK, Fran, I mean . . . really? After being at the police station?' My stomach rolls as her cigarette smoke wafts towards me. What I really want to say is, *did they tell you I lied? Did they tell you I'm not Anna Cox?* I wonder if I should say something now, or would that tip her right over the edge?

'I honestly don't know, Anna.' *No, they didn't tell her.* I have to say something, I have to tell her before they do.

'Fran, I need to tell you something.' My stomach lurches, and for a horrible moment I think I'm about to be sick. 'It's important. And I want you to know that I never meant for it to be like this . . . it was never anything personal.'

'What?' Fran squints at me through her cigarette smoke, her eyes narrowed.

'The thing is . . .' I gulp. 'My name isn't actually Anna Cox. Something happened in my past, something that wasn't my fault, and when I applied for the job with you I gave you a different name. I'm sorry.' I wait, sure now that she'll tell me to leave, just get out, and then it'll all be over.

'What? What do you mean?' She lowers the cigarette from her mouth as she frowns, her lips pursing. 'Anna . . . you're not Anna Cox?'

'No. God, Fran, I'm sorry, I know I've massively messed up . . .'

'Just shut up for a minute.' I watch as I see her trying to process what I've said, her lips moving as she mouths my words. 'If you're not Anna Cox, then who the fuck are you?'

I take a deep breath, knowing that once I tell her my real name there is no going back. 'Charlie. My name is Charlie Seddon.' And I pause, waiting for the penny to drop.

'Charlie Seddon?' Her eyes widen in horror as she looks me over, raking her gaze over my badly bleached hair, my skinny frame, so different to six years ago, making the connection between me now, and the photographs in the newspapers back then. 'Oh my God. *You're* Charlie Seddon? You . . .' She starts to pace, flicking the cigarette to the floor, her feet slipping slightly on the damp paving slabs. 'I can't believe this. *Charlie Seddon*. You absolute bitch.' She stops and glares at me, a muscle working in her jaw as she tries to control her anger.

'Fran, please. It didn't happen the way they said it did – I swear I never did anything wrong! And I would never have hurt Laurel, you believe me, right?'

Fran steps towards me, raises her left hand and slaps me sharply across the face. 'Don't you dare,' she shouts, her cheeks a dark, angry red. 'You lied to me – you made your way into our house, knowing what you did. We – I – trusted you, and all the time you were lying.' She bunches her hands into fists and I think she's going to hit me again, but instead she resumes pacing.

'You lied about who you were – you let me leave Laurel in your care, knowing what happened before. I can't believe you've got away with this . . .' she pauses for a moment as if remembering, 'but I got references for you! How? I got references from your old employers, the Emericks . . . so what? Did you get someone else involved in lying to me about who you were?'

'No,' I raise my hand to my face, the skin burning where Fran slapped me, 'I gave you the real Anna's old employers' name. I'm sorry, Fran, I'm so sorry. I swear I never did anything wrong – it wasn't my fault. Please, will you let me explain . . .' I can't help myself, I start to cry.

'All I ever wanted was to be a good mother to Laurel,' Fran says, ignoring my pleas as she still paces, her arms hugging her tiny frame, 'that's all I ever wanted was the best for her. And now I find that the one person I thought I could trust with her is just another liar – not only that, but a child killer as well. God, I feel ill.' A look of disgust crosses her face and she clutches dramatically at her belly.

'Then maybe you should have been there! If you were so desperate to be a good mother, maybe it should have been you looking after her, instead of being so busy all the time!' I shout, her spiteful, bitter words breaking through my thin veneer of control. I watch as her face crumples. 'I never killed a child, Fran. It was an accident, a horrible, heartbreaking accident, and it's something that I'll never get over. I loved – *love* – Laurel, and I would never do anything to hurt her.'

'And I'm simply supposed to believe you?' Fran gives a snort of laughter, hideously out of place after my outburst, as tears track their way slowly down her cheeks, 'because you're just *so* honest. You've betrayed me, Anna, Charlie, whatever you want to call yourself. I trusted you with the most precious possession I had, and you lied your way into the position. I don't know if I can ever forgive you for that.'

221

'I'm sorry,' I whisper for the hundredth time, but she doesn't reply.

Later, I am in my room, hiding from Fran after our conversation outside, if I'm honest, thinking over everything I have said to the police and wondering if there was anything more I could tell them, anything else that would point them in the right direction. I feel desperate to make amends for lying to Fran about my identity, desperate to make her understand how I really feel about Laurel before she asks me to leave. I can hear her pacing above me in the room she shares with Dominic, and the low murmur of her voice as she talks on the phone, presumably to her mother again, and I wonder if she is telling her mother that I'm not really Anna Cox, or whether she is voicing her concerns about Dominic, the way she did to me in the church.

I can't help but feel that he is hiding something, and the idea that he knows where Laurel is makes me go hot and cold, leaving a thick, heavy ball in my stomach, as I slowly fold T-shirts and sweaters and place them gently in my suitcase. There is no sign of Dominic yet, and I wonder how much longer the police will be talking to him for, that's if the police still have him at the station. I wouldn't put it past him now to go to Pamela, or some other willing woman, on leaving the station rather than come back home and face Fran's wrath.

I look up as my door is slowly pushed open and Fran stands there, her face unreadable.

'You're packing,' she states, and I carry on folding a cardigan, fussily shaking the fabric out to make it fold neatly, avoiding eye contact.

'I thought you'd want me to leave. I know I shouldn't have lied, but . . . it was too complicated to explain when I first met you and then I got attached to Laurel, and I was worried you would fire me if I told you the truth . . .' I trail off as I realise that she isn't shouting or screaming at me, she isn't telling me to leave.

'So, your name is really Charlie Seddon, not Anna Cox?' she says, and I nod. 'Archie Mackenzie died while he was in your care – do you see how that looks, now I know the truth about who you are?'

'That's why I couldn't tell you who I was – that's the only reason I lied, I swear. I promise you, Fran, I never hurt Archie. I left him alone for the shortest time, while I thought he was asleep. It was an accident.' I feel my eyes well up again. 'I've never left Laurel, not even for a second, not after what happened to Archie.'

'I have to ask you this, Anna . . . does the fact that you didn't give me your real name have anything to do with the fact that my daughter has been abducted? Does this mean that you know something about where she is?'

'Well, no, of course not,' I say.

'Right.' Fran tilts her head on one side as if considering something. 'You lied to me, Anna. You don't mind me still calling you that, do you?' Fran's tone is chilly. 'I'm not sure I can ever believe another word that comes out of your mouth, but I do believe despite your lies that you do genuinely love Laurel. Besides, don't you think I have more important things to think about, like where my daughter is? Whether I'll ever see her again? Almost everyone around me has turned out to be a liar, so the fact that you're a liar too shouldn't really come as that much of a surprise.'

'I understand if you want me to leave,' I say again, wincing internally at her harsh words, the thought of not being here if – when – Laurel comes home like a knife in my chest.

'Well, obviously I'd prefer it if you weren't here.' Fran looks at me. 'But I've thought about things and despite your history, despite what you say you didn't do, Laurel is the most important thing, not your name, or your history. Laurel will be upset if she comes home and you're not here, it might make things more traumatic for her. Right now, I'm slightly more concerned by the fact that Dominic hasn't come home yet. I mean,' she draws a tissue out from her pocket and dabs gently at her nose as she blinks, 'I don't even know Dominic anymore. I don't want to be alone when he comes home, because I don't know how he will react. I thought he might be cheating on me with that . . . whore. Pamela.' There is a vicious tone to her voice, as if even saying Pamela's name is difficult. 'But deep down, I was hoping it was all paranoia. That I got things wrong, that this was only a minor blip. Obviously, that's not the case. All I want now is for this to be finished. Over. I want Laurel back home, where she belongs, so the two of us can make a new start.'

I don't know whether she means herself and Dominic, or herself and Laurel, if – when – Laurel comes home, so I merely nod and say nothing.

Fran leaves, and such is my relief at the fact that she's allowing me to stay, for now anyway, that I remain in my room out of her way, just in case she changes her mind. I start to unpack the few things I had placed carefully into my suitcase, taking my time to hang them back up so I don't have to head downstairs anytime soon, even though I have no idea if Fran is even still home, it's so quiet. Such is the silence in the rest of the house that I almost jump out of my skin when my ringtone blares filling the room with Taylor Swift's 'Shake it Off' (Laurel's choice), *MUM* appearing on the screen. Sighing, I take a deep breath before I press the button to connect.

'Hi, Mum.'

'Oh, Charlie, what have you done?'

CHAPTER 22

My mother's words are laced with worry and disappointment and I have to swallow hard to squash down the emotion that rises up in me at the sound of her voice.

'Hi, Mum. Nice of you to ring. I'm not too sure what you mean by that, but I'm sure you're going to tell me.' I say the words, but I do know, of course I do, and my heart sinks like a lead weight.

'The girl. The missing girl in Surrey. Why didn't you tell me?' Her voice catches, and I hear her suck in, and I know she's smoking, even though she promised my dad she'd given up.

'I couldn't,' I say, my eyes smarting. 'And how did you know?'

'BBC online.' There's a pause. 'There's a breaking news banner on the website. A picture of you leaving the police station, and a headline that says, *Did the nanny do it?*'

'So, you're ringing to ask me if I had anything to do with Laurel's abduction?' A fist of hurt twists in my belly. I am still nothing more than a disappointment to her.

'No, silly girl,' she says softly, 'I'm calling to see if you're OK. To ask why you didn't tell me that you were home. Why you wanted me to think you were still in Killin.'

'Mum . . .' I battle for a moment to take a breath, the lump in my throat is so big.

She says nothing, simply waits for me to continue. I picture her in the house I grew up in, miles away from here, her dressing gown tied tightly around her waist, standing in the kitchen waiting for the kettle to boil as she did so many times before when I sneaked in late. She was always waiting for me, waiting to hear what I had to say. I don't know when that changed. Was it when I decided to skip out on a law degree and train to be a nanny? When I decided I was being stifled and I ran away to Scotland, to be with a lad I barely knew? Or when I was accused of killing a small boy, the press and the public picking over every aspect of our lives?

I start to speak, the words tumbling over one another. 'Do you remember, Mum, what it was like? When you came up to Killin, when they first said that I did it?'

'I remember,' she says, her voice heavy. 'Of course, I remember.'

'The way people reacted – spitting at me in the street, shouting and swearing at me, my face on the front page of the newspaper every day.' My voice breaks, but I push on. 'That day . . . the day they said I could go, that they believed I didn't do it . . . the day you came and met me . . . that man pushed you, told you that you were the mother of a murderer and that we'd both rot in hell. That was the day I knew everything had changed, nothing was ever going to be the same again if I came home.'

'You didn't have to lie to me though, Charlie, you didn't have to pretend that you were still in Scotland. You could have come home, I would have taken care of you.' My mother sniffs, and I know that I've made her cry, again, the way I have so many times before.

'I couldn't . . . I felt ashamed, I suppose. I know I didn't do it, and the police, the media, they eventually agreed that I was innocent but it wouldn't have mattered to anyone else. How could I come back and live at home, knowing the way people would react? The things they'd say to you? Or even do to you?' It was bad enough before, people threw eggs at my parents' house, vandalised my dad's car, refused to serve them in the local shop.

'I thought I would come home sometime, to you and Dad, but I just couldn't let you go through all that again. I only wanted to protect you. And then it got harder and harder to say anything, and I got the job here, but I was using the name Anna Cox and it was all so complicated, so I kept on pretending to you that I was still there . . .' I stop, not sure where to go anymore. 'I didn't want to disappoint you more than I already had done.'

'Charlie, you have never disappointed me – I might not have always agreed with your decisions, but it doesn't mean I'm not proud of what you've achieved. What happened in Killin – it doesn't change what I think about you. You're my daughter, and I love you, I know that you never meant for that boy to get hurt. None of that matters anymore. What does matter though is what's happened to Laurel – and what's going to happen to you. I'm worried about you, Charlie.'

'I know. I don't know what to do, what to think. We all just want her back. I can't think past that at the moment.'

'I understand that, Charlie, I really do, but you need to think about what is best for you. I don't want to see you caught up in all of this, not again. If it all becomes too much, I think you should consider getting away from things for a while. I'm sure the Jessops would understand.'

I glance towards my suitcase, still only half unpacked, and then to the birthday card on the bedside table that Laurel drew for me, what seems like a million years ago. 'I can't come home, Mum, I can't leave Fran. Dominic hasn't come back from the station yet, and things have been a little . . . fraught round here today.' As I say the words, the thought of going home, hugging my mum, sitting in the kitchen letting her fuss round me is all too tempting.

'You're not on your own, Charlie, you've never been on your own in any of it. We're here if you need us, me and Dad. Or, if you don't want to come home you can always go to Aunt Lou's holiday home – she's not been back there since Uncle John died and I'm sure she'd be grateful for someone to look after the place for her. Just a thought.'

I realise that she is giving me an out if I need one – if the press attention becomes too much, or if Fran decides she does want me to leave. I've managed to keep out of the way for the most part up until now, but now the press have caught wind of the fact that I was being questioned at the station, it's only a matter of time before they find out who I really am, before things escalate, exactly as they did in Killin.

'Thanks, Mum.' We say our goodbyes and I hang up, feeling better than I have in a long time. I have no more secrets left to keep, nothing left to hide now that I have been honest about what happened in Scotland, and I have confessed to being someone other than Anna Cox. Now all I have to hope is that the secret of whoever took Laurel will be revealed soon. That the truth will come out.

The next morning marks a month since we last saw Laurel. It is the first weekend in December, a weekend which would usually be spent trawling the local Christmas tree farm searching for the best possible tree. The first year I worked for the Jessops Dominic went out of his way to be there on this weekend, not wanting to miss the search for the elusive perfect tree, but for the past two years he hasn't; citing work as the reason for his absence. This meant that for the last couple of years I have been included on this most special occasion, responsible for holding tight to Laurel's hand to make sure she didn't run off too far amongst the trees. There is a bittersweet moment when I wake, and I forget that she isn't here before the heavy sense of loss returns. I think that maybe Fran will skip the ritual this year – if I, as Laurel's nanny, don't feel like celebrating, or even acknowledging a Christmas without Laurel I don't see how Fran will want to – but when I come downstairs she is in the hallway, pulling her boots on, the fur cuff leaving stray hairs on the bottom of her designer jogging pants.

'You're up!' she exclaims, giving me a thin smile. It's as though our conversation the previous evening never happened, like I never confessed my secret to her and everything is as usual, but despite her attempt at normality, her face is pale and the dark rings around her eyes tell me that she didn't sleep last night. Again. 'It's tree day, you didn't forget, did you?'

'No, but . . .' I watch as she reaches for her thick ski jacket, shoving her arms into it and pulling a grey woollen hat out of the pocket, feeling a little uneasy at the way she is behaving as usual. 'I thought maybe you'd want to give it a miss this year, seeing as Laurel isn't here?'

Fran stops, her blue eyes icy cold as she stares at me. 'She's not here *now, today*, Anna but she might be by Christmas Day.

She'd want a tree. And besides . . .' she clears her throat, 'it helps. To feel a bit normal, you know? After everything.'

I say nothing, but reach for my own jacket, my skin prickling uncomfortably as I note that she still calls me Anna. There is still no sign of Dominic, and Fran doesn't mention him. It feels wrong to be carrying on like nothing has happened, as though Laurel will come barrelling downstairs at any moment, demanding that I help her with her boots, singing Christmas carols in an off-key voice that always makes me smile. Fran is still the boss, whether Laurel is here or not, so I pull on my coat and follow her outside.

It takes all day to find the ideal tree. It's perfect winter weather – the sun is shining, and frost crackles under our feet as we arrive at the Christmas tree farm, eventually thawing to leave a clear, crisp day. My feet are numb as we eventually choose our tree, the tree that Fran declares 'The One' and she pays for it, arranging with the manager to have it delivered to the house. I've tried my hardest to engage with her today, to offer an opinion when asked, but I can't help feeling that this was all a pointless exercise, something to make Fran feel better, more normal. I am waking up to the fact that Laurel not being here is the new normal – might be the only normal that we know from now on. The idea of getting away from here, going home, or even further afield, is more and more appealing, but I'm concerned about broaching the subject with Fran just yet, especially after our row yesterday and while the media are still circling. I don't want to look as though I'm running away – I have nothing to run away from this time. Fran doesn't talk much on the way home, and I don't try to fill the silence.

As we approach the house we see DS Wright waiting on the doorstep, in the dusky twilight, her breath reaching out in smoky plumes as she runs a hand over her hair.

'Oh.' Fran stops, and I almost crash into her. 'DS Wright.'

'Fran. Can I come in?' She looks frozen, the tip of her nose a bright pink. Kelly stands beside her, her eyes looking everywhere except at Fran.

'Of course. Anna?' Fran looks at me, and I fumble in my pocket for the door key, avoiding Wright's eye as she registers that Fran still calls me Anna. Pushing open the door I stand to one side to let them both in, following behind them as they head into the living room. Wright stands until Fran gestures to her to take a seat. There is a strangely formal air in the room.

'Dominic isn't home yet,' Fran says, a slight frown creasing her brow. It's been too long between botox injections. 'Maybe we should wait for him. Anna, what do you think?'

I look to DS Wright, who gives a slight shake of her head, and say nothing.

'Mrs Jessop, Fran, there's something I need to tell you,' DS Wright says, shadows from the now lit lamp flickering across her face. 'Dominic won't be coming home. Not tonight. Not for a while, I should think.'

Something crosses Fran's face, an emotion that I can't put a name to before it is gone again, her features blank and smooth as she waits for Wright to go on. The only thing that truly belies her feelings is the way her fingers knit tightly together, what's left of her bitten fingernails digging into the backs of her hands.

'What's going on?' she asks, quietly, but I know. I know exactly what DS Wright is here to say.

'Fran . . . we've charged Dominic with the abduction of your daughter, Laurel.'

CHAPTER 23

I watch Fran as she blinks twice, slowly, her hands falling to her sides before she lowers herself into a nearby chair. She raises her hands to her mouth briefly, and I see her fingers shaking as she brings her hands back into her lap. I can feel my pulse thudding hard in my temple, and I wonder if Fran's heart is galloping the way mine is.

'Dominic?' Fran says, her eyes never leaving Wright's face. She gives a small nod and glances towards me, and I remember our conversation in the cemetery, when I wanted to tell her about the hair on his jacket, the suspicions I was harbouring about exactly where Dominic was the night Laurel disappeared.

'I'm sorry, Fran.' Wright nods her head towards Kelly, who stands to one side in the doorway. At her gesture she rushes forward and stoops down next to Fran, clasping her pale, lifeless fingers in her hand.

'Don't fuss over me,' Fran snaps, shaking her fingers free and getting to her feet. As she begins to pace she looks at me, shaking a finger in my direction. 'You had an idea this was coming, didn't you, Anna?'

I open my mouth, but nothing comes out. Yes, I was suspicious of Dominic, but I had nothing concrete to back my gut feeling up. 'I didn't . . . I mean, I don't . . .' I manage to stammer out, flicking my eyes towards Wright, a knot of terror building in my chest at the thought of everything I told DC Bishop in my interview, of her and DI Dove thinking I was in on it with Dominic.

'You said to me that day at the church,' Fran says, 'you had a feeling then, didn't you? That Dominic was lying about something.' Before I can reply she turns to Wright and carries on speaking, her words tumbling out over one another as she barely pauses for breath. 'Has he told you where she is? Did you find Laurel? Anna, come on, get your jacket, we'll need to go now and see her . . . we can see her, can't we?' Now she halts, her chest hitching. DS Wright looks uncomfortable, rocking slightly on her heels, and Kelly steps forward.

'Fran, Dominic hasn't told us where she is yet.' Kelly's voice is quiet, and she hesitates for a moment, her hand in the air as if to place it reassuringly on Fran's arm, before she thinks better of it, and lets her hand drop to her side. 'He's denying knowing anything about what happened to Laurel that night.'

'So how have you arrested him? Something must have happened to make you people think he's guilty? You don't simply arrest people with no reason.'

'There is something,' Wright says, 'a few things, in fact. We do need to talk to you about some things that have come to light. Are you OK to talk here, or would you rather . . .?'

'No. Here is fine. Anna, come and sit by me.' Fran pats the seat next to her distractedly and I slowly move towards her, my legs like lead. There is a strange numbness around me, as if I have lost all sense of feeling, and I realise that perhaps I am in shock.

'Fran, Dominic was supposed to meet you that night, wasn't he?' Wright says, flicking through a notepad that she pulls from her bag. 'But he didn't show up. Not until you had arrived back here with the police after leaving the site of Laurel's disappearance.'

'That's . . .' Clearing her throat, Fran tries again, the words seeming to get caught on their way out. 'That's right, yes. He said he would meet us at the field, as he had a list at the hospital until six o'clock. There didn't seem much point in us waiting here to meet him, as we would have missed the start of the bonfire, so I told him to meet us there. We argued about it, actually.' She blinks, pinching the bridge of her nose between thumb and forefinger as if to stop the tears. 'Do we really have to do this now? Shouldn't you be there, at the station, questioning him? Making him tell you where Laurel is? I can't bear this much longer.' Her voice breaks, and a single tear rolls down her cheek. 'I really need to know that she's OK.'

'We are trying, Fran, I promise. We need you to tell us as much as you possibly can in order to help us get the information we need. So, Dominic never showed up. Did he ever tell you where he was that night? Anna?' Wright turns towards me.

'He never told me,' I say, shaking my head. 'All he said was that he'd told you where he was, and that I shouldn't mention it to Fran. Sorry.' My stomach churns at the thought that all of this could have been dealt with, *Dominic* could have been dealt with days or even weeks ago if I had just told the police my suspicions. 'I thought perhaps . . .' I glance towards Fran, as she sits, head down, her fingers picking at her cuticles. 'I thought perhaps he'd gone to meet a woman.'

'Instead he . . . what? Snatched Laurel? Oh God, I feel sick,' Fran moans, leaning forward, clutching at her stomach.

'But if he took Laurel, how could he have known that she would follow Fran to the portaloos?' I ask, still not wanting to believe that Dominic, the man I've worked for, shared a house with for the past three years, the man who supported me all those times when Fran was being difficult, could be capable of something so horrific.

'This may not have been something that he planned,' Wright says, 'it may have been a spur of the moment decision, but in any case, Dominic doesn't have an alibi for the time frame in which Laurel went missing.'

'Where does he say he was?' Fran asks, her face clammy, tendrils of hair sticking slightly to her damp forehead. She looks ill, as though she might throw up at any minute.

'He has admitted that he arranged to meet Pamela, but then never showed. He says he was driving around, but he couldn't tell us exactly where. He said he was still upset with you, Fran, after your argument that morning. There isn't any CCTV along those country roads, so it's been difficult for us to trace his exact whereabouts that evening.'

'So, he doesn't have any sort of alibi at all?' I ask. It's looking more and more as though my instinct was right, and I rub at my arms, as a sudden chill runs over me as though someone has walked over my grave.

'No. It doesn't look that way,' Wright says. She sinks into the chair opposite Fran, leaning forward to catch Fran's eye. Fran is still staring at her feet, her eyes wide and unblinking, unwilling to meet DS Wright's gaze. 'There are a few other things that I need to speak with you about, Fran, relating to Dominic and his arrest. We found some . . .' Wright tilts her head to one side as she considers how best to put her next words, 'some disturbing images on his computer.'

'On the PC?' Fran finally looks up at DS Wright, her mouth a grim slash cut into her pale face. 'What kind of images? Pictures of Laurel?' She raises her hand to her mouth, pressing hard against her lips. Swallowing, I close my eyes, fighting back the nausea that scorches the back of my throat.

'The only pictures of Laurel were family photos, thankfully, but obviously we did do a thorough search as part of the investigation and we did take a further look into the files on the computer. We found several images depicting children.'

'Oh, God.' Fran gets to her feet, rushing from the room, and a few moments later we hear the sound of retching coming from the downstairs bathroom.

'I'll go,' Kelly says, leaving DS Wright and I alone together, the overpowering scent of lilies coming from the plug-in air freshener making me feel even sicker.

'I can't quite believe this is happening,' I say, shaking my head. A lock of hair flops over my forehead and I shove it back, impatiently. 'I mean . . . God, *Dominic*.' I let out a long breath. 'I mentioned it to DC Bishop in my interview but . . . I should probably tell you that there was a hair on his jacket, the morning after Laurel disappeared. A long, blonde hair. I thought maybe it belonged to a woman, that maybe that's where he'd gone that night . . . I didn't say anything. I should have though, shouldn't I?' Hot tears sting my eyes and I have to blink rapidly to try and quench them.

'You probably should have done – but it may not have made the slightest bit of difference. If the hair is Laurel's it could have been left there at any time. And Laurel was already gone by then.'

'You definitely believe Dominic took her?' Fran's voice makes me jump, and I turn to see her in the doorway, her face pale with a sickly sheen, one hand pressed against her belly. 'But he won't say where she is?'

'That's right,' DS Wright says, 'there's something I'd like to show you, Fran, if that's OK? It is potentially quite distressing to both of you, I should warn you.'

'OK.' Fran nods. 'Whatever it is, I just want to know.' Her voice breaks on the last word, and impulsively I reach over and take her hand, her fingers cold in mine.

DS Wright reaches into the satchel style bag she has at her feet and pulls out an A4-sized photograph, protected by a plastic wallet. 'I need to know if either of you recognises this.'

It's a sock. A tiny, pale lemon sock with a white lace frill around the ankle. I hear Fran inhale, and then she whimpers slightly. 'It's Laurel's. That's Laurel's sock, isn't it, Anna?' She turns to me with wide eyes and I nod in agreement.

'Yes. That's Laurel's sock . . . there's blood on it.' I raise my eyes from the photograph to meet DS Wright's eyes, my skin itching as though there are a thousand tiny ants marching over it. A dark crimson stain mars the perfect lemon yellow wool, a thick, ugly stain that tells of a deep, angry gush of hurt. I close my eyes as the room seems to swim about me for a moment, and I feel Fran's fingers grip my hand tightly, so tightly it hurts.

'So, you both can confirm that this is definitely Laurel's sock?'

'Yes,' Fran whispers, 'I put those socks on her that night before we left the house. She wanted to wear sandals because she loved showing off these socks, but I made her wear wellies instead.'

'But what about the blood,' I say, 'and where did you find the sock?'

'We found the sock in Dominic's car,' Wright says, and although she speaks with no trace of emotion in her voice, she blinks hard, telling me that she's finding this just as difficult as we are. 'It was tucked away underneath the passenger seat.'

'Hidden,' Fran says, 'he hid it there. He must have done, no one else drove that precious car of his. What has he done to my daughter? Where did the blood come from?' She is weirdly calm, not at all like the fiery, angry Fran that I've been used to dealing with for the past three years. It's as though all the life has drained out of her since Laurel has been gone, and now the news that Dominic is responsible has just pushed her over the edge.

'Dominic says that he has no idea where the sock came from, and that it could have been there from a previous journey that he took with Laurel in the car a few weeks ago. Although, obviously, Fran you contest that, saying that Laurel was wearing those socks on the evening that she went missing. Dominic also says that Laurel was prone to nosebleeds and that the blood could have been from a nosebleed. Did Laurel have any nosebleeds that day, or recently at all?'

I think hard for a moment. Fran looks away, waiting for me to answer, the ghost of my words asking her why she wasn't there for Laurel hanging in the air. She had been so busy with auditions and meetings that Laurel had seen fairly little of her in the weeks leading up to her disappearance. It had been me that had had practically sole care of Laurel in those last few weeks. 'No, not that night. Definitely not that night,' I say, 'in fact, I don't think she'd had one recently at all. Not since the summer. She tends to suffer dreadfully from hay fever from May until around the end of July, and that's when she seems to get the nosebleeds. She certainly hasn't had one recently.' There is silence as the full implication of my words sinks in. DS Wright gets to her feet, and starts to make her goodbyes, but Fran lays a hand on her arm.

'Wait. What happens now?'

'We will continue to press Dominic on where we can find Laurel, but I will be brutally honest with you, we're not sure that we will find her alive. You need to prepare yourself for the worst-case scenario.' She pauses at the doorstep, turning back to Fran. 'In light of the information you've given us today, we will be formally charging Dominic Jessop with the abduction of Laurel. I'm so sorry, Fran.'

We watch in silence as she walks away to her car, Kelly scurrying off to the kitchen to make more tea, no doubt.

'Will you excuse me, Anna?' Fran turns away, heading back up the stairs towards what was her and Dominic's room, and now I suppose is only hers. Slowly I close the door, leaning my back against it and feeling at least something is solid around me. I feel as though I'm walking through a flood, unsteady and unsure of everything around me. *Dominic.* It's hard to believe, and yet all the evidence stacks up. So why can't I shake off the feeling that something still isn't right?

CHAPTER 24

The next few days pass in some kind of weird, twisted blur, where nothing is right, and everything feels dirty and squalid. I think of all the time Dominic spent holed up in his office in the evenings, until well past midnight, after he finished his list at the hospital. Times that Fran and I both assumed that he was working. Was he really looking at images of children on his computer? The thought makes me feel sick, and I have developed an unnerving habit of washing my hands frequently throughout the day, so now they are chapped and sore, the skin so dry it has cracked across my knuckles. As I wander past Laurel's closed bedroom door, I think of all the times Dominic would go and tuck her in, on the rare nights that he was home in time to do so, and the laughter that would pour out from under the door as he read her Dr Seuss stories. I'm finding it tough to match up the man who would read story after story after a long day in the operating theatre, with the picture that the press is painting of a monster who abducted, and possibly murdered, his own daughter.

The press is another matter altogether. They have been back with a vengeance since the police turned up that morning to search the house, returning to the doorstep to call out and snap photographs the minute the front door is opened. It is a constant invasion of privacy and we've taken to using the back gate as an attempt to fool them, not that it's worked. The front page every morning has some take on Laurel's abduction. I made the front pages very briefly, once the story broke that I wasn't really Anna Cox – I've never been so thankful that I'd already confessed, to my family and to Fran.

Dominic's face has been splashed across every tabloid and broadsheet, dominating the online news and flashing across the screen every time we turn on the television, so now we don't bother at all. *MONSTER* and *PERVERT* are the words that have been used most commonly to describe him, and I've deleted the BBC news app off my phone in an attempt to avoid the news as much as I can. Fran has said very little over the past few days, and seems reluctant to discuss anything, although Kelly says we should try to keep her talking, as it's not good to bottle things up. I know Fran, I know she'll talk when she's ready.

The smell of bonfire smoke wakes me early one morning, and for one stomach-lurching moment I am back in the field, mud and straw beneath my feet, fireworks bursting above my head as I scream Laurel's name into the inky darkness, desperate to see her sparkly silver bobble hat heading towards me. I sit bolt upright, my hair sticking to my forehead and a prickling under my armpits as I realise I'm at home, and Laurel is still gone, and Dominic is still not talking on where we might have a hope in finding her.

I push myself to get out of bed, wandering downstairs in a thick hoody and a pair of jogging bottoms. It's the week before Christmas, and the sky is full of thick, heavy grey clouds that look as though they're bursting to dump a ton of snow over the country. Shivering, I step out of the back door to where the source of the bonfire smoke reveals itself. Fran stands in front of a roaring fire, methodically feeding scraps of fabric into it. She wears only a thin T-shirt and pyjama bottoms, and her feet are shoved into an old pair of flip-flops.

'Jesus, Fran, aren't you freezing?' I come and stand next to her, holding my hands to the warmth of the flames.

'I hadn't really noticed,' she says, pushing what looks like a pair of trousers into the bonfire, poking at it with a broken tree branch she's grabbed from the dead apple tree at the bottom of the garden. 'I suppose it is quite cold.' She looks around, as if noticing for the first time the thick clouds above and the brisk wind that bites at her bare skin.

'What are you doing?' I ask, softly. She looks so fragile, her thin arms bare, standing there in what must the clothes she slept in. She looks nothing like the Fran I knew from before – the fierce, demanding Fran, always perfectly made up, always too busy living in a fantasy world made up of adoring audiences, dashing leading men and thick pan stick make-up to pay much attention to what was going on in her own family, under her own roof.

'Burning his things. Dominic's things.' His name is like bitter poison on her tongue and she almost spits it at me. She throws a pair of leather brogues into the fire, shoes that must have cost Dominic a fortune, and they disappear into the flames in a cloud of ash and smoke. 'I don't want anything of his in the house.'

'What about the police? What if they need his things and you've burned them?'

'They've taken everything they need.' She pokes viciously at the flames again, her face hard. 'I can't sleep with his things in my house, Anna. I just want rid of him, to forget I ever met him.'

I wish that Kelly was here to help me manage Fran in this frame of mind, but Kelly no longer comes every day. Now that Dominic has been formally charged and is awaiting trial, Kelly has other families to deal with, and although she said she is only at the end of the phone, Fran hasn't contacted her once. She says she's relieved to see the back of her, that Kelly never helped anyway, she was merely there to spy on the family. I privately think that perhaps that was a good thing, if Dominic really is guilty of Laurel's abduction. 'Is he still not talking?'

'No,' she sniffs, and swipes at her face with the back of her hand, leaving a smear of sooty ash on the bridge of her nose. 'He still says he didn't take Laurel. Still refuses to admit to it and tell us where she is. I hope he rots in hell.' She jabs at the fire ferociously, and I step back as sparks shower the ground by my feet.

'And there's still nothing to show where he was that night?' I don't know why I'm poking the bear, so to speak, only I suppose I feel like maybe Fran will be less unstable if she would only talk about things.

'He says he was only driving around. He was thinking of leaving me, apparently.' She lets out a bitter huff of laughter. 'What utter bullshit. We had our ups and downs, of course we did, and I know now that he was cheating on me with Pamela – I'm not stupid. Maybe he would have left me eventually, but not that night. He's just covering his arse, trying to justify why he didn't come and meet us. Making up an excuse.'

'Fran, I—'

'Do you think he was planning on leaving?' Fran talks over me. 'I mean, really? Would he have left Laurel with nothing? I've been there, growing up with nothing, when my own father left. Maybe he thought that leaving me with no financial security wasn't enough. He had to take Laurel too, and make sure I really did lose it all. He probably thought he'd never get caught.' A strange light fills her eyes, and for a moment I feel desperately unnerved, convinced that she is a woman on the edge, close to losing it completely, and then it is gone, and she looks like the same old Fran again.

'I don't know, Fran. I feel like neither of us knew him at all.' I bat away that nagging feeling that arises whenever I try to marry up the Dominic I knew with the man portrayed in the media.

Fran throws the last of the pile of clothing into the flames, and I see Dominic's favourite golfing jumper, a pair of pyjama bottoms and his thick winter ski jacket go up in a plume of flames as the synthetic fibres catch alight. 'I'm going to go away for a while, Anna. It's time for you to move on, too.'

'Wait—' I process what she's saying. 'What do you mean you're going away for a while . . . you're leaving? What about Laurel?'

'That's why I'm leaving. For Laurel. She's lost to me, Anna, and I can't bear to sit in this house on my own, waiting for her to come home. Even if by some great chance they find her and she and I were reunited, do you honestly think that I could bring her up here? In a place full of the most hideous memories of the kind of man her father turned out to be?'

'But . . . no, I suppose not,' I say quietly. I suppose I had thought that I would move on eventually, but it still comes as a shock to hear Fran say the words. 'I simply thought maybe . . .'

'Maybe?' she prompts, frowning at me.

'Maybe you'd wait to see if Dominic did talk. But I can understand how you feel, of course. I'm sorry. I didn't think.' A hot flush creeps up my neck and I feel my ears start to burn. How embarrassing, to be so thoughtless, of course Fran wouldn't want Laurel to return to this house once she comes home. If she ever comes home.

Fran pauses for a moment, staring into the flames of the bonfire, and I wonder if the scent of the smoke has the same effect on her as it does on me. She takes a deep breath, holding it for a moment before she speaks. 'I've been in contact with Polly.'

'Polly, your sister?' Surprise makes my eyebrows shoot up into my hairline. 'That's . . . brilliant. How did she take the news about Laurel?'

'Not well, obviously.' Fran meets my eyes. 'I think you need to go home and be with your family for Christmas, Anna. I know we haven't really properly discussed the circumstances under which you came to work for us, but I do know you've spent every Christmas here with us, instead of with your family. Now they know you're back here – now we *all* know the truth about things – I think it might be best for you to go home for a while.'

'But you'll be here on your own,' I say hastily, not entirely sure that I do want to go home for Christmas. Although my mother says none of this matters, it will still be hard to go home and face her.

'I won't be here. I already told you I'm going to go away for a little while,' Fran says, shortly. 'I'm going to stay with Polly. She's renting a cottage in Norfolk, it's tucked out of the way and the press won't be able to find me there. I'm going to go and spend Christmas there, and then I think once Dominic goes to trial I'll sell the house and start afresh somewhere else.'

'Right.' I feel wrongfooted, off balance, and I snatch up the stick and start poking at the fire in an attempt to hide my feelings. Even though Fran and I were never the best of friends, not friends at all really, I suppose I assumed that I would stay on for a while, just to support her through the trial, but it seems she doesn't need me. 'I'll speak to my mother and let you know when I'm leaving.'

'Perfect.' Fran smiles at me, a quick, relieved smile, before she strides away towards the house, her arms wrapped around her body in an attempt to keep warm, leaving me alone, outside in the bitter winter chill.

I avoid Fran for the rest of the day, instead calling my mother and telling her I'll be home on Christmas Eve. She sounds pleased to hear from me, and I feel the burden of returning home lessen slightly. Perhaps it won't be as bad as I first thought it would, although the idea of Christmas without Laurel is difficult to imagine. I decide to only pack the bare essentials, at least giving me an excuse to come back to the house under the guise of collecting the rest of my things before Fran sells and I have to leave completely. I don't know why I feel so reluctant to let go, especially when not so long ago I was thinking about leaving. Now, when I think about never coming back, I think about how my memories of Laurel will fade and there'll be nothing left of her, merely the same old photos recycled on the front pages of the newspapers every year on the anniversary of her disappearance.

Shoving jeans and sweaters into a backpack, my phone buzzes and I grab it as a reason to stop packing for a moment. It's a text from Pamela. I pause with my finger over the delete button, wondering whether to simply trash it without even reading it. She's been interviewed by one of the red tops, giving her side of the story regarding Dominic, and I was witness to Fran cutting the paper into tiny shreds on reading it. Curiosity gets the better of me, and I stab at the phone screen, opening up the message.

'It's Pamela. I need to speak to you – please call me, or even text if you'd rather, so we can arrange to meet. I wouldn't ask, only it's important.'

Sighing, I hesitate only for a second, before I punch out my reply.

'When?'

CHAPTER 25

It is several weeks later before I manage to meet up with Pamela. Christmas was spent with my family, my mother over the moon to have me back at home again. Although things were a little awkward and stilted when I first arrived back, I kept a low profile from the neighbours, and by the time Christmas Day was over it was as if I'd never left for Scotland in the first place.

On Christmas morning I go to church, walking slowly through the rain to arrive towards the end of the service. I slide unnoticed into a pew at the back and wait for all the other parishioners to leave before I approach the altar, lighting a candle and saying a whispered prayer for Laurel. I wonder if Fran is doing the same thing, Polly beside her, or if she is curled up in bed, not wanting to face Christmas Day at all. I wonder if Dominic is thinking of Laurel today, too, alone in his cell.

Pamela texts me several times over the Christmas period, but it is the last week in January before I manage to arrange a time and place to meet with her. Part of me is nervous at hearing what she has to say but desperate to know what news she has, and the other half doesn't want to see her at all – she lied to me, tricked me, and I trusted her. I try to ignore the fact that Fran must feel the same way about me deep down.

We meet at a pizza restaurant in the centre of South Oxbury and I feel as though I have to watch over my shoulder in case Fran appears, even though she's told me that she's decided to stay on with Polly at her rented cottage in Norfolk for a little while. I enter the restaurant ten minutes later than we agreed, not wanting to be the first one there. Glancing around, I see Pamela sitting in a corner booth, tucked out of the way of the rest of the diners, a large glass of red wine in front of her even though it's barely midday. Weaving my way through the room, I tug off my scarf and reach the table before she's even realised I've arrived.

'Pamela.'

She looks up from where she is shredding a paper napkin across the table, her fingers worrying at the paper and leaving confetti-like shreds all over her skirt. 'Oh, Anna. I didn't think you would come. You didn't seem too keen to get together.' Her tone isn't bitchy, or snarky, she just sounds incredibly tired.

I slide into the seat opposite and look at her more closely. Her skin is pale and blotchy, spots breaking out in a little rash between her eyebrows. Dark circles ring her eyes, a faded bluish-purple, and her hair, usually styled and bouncy, hangs limply around her face, her fringe ever so slightly greasy. In short, she doesn't look too dissimilar to the way Fran looked when Laurel disappeared.

'Sorry. It . . . feels a bit strange, you know. How are you?' I feel I have to ask the question, even though it's clear from what I see in front of me that she isn't coping too well.

'Oh, you know. It's difficult, but I have to be there for Dominic, especially now Fran has abandoned him.'

'I wouldn't say abandoned as such, he took Laurel and is refusing to tell the police where she is. Fran has accepted that Laurel won't be coming home alive now, but the decent thing would be for Dominic to confess to everything and at least let Fran bury her daughter. He owes her that much.'

'*Owes* her?' Pamela screws her face up as she screeches the words out, before looking around the restaurant and lowering her voice. 'He doesn't owe that bitch anything. He didn't do *anything* to Laurel, Anna.' Her cheeks flush, and she fumbles for the wine glass in front of her, taking a healthy swig and leaving her lips stained with purple.

'Oh, Pamela, come on. I know you still love him, but even you have to admit that things simply don't stack up when it comes to Dominic. He doesn't have an alibi . . .'

'No, he doesn't, but those roads aren't covered by any CCTV. He didn't stop anywhere, he was merely driving around trying to pluck up the courage to tell Fran that he didn't want to be with her anymore. He was going to tell her that he wanted to be with me.' Pamela sips at the wine again, more sedately this time, as the waiter approaches our table.

'Just coffee for me, please.' I wave him away and turn back to Pamela. 'Pamela, think about things rationally. The person who saw Laurel getting into a car picked Dominic's out of a range of photos. And there's the sock – you know about the sock, right?'

Pamela blinks. 'It was a nosebleed. Dominic told me Laurel had a nosebleed and I believe him. He *didn't do this*, Anna. Are you really going to let him go to prison for something he had no part in?'

I grit my teeth, trying not to give in to the frustration that courses through my body. The woman is delusional, she has to be. And to think that when I first met her I thought she was so calm, so together, so . . . everything that I wanted to be. 'She didn't have a nosebleed, Pamela. And even if she did, it wouldn't have been Dominic who dealt with it in the first place, it would have been me. Dominic was never there.'

'Please, Anna, please try and see things from my point of view. Why would Dominic hurt Laurel? She was his daughter, he loved her. He's not a violent man, he couldn't do something like this. You forget, I *know* him.'

I cast my mind back to the events of the days following Laurel's disappearance and I have to beg to differ. I remember the way Dominic grabbed Fran's arms, forcing her back against the kitchen worktops. The way Fran whispered to her mother on the phone about his unpredictable behaviour, the way he threw his glass, smashing it to smithereens, and I can't agree with Pamela that he isn't violent.

'You used to know him. You weren't there, Pamela. You didn't see the way things could be in that house.' I reach down to pick up my bag, ready to leave even though my coffee hasn't arrived.

'Fran hated Dominic,' Pamela says, clutching me by my forearm, dragging me back to a seated position. 'She knew he was unhappy, she knew he was going to leave her and come back to me. That woman is poison, Anna, and she knows that Dominic could never, ever do something as awful as what they're saying he did. He's not perfect, but he's not a killer. I understand that she's devastated by Laurel's disappearance, but will you really support her in letting Dominic go to prison? Whoever really took Laurel is still out there, Anna, you know that.'

'No, Pamela.' I shake her off and get to my feet, ready to make eye contact with the waiter if I have to. 'I don't need to listen to this. Fran isn't perfect, far from it, but she wouldn't let Dominic go to prison if she didn't believe that he did it. Despite the fact that things weren't perfect between them, she loved him. And the police would never have charged him if they didn't have the evidence to back up the claim that he was responsible.'

'He'll die in there, Anna.' Pamela's voice breaks and tears begin to stream down her cheeks, as she wipes her nose on her sleeve. 'You should hear the things the other prisoners say to him, what they threaten to do to him. He's innocent, Anna, I swear.'

'What is that you want me to do, Pamela? Why have you asked me to meet you here?'

'I want you to help me prove that Dominic is innocent. We need to get him out of there, Anna, I know he didn't do it, but I need *something* to give to the police to prove that it wasn't him who took Laurel.'

'Pamela, I have to go.' I step past her and make my way through the tables back towards the front of the restaurant, desperate to get outside and breathe some fresh, clean air.

'She's not so innocent.' Pamela grabs my arm as I reach the front door, hissing in my face, 'Do you really think she had nothing to do with any of this? This is as much her fault as it is anyone else's.'

I tug my arm free, tearing the sleeve of my jacket and hurry away, almost running in my haste to get away from Pamela and her toxic ideas.

Before I realise it, I find myself at the junction at the top of the road to the Jessops' house, my indicator flashing left to turn in. The road is quiet, empty, all the residents at work or at school and I find a parking space only a couple of doors down. Standing by the front gate, I slide my fingers into my pocket to feel the sharp, cold edges of my door key. I might tell myself that I didn't plan on coming back to the house, but deep down I must have known I would – why else would I have snatched up my door key from where it has laid on the small table next to my bed in my old childhood bedroom?

Curtains twitch at the house next door, and I turn away, towards the end of the road so the nosy old woman next door can't see my face, although I'm probably too late. I'll have to let Fran know I'm here. Fumbling in my bag I pull out my phone and dial Fran's number.

'Anna? What is it?' Fran's voice is sharp, almost unfriendly, and I think that perhaps she thinks I am phoning with bad news.

'Hi, Fran, it's nothing. Are you still with Polly, or are you home? It's just . . .'

'I'm still with Polly,' Fran sighs, 'I can't face going home yet, I'm not sure I'll ever be able to go back.'

'The thing is,' I pause for a moment, not sure how she'll react when I tell her I'm standing in front of the house and I want to go in, 'I'm here, actually. At the house. I wondered if I could pop inside and get the last of my things, before you . . . if you decide to put it on the market, I'll need to get my things back.'

'Oh,' Fran says, 'well, if you must. I mean, of course you must get your things back.' She sounds distracted, as though she's not really paying attention to what I'm saying. 'Of course. Do whatever you need to. Listen, Anna, I must go. Pop the key back through the letterbox, won't you, when you're done?' And my phone beeps three times in my ear and goes dead. She's hung up.

OK. I turn towards the house, the curtains in the window next door hurriedly falling back into place as the nosy neighbour hides from me, and I give her a broad grin as I walk up the path and slide my key into the lock.

It slips in easily and I pause for a moment, my pulse starting to flutter as I realise I am nervous about walking back into the house after so many weeks away. I take a deep breath and push the door open, a huge pile of mail behind it catching on the mat, meaning I have to use my shoulder to force a gap wide enough to get in. The air smells stale where the house has been closed up for almost two months, and dust motes dance in the air as the sunlight streams into the living room through the window. I stoop down to collect up the post, a thick sheaf of pizza delivery leaflets, political canvassing, some bills, and three thin sheets of writing paper, neatly folded in half. I throw the other pieces onto the tiny telephone table and with a guilty lurch, open the first sheet of paper.

It's an apology from Ruth, saying sorry for the way she behaved, and could Fran find it in her heart to forgive her? I fold it in half and lay it on top of the post pile, before opening the next. It's more of the same – Ruth tells Fran in slightly more detail this time how sorry she is, and how all she ever wanted was to help. I open the third, expecting to see more apologies, but this one simply reads, 'You never deserved her anyway,' although whether she's referring to herself, or to Laurel I have no idea. The woman is delusional. I screw it up, and then after a moment's pause, reach for the other two and screw them up too, stuffing them deep into my pockets. Fran doesn't need to see these, just like she doesn't need to know what Pamela has been saying.

As I comb through the rest of the mail, selecting out only the things Fran will need to deal with and discarding all the rest, I notice the light on the old-fashioned answer machine is flashing. I hover over the machine, unsure whether I still have the right to press the play button and take the message for Fran. I wouldn't have hesitated before, it was just part of my job, but I don't fit in anymore, and I don't belong here in this house, not without Laurel. As I hover, finger poised, the phone shrieks into life, the ringtone making me jump and I snatch up the receiver in an instinctive gesture.

'Francesca?' The voice on the other end of the phone is plummy, and the line hisses slightly, as if they are calling long-distance. 'Is that you? Why haven't you been answering the telephone?'

This must be who has left the messages for Fran. The light still blinks at me out the corner of my eye. 'I'm sorry. Fran isn't here at the moment. This is Anna, can I take a message?'

'Where is she? I've been trying to get hold of her for weeks.'

'Err . . . she's staying with her sister, I believe. I can give her a message, Mrs . . .?' I pause, waiting for her to tell me who she is.

'This is her mother. And did you say she's staying with Polly? That's impossible, Fran and Polly don't speak.'

'Well, after everything that's happened with Laurel, they seem to have patched things up. Fran said Polly invited her for Christmas to get away from the press, and she's decided to stay there for a little while. She's finding it a bit difficult to come back to the house.'

'What do you mean, what's happened with Laurel? And what about the press? I'm sorry, miss, but I really have no idea what you're talking about.'

'You don't . . .?' I stutter, not sure whether I heard Fran's mother correctly. 'You don't know what happened with Laurel?'

'No, I just said that.' She is sharp, impatient, and she sounds, for a moment, exactly like Fran. 'I haven't spoken to Francesca since the beginning of the summer. She called me to say she would be away for the summer, and then I took a cruise along the Nile and have only been back for three weeks. I've been calling her constantly since then, and she's been ignoring my calls.'

Fran was never away – busy, yes, but not away – and now her mother is telling me that she hasn't spoken to Fran since early summer. I lean back against the wall, a slightly sick feeling rising in my stomach as it flips over.

'I'm so sorry, we seem to have our wires crossed somewhere. Like I said, Fran isn't here at the moment, and I think it's best she explains things to you. I can give you her mobile number.' I read out Fran's number from my phone, stumbling over the numbers and having to repeat them several times before Fran's mother has the correct number. Finally, she hangs up and I slide down the wall, twisting to end up sat on the bottom stair.

Fran's mother hasn't spoken to her since the summer. Yet, several times over the first few weeks of Laurel's disappearance, I would find Fran whispering into her phone, and she would always tell me it was her mother she was speaking to. I think hard, Fran's voice coming to me as I hovered outside her room, '. . . *it will be OK. I promise. I can deal with this.*' If she wasn't talking to her mother, then who was she talking to? Is Pamela right after all – has Fran been lying to everyone all along?

CHAPTER 26

The light is fading in the hallway, the sun lowering in the sky to leave the usually airy space dark and gloomy as I sit on the bottom stair, stiff from holding the same position for goodness knows how long. The idea that Fran has been lying has my brain fizzing, my thoughts jumping all over the place. I force myself up to standing, my knees twinging, stiff and sore as I do, and I head into the kitchen where I run the cold tap, holding my wrists beneath the icy water for a moment before leaning over and splashing my face, droplets rising up and landing in my hair. *Has Fran really been lying all this time? Does she know something about Laurel's disappearance?*

I scrub my face dry with a clean tea towel, the rough fibres scratching at my skin and leaving my cheeks red and hot, and my brain still just as confused as it was before. Heading upstairs, I enter my old bedroom, everything is exactly as I left it, even down to the used coffee mug on the bedside table that I had forgotten to bring down before I left. I move it to the windowsill, turning my nose up at the thick layer of mould that floats atop the dregs of coffee. Turning my attention to the wardrobe, I drag out the small suitcase that I left in the bottom and start to throw in the few items of clothing I left behind – a hoody, some thick socks, several thin summer dresses – all the time telling myself that I'm wrong. That Pamela is wrong. That Fran's mother simply got her dates confused – maybe she's losing track of things, now that she's elderly.

At that thought I stop, lowering myself on to the bed, a thin summer cardigan in my hands. *Come on, Anna. Even if she is elderly she's not likely to forget that her granddaughter has gone missing.* It's no good. I can't ignore this, something about Fran isn't right, and I need to find out what it is – especially if it means that Dominic didn't do this after all. Shoving the cardigan into the suitcase, I yank the zip closed and drag it to the top of the stairs. Once I'm finished I won't ever return to this house, not even if they do find Laurel. For all the expensive décor, the luxury candles dotted around, the ridiculously expensive gadgets, this house isn't a home – it's toxic, a bed of lies, and now I can't wait to get away.

I lug the suitcase down the stairs, bouncing it off every step, and place it by the front door, before heading towards the kitchen. I don't know what I'm looking for – but I know there must be *something* here, something that will tell me whether my new instinct is right about Fran. Rifling through the kitchen drawers I find nothing, so I turn my attention to the cupboards, pulling out half empty boxes of cereal, shoving my hands inside to make sure nothing is hidden there. I find nothing – apart from a heap of takeaway leaflets shoved in the bottom drawer.

The kitchen bin sports a brand-new bin bag, and I know the outside bins will have been taken away weeks ago. Disheartened, but not ready to give up yet, I head down the hallway to Dominic's office, hoping against all hope that the door won't be locked. It's not – the handle turns easily in my hand – and I enter, the air thick with dust, as though the room hasn't been used for years. As I lay my hand on the door handle I have a flashback to a few nights after Laurel disappeared, Fran's voice coming from the other side of the door. Why was she using Dominic's office? At the time I thought perhaps she merely wanted a bit of privacy, to talk to (*someone*) her mother in peace without me or Kelly overhearing. Now, I can't help but wonder if she was up to something a little more sinister.

I think back to when DS Wright and Kelly told us that Dominic has been arrested, that images of children had been discovered on his computer. I remember the way my stomach lurched, and my hands started to shake as the shock of adrenaline pulsed around my body, making my lips feel numb and the floor unsteady beneath my feet. Fran had seemed so calm, and I reasoned that that was her shock reaction – everyone reacts in different ways after all – but what if she seemed so calm because she *wasn't* actually that shocked? Because, maybe, she already knew what they would find on Dominic's computer. That maybe she was the one who had put them there. If your husband was accused of something so completely hideous, so wrong, would you simply accept it? Or would you defend him? The more I think about it, the more I feel uneasy about her reaction.

I sink into Dominic's luxury leather chair, feeling the worn area made by the shape of his body, my head starting to throb at the temples as I pull open the drawers, rifling through all the bills and paper, nothing standing out to me. The papers spill out and I shove them back into the drawer, carelessly, telling myself that if Fran notices she'll just think it's a result of the police search. Leaving the office, I pull the door tight shut behind and head for Fran and Dominic's bedroom, my feet heavy on the stairs as I make my way up there. I'm still telling myself this is ridiculous, that Fran wouldn't ever do anything to harm Laurel, and she certainly wouldn't see Dominic in prison for something he didn't do, but Pamela's words seem to shout even louder in my head — *she's not so innocent.*

At their bedroom door I pause, still a healthy amount of respect for their privacy making me reluctant to enter their private domain. I give myself a shake and push the door open, slightly shocked at the mess that confronts me.

At first I think maybe the police didn't tidy up after they searched the house last time, but I know that Fran would never have left it like this for so long, not unless she was leaving in a hurry, which it now seems like she did. It's as though she threw some belongings into a bag and ran out, the minute I left the house before Christmas. Tights and underwear litter the blue and gold bedspread, and while her hairbrush and straighteners are missing from the top of the dressing table, her make-up still covers the top, the lid removed on a bottle of foundation, leading to a small, dried patch of porcelain etched into the wood.

Without thinking about things too hard, I yank open her drawers, pulling out T-shirts, knickers, scarves, shaking them out to make sure I don't miss a thing. I find nothing, not even a hidden diary, until I reach under the mattress and my fingers brush against what feels like a slip of paper. Reaching further in, until my armpit is pressed up against the edge of the bed frame, I manage to snare the paper in my fingers and pull it out.

It's a receipt, from a local supermarket for a large bar of milk chocolate and a pint of milk. Nothing exciting in that, but when I turn it over, there is 'P' scrawled across it in biro, with a postcode written underneath. *P. Polly? Or Pamela?* I turn the thin piece of paper over and over in my hands until it becomes damp.

Pulling out my phone, I type in the postcode and wait for the screen to load. It brings up a Google map, a red pin indicating the location of the postcode on the map. I zoom in, noting down the road name and the location. *Norfolk.* Exactly where Fran said Polly was staying. So, Fran must have always intended to go and stay with Polly, and by hiding this under the mattress, she didn't want Dominic to know about it.

I don't know what to think – was Fran planning on leaving Dominic, even though she seemed to be terrified that he would leave her? Or did this come about after Laurel's disappearance? Although I now think I have found where Fran is staying, it still doesn't tell me whether Pamela is right when she said Fran isn't so innocent. And I still can't shake off that feeling that something isn't quite right – and that Fran hasn't been entirely truthful.

I leave Fran and Dominic's room and head back down the narrow flight of stairs to the landing, bypassing my own bedroom door and heading for Laurel's. As I push the door open, I think I catch a faint whiff of her baby scent, and my stomach clenches with longing. Her dressing gown, pink and fluffy, hangs on the back of the door, and Bom, her stuffed tiger, sits next to her nightlight, almost as though she's about to come running in from her bath, ready to go to bed.

Fighting back hot tears, I blink rapidly, and get back to the task in hand. I still have that itchy feeling at the back of my brain that tells me somebody said something, or I saw something, something that wasn't quite right and that I can't put my finger on. Something that could tell me once and for all whether I am barking up the wrong tree. Whether Dominic is innocent or guilty.

Fumbling through Laurel's toy box, I try hard not to get distracted by the items I find, memories of pretend tea parties, building Lego houses, dressing dolls in radical outfits assaulting me from all sides, and making me only all too aware of my grief. There is nothing, so I move to the chest of drawers, the one Dominic brought home from Ikea and that Fran then decided to paint in Farrow and Ball – the one that I once caught Laurel about to stick stickers all over and had to rescue before Fran noticed. I dig in to the top drawer, scrabbling through vests, tiny pairs of pants and socks, before I see it, and I freeze, the hot, acid burn of bile scorching the back of my throat.

This is it – this is what I was looking for, the thing that I couldn't quite put my finger on. A tiny lemon yellow sock, with a white lace frill around the ankle.

I hold it between finger and thumb as I sit down on the edge of Laurel's bed, swallowing hard to keep from being sick. The sock is slightly grubby at the toe, a thick smear of dark grey dust marring the seam. Almost as though it's been hidden somewhere else for a while, out of sight, out of mind. *Like, stuffed under a church pew somewhere?*

The thought comes unbidden to mind, and I see Fran perched on the end of the church pew, Kelly's voice saying she went there a lot for some peace. I run my fingers gently over the fabric, finally piecing together what it was that I couldn't put my finger on.

I think back to that day, the day when DS Wright told us Dominic had been arrested. That they had found a tiny yellow sock in his car, hidden away. Fran saying that she had put the socks on Laurel that Saturday night . . . only, she didn't. *I* was the one who got Laurel ready that evening – Fran was busy on the phone, and Laurel didn't want to wait, she wanted to get to the field early, so she didn't miss the start of the bonfire. *I was the one who shoved Laurel's feet into her boots, I was the one who bundled her up into her coat. There was no argument between Fran and Laurel over wearing sandals, not that I heard, and Fran was banking on me being so shocked by Dominic's arrest that I couldn't piece it together.*

I bring the sock to my nose, hoping to inhale some of Laurel's scent, but it doesn't even smell of laundry soap anymore, it's musty and stale. I think of Fran, coming back into the kitchen from the garage with a bottle of wine in her hand, a guilty look across her face. Was that when she did it? Was that when she planted Laurel's sock in Dominic's car in an attempt to prove him guilty of hurting Laurel?

A cold shiver runs down my spine as I realise exactly how calculating and clever Fran has been. A grieving, desperate mother on the surface, able to convince everyone, including the police that Dominic was guilty of the most heinous crime. But what has she done with Laurel? And how did she manage to pull this off, in a field full of people, when she only left me alone for a matter of minutes? More to the point, how can I make this right again?

Looking up, my eyes light on Bom, sitting serenely next to the night light. I know what I need to do. I tuck the sock into my pocket, pushing it deep down and then smoothing the pocket flat so there is no chance of it falling out, and snatch up the tiger. I check that I have the slip of paper bearing the postcode to Polly's cottage and lug my suitcase out to my car. Returning to the house, I double lock the front door, and hurry back down the path to where my car is parked.

Turning on the ignition, I wait for the sat nav to fire up before I enter the Norfolk postcode, the screen telling me it is 180 miles away, and will take me approximately three hours and thirty-seven minutes to reach my destination. I check my watch. I should be in Norfolk by nine o'clock this evening. I put the car in drive and pull out on to the main road, taking a deep breath as I do so. I'm going to do it. I'm going to confront Fran.

CHAPTER 27

It's been years since I drove this far – I didn't drive at all in Scotland, and I've only driven short distances or used public transport with Laurel since I started working for the Jessops, seeing as Fran didn't like the idea of Laurel going out in my clapped-out old banger, and Dominic wasn't likely to let me use his car. It's dark before I've even hit the road, and by the time I am approaching the A140, the road that will lead me directly to Fran, I am battling a terrible headache, and my eyes are feeling the strain of concentrating for so long. Finally, the sat nav tells me to turn left, and that I am almost at my destination.

I dutifully follow the instructions, turning left on to an unlit track. The track is rutted and bumpy, full of potholes, and I flick on my full beam in order to be able to see more than a few metres in front of me. Doubt nags, and I wonder whether I punched in the wrong postcode, as now I have left the narrow country lanes behind there is nothing ahead of me, apart from more bushes, more trees, more shadows. Deciding that I must have made a mistake somewhere, taken a wrong turn perhaps, my mind full of Fran, Laurel, Dominic and the discovery of the yellow sock – something that makes my stomach flip every time I think about it – laid carefully next to me on the front seat, I decide to push on until I find a space to turn around when I see it.

Further ahead, a single light is visible through the trees. Maybe I didn't put the postcode in wrong, after all. My heart beating a jumpy tattoo in my chest, I carry on along the rough track until the cottage comes into view. There is a dark-coloured car parked in front of the stone cottage, and for one brief, heart-stopping moment I think it is Dominic's car, before I realise that it's a slightly different shape, a Volkswagen badge gleaming on the back as my headlights flash across it. I pull up next to it, and tucking the sock into my jeans pocket, I snatch up Bom, Laurel's stuffed tiger, and step out of the car.

It feels good to stretch after more than three hours hunched over the steering wheel, and the air is briskly cold against my face after the warmth of the car heater. There is the faint smell of the sea on the air, even though it feels as though I am tucked away in a forest, and I breathe deeply for a moment, trying to clear my head before I step forward, until I'm standing under a tiny porch light and raise my fist to knock on the door.

There is no answer, and I flick my wrist round to check the time on my watch. Ten past nine. I made good time, the hour of night meaning that I didn't hit any traffic on the way up. It's still early – Fran has always been a night owl, often out at events and shows in the evenings, not returning home till the early hours of the morning, then sleeping the day away, sometimes only waking just before Laurel came home from school. Maybe this isn't the right place – maybe Fran isn't here at all, and the postcode and the initial had nothing to do with Polly. *No. There's no such thing as coincidence.* I raise my fist and bang on the door again, and this time I hear scuffling behind the door, a whispering, as though there is a debate as to whether the door should be opened or not. Just as I am wavering, sure that I have got the wrong place, the door creaks open and I see Fran peering out, lit by the soft lamplight behind her.

'Anna!' She steps forward, pulling the door closed behind her, one arm behind her back. 'What . . .' She frowns, a red flush creeping up her neck before she clears her throat. 'What on earth are you doing here?'

'I . . .' I stutter, words not ready to come. I hadn't thought about what I would say when I saw Fran, my thoughts jumbled and tangled and as I see her in front of me for the first time in weeks, I falter, not sure that she could ever have done the things I've been accusing her of in my mind on the journey here. 'I went to the house today.' It feels like days ago already. 'I found this.' Remembering that I am clutching Bom against my chest, I hold him out to her like some sort of offering.

'Oh.' Fran blinks. 'I forgot all about Bom.' She takes him from me, almost snatching him out of my hands.

'Fran, listen . . . I need to talk to you, it's important.' The words burst out before I can stop them. I've come all this way, I need some answers.

'Thank you, Anna, I appreciate you driving all this way just to hand over Bom, but you really didn't need to. You should be heading back. It's getting late.' Fran's voice is icy cold, and it's as though I haven't even spoken. She steps back, ready to push the front door closed.

'What? Fran, I need to talk to you, it's really, really important. You can't make me leave.' I step forward, planting my foot between the door and the frame.

'Anna. Just go. Please. At least respect my privacy now Dominic is gone. For Laurel's sake.' Glancing behind her she moves back as though to slam the door. *She's not so innocent.* The sound of Laurel's name on her lips ignites a spark of rage deep down in my belly, and without thinking I throw out a hand and shove hard, sending Fran stumbling backwards into the dimly lit hallway.

I step inside, the warmth of the open fire in the room to the left reaching my cold cheeks and making them burn a bright pink. 'That's what I wanted to talk to you about, Fran.'

'What do you mean?' She looks at me warily, one hand to her throat.

'We need to talk about Dominic. About what happened the night Laurel went missing. About all of it.'

'Why? You know what happened, for God's sake, Anna, Charlie . . . *whatever you want to call yourself*, you were there!' She looks past me to the stairs before she lowers her voice. 'You were there,' she hisses, 'there's nothing to talk about.'

'There is though, Fran,' I say quietly, convinced now that Polly must be upstairs. I keep my voice down, not wanting her to come down and throw me out. 'Things don't add up.'

'What do you mean?' Her hand flutters up from her throat towards her mouth, but I am not fooled. I know that this is Fran, the actress, in front of me now. Not Fran, the concerned mother, who kept all of us fooled. Not Fran, the betrayed wife. I know better now – I know she's lied. I dig in my pocket, my fingers closing around the fabric of the sock, and I pull it out, laying it flat on the palm of my hand.

'I found this, Fran. Hidden in the back of one of Laurel's drawers. You can see by the grey dust on it that it was hidden somewhere else before that. My money is on somewhere in the church, you know, the church that gave you *such comfort* while Laurel was gone. You couldn't risk leaving it there once you decided to leave Oxbury.'

Fran's face turns a chalky white. 'Anna, I can explain . . .'

'Really, Fran?' I shake my head. 'How can you talk this one away? What did you do? Hide it until the police had searched the house again, and then put it back?'

'Look, Anna, you don't understand. You don't know what it was like for me, living with Dominic, how much of a brute he was to me . . .' Fat tears form in her eyes, but all I can think is *crocodile tears*. 'You were in your room every evening, and he was so careful to hide the kind of person he really was . . .'

'What happened to Laurel, Fran? What do you really know about what went on that night? Because I know things didn't happen as you'd have all of us believe. I'll admit, I believed Dominic was guilty for a while – there was too much evidence against him. You made sure of that. But then . . .' I trail off, distracted by something that has caught my eye through the open door of the living room behind Fran. 'Wait a second . . .' I push past her, knocking her hard against the wall, barely registering the satisfying thud her head makes as she knocks it hard against the plaster. The heat of the small room makes sweat prickle on the back of my neck, the open fire roaring as it engulfs logs whole. I cross the room in two steps, my hands to my mouth as I realise that I really did see what I thought I did. I snatch up the item from the top of the bureau it rests on and turn to Fran.

'She's here, isn't she? Laurel is here.' And I squeeze the sparkly silver bobble hat tight between my fingers.

My ears roar as though I am underwater, the rushing filling my head and I think for a moment that I'm going to faint. Fran watches me from the doorway, without speaking.

'She is here, isn't she?' I say again, my voice barely above a whisper.

'Yes, she's here,' Fran says, and she is cool again, no trace of the fear that crossed her face when she realised it was me on the doorstep, although her fingers tremble slightly as she holds out a hand towards me. 'I can explain everything.'

'I hope so, because I really want to hear it.' My voice is steady, and I manage to blink back the tears of relief that sting my eyes at the knowledge that Laurel is OK, that she wasn't taken by strangers.

'That night . . . the night of the bonfire,' Fran says, meeting my eyes, 'it was the perfect opportunity. I could get Laurel away and no one would ever suspect that I had anything to do with it. She's OK, you know that, right? I wouldn't have ever hurt her.'

'How, though?' I say, thinking back to that awful night. 'How could you have possibly done this? And why? I don't understand why you would even want to do something like this.'

'It wasn't so hard once I thought about it all.' She sounds thoughtful. 'I knew Dominic was having an affair. With Pamela, I suspect. I saw the texts on his phone. I knew what would happen once Pamela got her claws back into him – he always loved her, you know? I was always a poor second to his precious Pammy, and Lord knows if I hadn't got pregnant with Laurel we never would have lasted.' She gives a rueful laugh. 'Thing is, I loved Dominic so much, until I started to hate him, that is.'

'But . . . you could have simply left. Taken Laurel and started again.'

'Ha!' Fran snorts. 'I know what happens when people get divorced, Anna. I watched it happen with my parents. My father left, and he took it all, he left my mother with nothing. There was no way I was going to end up destitute while Dominic and bloody Pamela were living it up. And how long before Pamela decided she wanted Laurel too? You know Dominic wanted her to have an abortion?'

'Yes, she told me that, that day when I confronted her, but honestly Fran, this is . . .'

'Don't tell me what this is!' she hisses at me. 'You have no idea. Dominic was violent to me, he hurt me, and I couldn't risk him hurting Laurel too, so I had to get rid of him.'

I say nothing, as she rambles on, convinced by her own lies.

'I was in touch with Polly, but obviously I couldn't tell Dom that. I told her how he was, and she told me she could help me. We met in London a few evenings, just to get together the logistics of the plan. She would hire a car that looks vaguely similar to Dominic's and she would wait in the lane on the night of the bonfire. I was to text Dominic from an unknown number and make out as though the message was from Pamela. I knew he'd go running, and when she didn't turn up, well . . . I didn't know he'd already arranged to meet her.' Her face darkens. 'There was every chance that things would go wrong, but then I would simply claim that Polly had come back, and I was delighted to see her, that we had decided to bury the hatchet. Instead, when Laurel followed me to the toilets, it was the perfect opportunity. I handed her over to Polly through a gap in the fence, and it was sheer luck that a witness saw Laurel getting into a car that could have been Dominic's. In the dark, and from the back, a VW Touran looks a similar shape to a Porsche Cayenne. It almost went horribly wrong when she said it was dark-coloured instead of silver.'

I could testify to that – hadn't I thought it was Dominic's car on the drive when I first arrived? 'But, Fran, all of this . . . hurt and upset. I honestly thought Laurel was dead. And Dominic . . . you'd really let him go to prison for something he hadn't done? All because you thought he would leave you?'

'But he would have been guilty, Anna,' Fran snaps, 'he would have been guilty of ruining Laurel's life when he swanned off with his fancy piece, and left her to a lifetime of scraping by, always making do. And then what if he'd come back for her? Lured her away from me with all his false promises, to go and live with him and Pamela, leaving me all alone? I had to punish him, to make sure he was off the scene for good. I took the yellow sock that day, while you were out at the supermarket. Laurel did have a nosebleed that morning, but you weren't here to see it. I just held the sock against her nose for a moment, sufficient to give a big enough stain. I knew the fresh flowers in the hallway would get her hayfever going, and even though I hated myself for effectively giving her a nosebleed, I had to do it. All I had to do then was hide it in his car.' She raises her eyebrows. 'I thought you'd caught me that day, coming out of the garage. I grabbed the wine in a panic. I was the one who put those hideous pictures of those poor children on his computer – that was Polly's idea. She said it would make sure they really were suspicious of his motives.' She gives a sad smile, and for a brief second, I almost feel sorry for her, until I think about how cruel, how calculating she has been.

'Can I see her? Can I see Laurel?' I say, nausea making my stomach roil and saliva spurt into my mouth. I had no idea how wicked Fran could be, and all the time I was living under the same roof as her. 'Just one last time. Please.'

'Absolutely not. No, Anna, I can't let you do that.' She shakes her head, her perfect bob bouncing above her shoulders.

'Really?' I slide my mobile from my pocket and wave it in her direction. 'I want to see her, Fran. I want to see for myself that she's OK. Otherwise I think I should probably call the police now and have them come and see what really happened to Laurel.' My pulse thunders in my ears as I hope that she doesn't call my bluff.

'OK, OK,' she sighs, as if dealing with a demanding toddler. 'There's no need for that, Anna. You don't need to call anyone. But you look at her from the doorway – you don't go in, and you don't touch her.' Fran turns, and I follow her up the narrow, twisting staircase to the top landing. She pushes open the second door, revealing a single bed, lit by a small pink nightlight. Ignoring every word she just said, confident that she won't stop me, not if it risks waking Laurel, I take Bom from Fran's arms and creep across the carpeted floor, leaning over the small bed to see Laurel's sleeping face, her hair a bird's nest tangle of blonde curls. I tuck Bom in next to her, as I'd done so many times at the house in South Oxbury and return to the doorway.

As I reach the top of the stairs, I look around, wondering where Polly is. The door to the room next to Laurel's is tightly closed, but the one at the end of the landing is slightly ajar, and I see the edge of Fran's dressing gown hanging on the back of the door. The door next to Laurel's room is slightly open, revealing a glimpse of a bathroom inside, a bottle of Matey on the side of the bath.

'You need to go,' Fran whispers, ushering me down the stairs. 'I should never have let you in here.' I don't remind her of the fact that she didn't let me in, I forced my way in.

At the bottom I turn back to Fran, eyeing her closely. There is none of the stress I have seen etched into her face over the past few weeks – stress that I now know was from keeping her biggest secret ever, not from worry about where her daughter might be. Her skin is smooth and unlined, and the dark circles beneath her eyes have disappeared. I think of Dominic, dishevelled and unshaven, gaunt from sudden weight loss, and I know that Fran will be gone from here by the morning, Laurel too.

'I have to tell the police, you know that, Fran, don't you?' I say, my eyes never leaving her face. 'It's the right thing to do. Dominic can't spend the rest of his life in prison for something he didn't do.'

Fran's eyes go wide for a moment, before she gives a soft laugh. 'Oh, Anna, you silly girl. You really don't know, do you?'

The air around us thickens for a moment, and I cock my head on one side, trying to figure out what she means.

'I don't know what?' I say eventually.

'Hmm, I suppose the news hasn't broken quite yet.' She turns her wrist to check her watch, and then leans over to turn on the television, the BBC *News at Ten* appearing on the screen. 'I had a phone call from the police. Very distressing.' She turns up the volume, and a news reporter stands in front of the prison Dominic is being held at on remand, the cold making his nose red and his eyes water, as he reports that alleged child abductor Dominic Jessop was found dead in his cell earlier today.

'What . . .? Fran, what?' I turn to her, bewildered, shock making me stumble over my words. 'What happened?'

'He was attacked in his cell, by another inmate. They don't like people who hurt children in prison,' she says remotely, leaning forward to flick the television back off. 'The police called to tell me after dinner this evening. Obviously, Dominic didn't make it, so now there's no need for a trial.'

A low moaning fills my ears, and it takes me a moment to realise that the strange noise is coming from me. 'Oh God, Fran, this is awful, I have to go, I have to tell the police.' I get up, fear and shock causing me to trip over my own feet, and I stagger, knocking my shins against the coffee table and making me hiss with pain.

'Anna, don't be so ridiculous.' Fran grasps me tightly by the upper arms. 'If you go to the police now, what do you think will happen to Laurel?' She tightens her grip and I wince, her fingernails digging deep into the skin on my upper arms, as she drags me towards the front door. 'I'll tell you, shall I? If you tell the police what I did, they'll arrest me. Dominic is dead, Anna, so what happens then? Laurel will be left without any parents, she'll be taken into care. Is that what you want for her?'

'But . . . what you did . . . it's wrong, so wrong, you can't be allowed . . .' I cry out, as she slaps me around the face, her palm meeting my cheek with a crack.

'*Think*, Anna,' she hisses, her face pushed right into mine, as she shakes me hard. 'Do you love Laurel? Because if you do, you won't go to the police. You won't let them take Laurel into care. Understand?'

I shake my head, my whole body shaking as fear and adrenaline overtake me. 'I won't say anything, I promise. Please.' Fran hustles me towards my car, opening the driver's door and pushing me towards the seat.

'Remember, Anna, not a word to anyone. Otherwise Laurel will be taken away for good. Forget you came here. Forget you saw me, forget about Laurel. Forget all of it.'

EPILOGUE

Moonlight sends a shaft of silvery light between the gap in the thin curtains, into Laurel's bedroom, an eerie glow passing over her face, making her skin appear white and ghostly. My heart twists at the sight of her, relieved to be with her again after so many weeks apart. *My girl*. She can't stay here now though, that much is obvious.

I start to creep across the threadbare carpet, careful not to wake Polly in the room next door, sure that the thundering of my pulse will wake the entire household. Reaching down, I gently pull the duvet away from where it is tucked under Laurel's chin and scoop her awkwardly into my arms. Stirring, she murmurs slightly, snuggling closer into my neck. She's always been a heavy sleeper, ever since she was a baby, and she settles back into my arms almost immediately. I want to cry as I breathe in her familiar smell, of baby shampoo and biscuits, and I drop a tiny kiss on the top of her head, sure now that she won't wake up, before I creep back towards the bedroom door. Those weeks without her felt like a lifetime.

I hesitate for a moment at the top of the stairs, my arms already beginning to ache with the weight of Laurel's solid little body in my arms, feeling a slight pang of guilt at uprooting her, pulling her away again from what she's become used to, before I give myself an internal shake pushing the thought away. I'm doing the right thing, taking her away from here tonight. It's for her own good. Her own safety.

Carefully I start downstairs, testing each stair with my foot before I put my weight on it fully, anxious in case the floorboards creak. Polly is asleep merely feet away, and any tiny noise could wake her. I make it downstairs without a peep, my heart galloping in my chest, and carefully slide open the front door, careful not to bang Laurel's head as I squeeze through the gap.

The wind picks up as I tiptoe across the gravel to where my car waits, the doors already unlocked in preparation for my journey, and I freeze as the outside porch light pings on, sending a warm yellow glow across the gravel driveway towards me. My pulse flutters an insistent beat in my temples, my fingers slick with sweat, and I shift Laurel uncomfortably in my arms, as my biceps start to burn with the effort of carrying her. A fox darts across the path from the front door, his movement the action that set off the automatic porch light, and I curse myself for not thinking to turn it off before leaving.

I wait for a few seconds, my breath frozen in my chest, sure that Polly will appear in the doorway at any moment, shouting blue murder. Nothing happens. The light pings off again, and I am swamped with darkness, thick and velvety, surrounding me like a cloak. My heart rate returns to normal, and moving quickly, I tuck Laurel into the car, covering her little body with the blanket that I left there expressly for this purpose. Sliding into the driver's seat, I take a huge, shaky breath, wiping my slick palms on my thighs, the thick denim of my jeans soaking up the dampness before

I push the car into neutral and let it gently coast down the driveway onto the dirt track, until it is safe for me to start the engine. I don't look in the rear-view mirror as I drive away. I don't ever want to look back from this moment on.

Laurel sleeps all the way as I drive as close to the speed limit as I dare, along the A11 before picking up the M20 at Dartford. It's still full dark as we head towards our destination, the night sky clear and sprinkled with thousands of tiny stars, barely visible in the light pollution from the street lamps. My eyes are feeling gritty and dry from tiredness, and I want to weep with relief as I see the first motorway sign for the Eurotunnel.

A short while before we reach our junction on the motorway, I spy a service station, dark and secluded with only a few lorries parked up for the night. It's closed, the early hour meaning no one will be around just yet, so I park in a space at the far end of the car park, glancing around to make sure I am not spotted by some early bird trucker, before I lean into the back seat to check on Laurel. She is still fast asleep, her breath whistling slightly in and out, her hair ruffled and tangled. I tuck the blanket around her completely, so that should anyone peer into the back seat it looks as though I have a pile of old rugs on the seat, no child to be seen anywhere. I straighten up and check my watch. I have twenty minutes until check-in closes. Stepping back into the car, I inspect the back seat once more, and reassured that no one will see any sign of Laurel, I pull back onto the motorway.

My stomach gives a tiny lurch as I see the motorway sign I've been waiting for, and I indicate left, pulling into the slip road and following the signs. I've booked our journey online, so I don't need to stop at a manned booth, and once my ticket is printed I head towards passport control. This is it. Make or break time.

'Passport please, madam.' The border control guy already seems bored, and I'm catching the first train out of Folkestone this morning. I try not to let my fingers tremble as I hand my passport over, doing my best to rustle up a ghost of a smile. 'Anyone else travelling with you?' He leans over and gives the back of the car a cursory once-over.

'No,' I say, my throat dry. 'Just me.' Laurel's passport is back at the house in South Oxbury – not that I could have ever used it to travel, not with the whole country knowing her name. I hold my breath as he peers at my passport once more, his eyes going from my face to my photo and back again.

'Have a safe trip.' He waves me through, and I almost want to vomit I am so relieved. I give him a shaky smile and pull away, as calmly as I can, heading towards the train, and Calais.

By the time the train reaches Calais, I have managed to snooze for half an hour, waking only as the guy on the train scans my ticket, worry gripping my stomach as I pray that Laurel won't wake. She doesn't, and as I drive off the train and on to the motorway, the sky is lightening, tiny, wispy clouds dotting the deep blue, with streaks of pink and orange marking the sky as dawn arrives, announcing a new day. The first day of the rest of our lives.

A sense of calm washes over me, as I look in the rear-view mirror at the little bundle on the back seat. I did it.

I got her away, to keep her safe with me. Tears spring to my eyes, blurring my vision and I have to blink them away, quickly. The roads are empty, and I put my foot down, eager to get as far away from England as I possibly can. I am humming along to the radio, the music turned right down low, when I hear Laurel moving around in the backseat. As I glance in the rear-view mirror, her tousled head appears from the beneath the blankets, and she looks crumpled and confused for a moment, her cheeks flushed with sleep. She frowns for a minute, obviously bemused by waking up in a car, and then her eyes meet mine in the mirror and she gives me a little grin, and I see the gap in her teeth where she's lost a bottom front tooth.

'Hello, sleepyhead,' I smile back at her, giving her a little wink.

'Hello, Anna,' she smiles back, 'where are we going?'

I know what you're probably thinking. That I'm no better than Fran, that my behaviour is even more appalling if anything, but I'll fight you on that. I'll defend my actions to the end. You didn't see the look on Fran's face when she spoke about Dominic that night – it was the face of a woman deranged – unhinged, for sure. The woman is a sure-fire psychopath. There was no way I could leave Laurel with her. I didn't know what would happen to her – would Fran someday decide that Laurel had slighted her the way she thought Dominic had? What would happen then? There was only one course of action for me, as I saw it, so I took the first opportunity I had, waiting until all the lights had gone out in the cottage before I gently broke in through the old front door. A lifetime of losing my keys served me well.

I'm taking Laurel to my aunt's house in France. We'll be safe there – Fran doesn't even know the house exists, and I've already told my mum I'll be here, and that I'm writing a novel, that I need peace and quiet. I'll teach Laurel to speak French, and we'll get by on the little money I have saved. She'll grow up in a safe, healthy environment, where she won't have to watch what she says, or tiptoe around, terrified in case she starts a row. She'll be loved. I'll be nervous for a while, of course I will, but it will soon settle down once we're accepted as part of the village. I turn into the secluded lane that leads to my aunt's house, a ramshackle farmhouse built over a hundred and fifty years ago.

Pulling up next to the house, I pause for a moment, allowing myself to think briefly about Fran, and whether she is awake yet. I wonder if she's realised that Laurel is not in her bed, if she ran into Polly's room to wake her. And I wonder what she will do about it – after all, it's not as if she can report Laurel missing, is it?

ACKNOWLEDGMENTS

This book has only made it out into the world thanks to a cracking team of brilliant people – Kate Mills, Lisa Milton, Celia Lomas and Victoria Moynes, to name a few. Thank you so much for all your input and work . . . I still feel so incredibly lucky to part of such an amazing team.

Thank you to my lovely agent, Lisa Moylett, and all of the team at CMM who work so tirelessly to make sure my books are the best they can possibly be, reining me in when things get a little bit off the wall (sorry!).

I needed extra help when writing this book as, for the first time, the story involved some aspects of police procedures. It's safe to say that I know approximately nothing about that, so any mistakes are purely mine . . . but writing and plotting was made a lot easier with input from Rebecca Bradley, Janine Jury and Shirley O'Dwyer. Thank you ladies, for all your assistance!

Massive thanks to Rachel Dove for her generous charity donation, in aid of The Zuri Project – the character DI Jayden Dove is named in honour of her son.

Natalie, Charlie and Christie – thanks for keeping me alive up a mountain while I was waiting for edits on this book . . . maybe we could do something more relaxing next time?

And finally, thank you to Nick, George, Missy and Mo. For everything, always.

Turn the page to read an extract from the gripping thriller,
The Party complete with a twist you won't see coming . . .

Don't you ever wonder what would have happened if you hadn't made that particular decision? If you had decided to go right, instead of left? If you had said no, instead of yes? It's strange how one, tiny, sometimes seemingly insignificant decision can have a knock-on effect on life ... like a cleverly constructed domino chain, crashing down into a broken and ruined pile of rubble. Maybe if I had been a little bit stronger, if I hadn't had that one moment of weakness, where I threw caution to the wind and just did what I *wanted* to do, as opposed to what I *should* have done, maybe then, none of this would ever have happened. Life would have gone on as usual, with no tears and recriminations. Nobody would have been hurt. Nobody's life would have been ruined. There wouldn't have been any lies, or betrayal, and we all would have carried on living our lives, completely unaware that everybody has two sides to them, completely oblivious to the fact that the people surrounding us carry their own secrets, locked deep inside them. It's easy to look back and say none of this is my fault, that I am exempt from blame, but deep down, I know that's not true. All of this – everything that has happened – all of it starts with me. And so now, I have to do what needs to be done. I have to finish it, once and for all.

1

NEW YEAR'S DAY – THE MORNING
AFTER THE PARTY

Something happened. Something bad. That's the first thought that swims vaguely through my mind as I struggle my way into full consciousness. Followed by the realisation that, *I don't know what, but I know it's not good.* My head hurts. I try to open my eyes, the feeble wash of winter sunshine that tries to force its way through the lining of the curtains making me squint in pain. My head hurts and I feel really, really sick. I close my eyes again, willing the thud at my temples to die down and let me go back to sleep, before I crack one eye open again, a vague sense of uneasiness making me reluctant to keep them closed.

Where am I? Peering out from under the duvet cover, the room is unfamiliar to me and I swallow down the nausea that roils in my stomach. In the dim light, I can make out a large chest of drawers pushed against the wall, the top of it free of any clutter, and a mirror hanging above it. A generic picture hangs on the opposite wall, and there is no sign of anything personal – no photos, no make-up, no clutter that tells me that this is someone's bedroom. A spare room, then, and I seem to be alone, which is good, I think.

The same thought drifts through my mind as when I woke, that something happened last night, something that makes me feel somehow dirty and indecent. Scratching at my arms, I roll on to my back before pushing the duvet away from my clammy face, sweat making my hair stick to my forehead. The touch of fabric against my skin makes me stop for a moment, pausing in my quest to get comfortable, that and the fact that every muscle in my body seems to hurt. Sliding a hand under the covers I feel around – yes, my top is still on. No bottoms though, the fabric against my bare legs is that of the cotton sheets I'm lying on, not my trousers, or pyjama bottoms.

Something bad happened. My heart starts to hammer in my chest as I run my hand over my thighs, wincing at the sharp pain that lances me. Frowning, I push the duvet down, exposing my lower half to the warm air emitted from a large radiator under the window, and struggle my way into a sitting position. *Slowly, Rachel, go slowly.* As I push up on my elbows to shove my way up the pillows behind me, a surge of saliva spurts into my mouth and I swallow hard, desperate not to be sick. The thumping in my head accelerates and black dots dance at the corners of my eyes.

Closing my eyes again I wait a moment, drawing in a ragged deep breath and letting it out slowly. *I've never had a hangover like this before.* The nausea fades, and I run my hands over my lower half again, the skin on the inside of my thighs feeling bruised and sore. I slide my hands between my legs, and my heart beat doubles as I realise the bruised, raw feeling extends to there too. *Oh, God.*

I lean back against the cool of the pillow, eyes closed again against the watery light, trying my hardest to remember what happened last night. There's nothing, not a single thing that I can hook my memory on, just that uncertain feeling that something happened to me last night. It's like there's a gaping hole in my memory, a black bottomless pit that has sucked away any recollection of the previous evening. *Gareth*. What about Gareth? Where is he? I have to get home. I have to see Gareth; he'll be worried (*angry?*) that I didn't come home last night.

Steeling myself, I swing my legs round and out from underneath the duvet, pressing my feet to the floor as dizziness washes over me. My mouth is dry, so dry it hurts to swallow. Spying a plastic water bottle on the floor, half-hidden under the bed, I lean over, another wave of nausea making my mouth water, and take a sip. It tastes stale and dusty, as though it has been there for a long time, but it relieves the scratchiness of my throat, squashing down the bile that sits at the back of it. Placing the bottle back down on the floor, the sleeve of my top rides up to reveal a thick, purple bruise on the underside of my bicep. I poke at it, hissing as the tender skin shrieks out at my touch, the muscle sore and delicate. I wrap my fingers around my arm and see that the bruise is a perfect thumbprint, as though someone has grabbed me roughly. *Remember, Rachel.*

I slide my body slowly down the bed frame until I have sunk onto the immaculate carpet, the thick pile tickling the undersides of my bare thighs, my head pounding in time to a rhythm that no one else can hear. Scrubbing my hands over my eyes, I take a deep breath and look up – I am naked from the waist down, and that needs to be rectified before

I can go anywhere. *I need to get out of here.* Something flutters in my stomach at the thought of the door opening and someone walking in, finding me like this, half naked and vulnerable. Getting to my knees, and squashing down the horrid, shameful thoughts that lurk at the outskirts of my mind at the soreness in my thighs, I crawl towards a tangled mass of black, bunched into the corner of the room, against the mahogany of the chest of drawers. Reaching out a hand, I pull the bundle towards me, unravelling it to reveal my black wet-look leggings. *Thank God.* Relief floods my veins as I recognise the snarl of black fabric as my own clothing, but that fades as I shake them out, searching for my underwear. It's not there. I turn the leggings inside out and back again, hoping that I've pulled everything off in a drunken state last night, but my underwear is definitely missing.

And are you sure that YOU took them off, Rachel? A stern voice whispers at the back of my mind, *the bruising on your thighs . . . the fact that you can't remember anything . . . what does that tell you?* I hunch forward over the bundle of cloth in my arms, fighting back tears and the ever-present urge to throw up. *What the hell happened to me last night? What did I do? And who else was involved?*

On shaking legs, now clad in yesterday's leggings, the plasticky fabric clinging uncomfortably to my clammy skin, I gently push open the bedroom door and venture out into the hallway. The murmur of low voices wafts up the stairs towards me, uncertainty making me waver on the landing, not wanting to go and face whoever is down there. At least now though, I have some idea of who it will be – a family portrait hangs at the top of the stairs, and I recognise the tiled hallway and stained-glass windows of the front door below. It's a house that I've only ever visited occasionally, and I've never ventured upstairs, which goes a long way towards explaining why I was confused when I woke up this morning. White Christmas lights glitter around the front door, and the scent of pine from the Christmas garland that circles the banister catches at the back of my throat. A tacky silver banner hangs drunkenly across the wall of the entrance hall, loudly proclaiming for all to have a 'Happy New Year'. The glitter of the lights makes me dizzy and I squeese my eyes closed for a moment, gripped by vertigo, certain I am about to lose my footing and tumble down the stairs. The dizziness passes, and slowly I make my descent, one hand brushing the wall to keep my balance, as I still feel ridiculously hungover – more than I would ever have expected, the insistent throbbing in my temples making me long for my own bed, and the safe comfort of my own home. My silver sandals dangle from the other hand, found in the opposite corner of the bedroom much to my relief, although I think I would have walked barefoot if necessary.

As I reach the hallway, the tiles almost painfully cold beneath my bare feet, the chatter of voices gets louder, as though a door has been opened. I scoot across the cold tiles into the front room, where all the evidence of a party lies, scattered and ground into the carpet. A Christmas tree, looking worse for wear now, its needles dropping and littering the carpet, shines gaudily in the corner of the room, almost seeming out of place in the grim aftermath of what must have been a raucous party. Several empty wine bottles line the mantelpiece, and glasses litter the coffee table, some empty, some with the dregs of boozy Christmas drinks in the bottom. The table is usually polished to a shine, but now it is marred with glass rings on the wood, crumpled napkins, and several paper plates with the remains of buffet food smeared over them. I fight back the nausea that rises at the sight of left-over canapés, the faint smell of warm seafood hitting the back of my throat. A hefty splash of red wine scars the cream rug in front of the still smouldering open fire, and there are tiny shards of glass glinting on the hearth, where someone has made a drunken attempt to sweep away a broken wine glass. I breathe lightly through my mouth, as the scent of red wine and a hint of stale smoke rises up from the damaged rug. The curtains that line the wide front bay window have been left open, and wintry sunlight glints on a frost-covered garden, watery rays streaming in and highlighting the dust motes that dance in the air.

Turning away from the window, I catch sight of myself in the mirror that hangs above the fireplace, and double take; sure at first that someone else is in the room with me, my reflection looks so unfamiliar in that fleeting glimpse. Stepping closer, avoiding the still damp wine stain, I peer into the glass. I was obviously one of those partaking in the red wine last night – a faint purple stain marks my lips. I run my tongue over my teeth, cringing at the furry feel of them. My face is pale, my long, dark hair framing it in a tangled mess. I run my fingers through in an attempt to smooth it. My eyes look too big for my face, ringed as they are by dark circles. In short, if I thought I felt like shit, I look worse. My belly rolls over as the scent of frying bacon hits my nostrils, and I bend to slide my sandals on to my feet, intent on leaving and getting home before anyone realises I'm still here.

'Rachel!' A deep, hearty voice behind me almost makes me overbalance, one sandal on, as I wobble precariously on the other foot.

'Neil.' I place my foot back down on the floor, the bruises twinging at the strain in my thigh, and inwardly sigh at not getting out before I was seen, unwilling to engage in conversation when I am so unsure of the events of the previous evening. 'Sorry, I was just . . .'

'I didn't know you were still here!' Jovial, and with no hint of a hangover, Neil grins at me, and gestures towards the kitchen. 'We wondered where you got to last night . . . end up in the spare room, did you? Come on through, Liz is in the kitchen, and I've got coffee and bacon on the go.'

My stomach gives another undulating roll at the thought of the greasy, salty meat. I give a small shake of my head and open my mouth to say, '*I'm sorry, I should go,*' but Neil holds out an arm and gestures for me to go first, and despite the ache in my head, the rolling nausea in my stomach, and the underlying fear that streaks through my nerve endings thanks to my black hole memory, I have no option other than to walk across the cold, tiled floor into the kitchen. I have obviously stayed here without my hosts knowing – *so who undressed me?* I remove the one silver sandal that I'm wearing and pad through into the open-plan kitchen dining area, the bright sunshine that pours in through the patio doors at the back of the room making me feel even more nauseous, if that's at all possible. My neighbour, Liz, sits at the kitchen table, sipping intermittently from a travel mug that sits on a coaster in front of her. She turns as I enter the room.

'Look who I found.' Neil pulls out a kitchen chair and motions to me to sit down, before walking over to the hob and flicking the gas on. He dumps more bacon in the pan and I have to swallow back the saliva that fills my mouth.

'Rachel!' Liz smiles and waggles her fingers in my direction. I slide into the chair next to her – she smells of bacon fat and stale coffee, and I have to hold my breath as she gets close to me. 'How are you feeling this morning? A little worse for wear?' She chuckles, but her face is pale and devoid of make-up, unusually for her. 'I think we all are. Some party, eh?'

'Yes. Some party.' I shift uncomfortably on the kitchen chair, the hard wood of the seat pressing against my bruises.

'Bacon sandwich?' Neil holds out a plate to me, and I try and fail to stop myself from recoiling. 'No New Year's diet actually starts on New Year's Day, does it?'

'No, thank you. Could I just have a glass of water, please?' I don't want to be rude, but I'm not sure I could keep the sandwich down if I ate it. My throat is still painfully dry, and I feel as though my entire body is craving a cold glass of icy water.

'Here.' Liz fills a glass from the water dispenser built into the fridge, her fingers leaving a trail in the condensation on the surface as she hands it to me, and as I reach out to take it from her, I get a flashback. Last night, Liz opening the door to me, a glass in her hand, the smile on her face much the same as it is now – slightly smug, a mildly boozy air about her. I feel the frosty air on my bare arms, as she opens the door and pulls me inside; warm, sweaty air enveloping me, the beat of the music – something Christmassy? An old song, perhaps – thumping through the house. The smell of cloves and woodsmoke in the air – Liz has the open fire lit, even though the house is sweltering. I shake my head to clear the image, setting the bells clanging inside again, and sip at the water.

'Thank you . . . for letting me stay, I mean.' I sip again at the water, as Liz pulls a chair out across the table from me and sits back down. I try not to wince at the harsh scraping noise the chair makes as she drags it across the tiles. Neil hums under his breath as he slaps bacon between two slices of bread and drops the plate in front of Liz. 'I didn't mean to impose.'

'Oh, don't be silly, you're not imposing.' Liz takes a bite of her bacon sandwich, before dropping a Berocca tablet into her own glass of water. She offers the packet to me and I take one, gratefully, dropping it into my glass and watching the bubbles start to erupt. 'I didn't realise you'd stayed to be honest; I thought you must have left with Gareth.' *Oh shit. Gareth.* He's going to be furious, I should imagine.

'Well, thank you. For the hospitality, I mean. I don't really remember going to bed.' I watch her carefully, hoping that she'll tell me who it was that must have helped me upstairs. *Who bruised my arms, and my thighs, and . . . worse? And did I go willingly?* Liz gives nothing away, sipping at her travel mug and still munching on her sandwich, taking each bite with relish.

'God, I don't think many of us do.' She gives a huff of laughter through a mouthful of food, a stray crumb flying from her mouth and landing on her plate. It makes me feel

298

sick. 'Never let it be said that the Greenes don't know how to throw a party.'

'Right.' I look away, wanting to ask her if she saw anything, but not wanting at the same time, afraid of what she might say. 'Was I . . . was I bad? Like, drunk?'

'Oh darling, we were all tipsy. I don't remember you doing anything you shouldn't have, if that's what you mean. Gareth left early, and you wanted to stay for another drink, no harm in that. It was New Year's Eve, after all.' She pushes her plate to one side, and makes to take my hand but I pull away, grabbing at my glass of water. *No harm. Only, I think maybe there might have been.*

'It's bloody New Year! Gareth needs to lighten up,' Neil says, as he slides his own sandwich onto a plate. 'Rachel, it's lovely to see you, and if you're sure I can't tempt you with my fried pig slices, I'm going to slope off and watch last night's Hootenanny.'

I wait for Neil to leave the room, headed for Jools Holland and a mild food coma if the amount of food on his plate is anything to go by, before I speak again.

'Did we . . . did we argue, do you know? Me and Gareth?' I pick at the skin around my nails as I ask, not wanting to make eye contact with Liz, as I feel as though I'm confessing to being absolutely hammered last night. *You're a disgrace.* The words float through my mind, spoken by someone else, an unseen, unknown someone, and I feel a hot flush of shame. 'I know he must have left without me, but I just wondered if we'd had a disagreement about things and that's why he left.' I raise my eyes to look at her, as she sips from her travel mug again, gripping it tightly in her hands as if afraid I might snatch it away.

'No, not that I'm aware of,' Liz says briskly, but her eyes slide away from mine, and I get the feeling that maybe she's not telling me something. 'He's probably at home wondering where you are.'

'Oh God, probably. I need to go. Thank you for . . . everything.' The urge to leave overwhelms me and I push back the chair roughly, slipping my sandals back onto my feet, the straps rubbing across the top of my foot. Startled, Liz gets to her feet but I hurry out of the front door before she can speak again, calling out a goodbye to Neil, and step out into the cold January air. Frost glitters on the front path, and I carefully make my way across the square to my own house, where I can make out the glow of the Christmas tree lights through the front window, calling me home. Home, to Gareth. Hoping that he can shed some light on what happened last night – why I can't remember anything . . . and why my body feels as though something, or someone has broken into the very core of my being.

Want another thrilling read from Lisa Hall?

Grab the 250,000 copy bestseller
BETWEEN
YOU AND ME
Everyone has a secret...

Looking for a new gripping read from Lisa Hall?

TELL ME
NO LIES
Don't. Trust. Anyone.

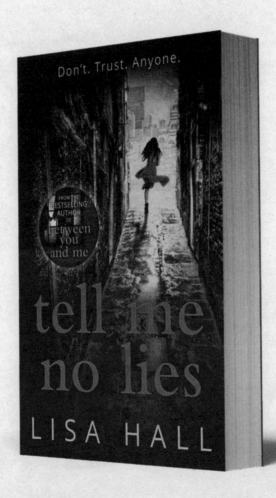

ONE PLACE. MANY STORIES

Bold, innovative and
empowering publishing.

FOLLOW US ON:

@HQStories